the reappearance of
Sam Webber

the reappearance of Sam Webber

Jonathon Scott Fuqua

CANDLEWICK PRESS
CAMBRIDGE, MASSACHUSETTS

First Candlewick Press edition 2001

Library of Congress Cataloging-in-Publication Data
Fuqua, Jonathon Scott.
The reappearance of Sam Webber / Jonathon Scott Fuqua.
—1st Candlewick Press ed.
p.   cm.
Summary: Since his father's disappearance and his move from a
safe neighborhood, eleven-year-old Sam gets help from his new school's janitor
and other adult friends in dealing with frightening new experiences.
ISBN 0-7636-1424-6
[1. Single-parent families—Fiction.   2. Janitors—Fiction.   3. Fear—Fiction.
4. Schools—Fiction.   5. Baltimore (Md.)—Fiction.
6. Afro-Americans—Fiction.]   I. Title.
PZ7.F96627   Re 2001
[Fic]—dc21   00-057185

First published in 1998 by Bancroft Press, Baltimore, MD

2   4   6   8   10   9   7   5   3   1

Printed in the United States of America

This book was typeset in Fairfield Light.

Candlewick Press
2067 Massachusetts Avenue
Cambridge, Massachusetts 02140

To Julie and Calla. I love you both.

missing person
missing person

My father, Big Sam Webber, disappeared the summer I was eleven years old. No one knows what happened to him for sure, if he was murdered, kidnapped, forgot who he was or just decided to run and never look back. When he was first gone, I hoped for murder or amnesia. I didn't want to believe that he would choose to leave. But the evidence always pointed to flight, that he gave up on my mom and me.

The police found his rusted old car at Dulles International Airport, down in Washington, D.C. It was in hourly parking and had rung up a giant bill over a two-week period, an amount that would've left me and my mother broke if we'd had to pay it. Luckily, we didn't. The police got it out, towed it somewhere, and blew dust all over it for fingerprints. Big Sam's were the only ones found on the worn steering wheel and scratched door handle. Kidnapping wasn't ruled out of the picture, mostly, I think, for my sake. He was what the police call a missing person, and he still is.

About a month after he disappeared, a pretty black police officer came by our house. She had a soothing smile and a gentle voice that whooshed out of her mouth like a scoop of sand. She asked me questions about my father. She wondered if Big Sam had ever mentioned leaving, if I'd ever gone to the track with him, seen him place a bet on something. Had I ever heard anyone threaten him, or did he sometimes seem lost?

I'd seen a little of all of those things, but nothing big enough to catch her attention. The thing is, remembering back to normal times made me feel horrible. And when we were done, she took me in her arms, held me against her so that my forehead scraped red on her shiny silver badge.

"It's going to be okay," she promised me, as if she could see into the future.

Just a few months later, I found out she couldn't.

When the savings were all used up, my mother sold the car. Then a couple of weeks after that, we started looking around for a cheaper place to live, somewhere closer to her job. We eyeballed a neighborhood called Charles Village, a few blocks off Baltimore's main north-south drags, Charles and St. Paul Streets, beside the best bus routes in the city and not too far from the Rotunda, a fancy shopping center with a Giant Supermarket crammed on the side.

Other not-so-okay things happened, too, like the way my name changed. Before my dad left, everyone, including my mother, had called me Little Sam. Together, my father and I were Big and Little Sam Webber, like I was a small part of him and he was a larger part of me. But when he'd been gone for a while, my mom suddenly started calling me Samuel. I think the name Little Sam reminded her that there had been a big one out there somewhere, and remembering that turned her into a wreck. So I tried not to get too upset over the change, but it bothered me. The part of me I had always liked the best was suddenly the very worst portion of all. Still, for my mom's sake, I got used to it as fast as I could. Everyone calls me Samuel or

Sam now. I wouldn't know what to say if someone called me Little Sam again.

When my father was still around, he was a Baltimore Gas & Electric employee, one of those guys who looks for weird-smelling fumes. He'd driven a car back and forth across the city all day, a little dusty-blue sedan, shoe-box shaped, with a bright BG&E logo painted on both front doors. It was a mess inside. It always had coffee and soda cups rolling around and crushed under the seats, plus greasy yellow McDonald's cheeseburger wrappers floating about. He loved that kind of food. My mom used to say that if he could have his way, he'd eat every meal at a fast-food restaurant, which didn't seem like such a bad idea to me.

Starting when I went into the first grade, my dad always tried to pick me up from school. No matter what his day was like, he'd swing by in the afternoons to get me and chauffeur me home. He worried that I was too shy, too small, and that bigger kids would pick on me if I was stuck taking the bus. He was right in most ways, too. I was shy, practically a runt, and oftentimes bigger guys tried to push me around. Even still, I knew I could do OK. But my dad never was convinced. See, he had been a huge kid. I've seen pictures of him, and his arms bulged like rubbery car bumpers. Being tough, he'd picked on runts like me when he was in school. He knew how cruel bullies could be, and he worried.

The truth is, my dad worried way more than normal. He suffered horrible headaches that his doctor said were caused by grinding his long flat teeth together. He chewed his cuticles raw, and cracked his knuckles about a thousand times a day. His worrying wasn't just for me, either; he worried about my mother, too. During the cold months, he didn't like her waiting in the dark for rickety crosstown buses. They didn't come by nearly as frequently as the ones rolling up and down Charles and St. Paul Streets, and he thought that she was vulnerable to something bad, standing along the side of the road as she did. So even though he was usually exhausted and sad in the winter, he picked her up at Junie's Florist, drove her home, then went downtown to drop off his work car. On the days he was feeling good enough, I begged to go with him, because it was nearly a perfect trip. Shimmering McDonald's cheeseburger wrappers swirled about us—bright, wrinkly birds—while colorful paper cups stamped with flashy lettering slipped and rolled beneath our shifting feet. And together, amid all that movement, we scampered into the magical city—buildings lit, Baltimore's skyline sparkling like a forest of Christmas trees, helicopters and jetliners streaking above.

He also worried about money. He and my mother tried to talk softly so that I wouldn't hear, but I knew what was going on. Their paychecks only went from week to week. We couldn't even afford to get a scruffy dog. When I asked about one, my dad usually asked me back who was going to pay the veterinary bills. Because I'd been listening in, I figured they couldn't, so I dropped the subject until I felt like I'd explode without a sad little mutt around the house to hug and walk, to be friends with.

My mom says my dad lived with the knowledge that we should have moved to a less fancy neighborhood than Rodger's Forge. The thing is, he didn't want me to get stuck in one of the rougher inner-city schools. More than once, I heard him tell my mother I wouldn't last two minutes in the places he'd gone. A kid like he'd been would have pummeled me for sport.

The Gordons, Ditch and Junie, owned the flower shop my mother started working at when she first dropped out of college. They'd never had any kids, so they treated my parents, who were kind of alone in the world, like they were theirs. As a matter of fact, when the Gordons came over, they didn't even knock on the door; they just opened it right up.

[4]

After my dad disappeared, not one thing seemed normal except for Ditch and Junie. They even helped my mom and me find a new, cheaper place to live. Junie spotted a few ads in the *Baltimore City Paper* and went ahead and set up some appointments. The thing is, when we went to see the apartments, I thought she'd overestimated how bad off we were. I mean, to me, they were for poor people.

The place my mom chose took up the entire second floor of a two-story rowhouse, and even though that might sound like a lot, it wasn't. Without any furniture, it was still cramped. A long skinny kitchen was in the back, crammed tight with a giant rounded refrigerator and cabinets that, for a time, smelled like wilted lettuce. Hanging off it was a shabby Baltimore bay window that somebody had added a few years before. It leaked like mad during storms. The narrow room right beside the kitchen was mine. The floors in it were scuffed a chalky brown, and the walls were so drippy with paint that they looked like they were drooling. Just looking in it made me feel low. Then there was the gloomy hallway, dark as a narrow cave, punctured by doors to a bathroom, a closet, the stairs, and the big front room, which was my mom's.

The front room overlooked the street, Abel Avenue, and the tar-drizzled front porch roof. It was the only place in the whole apartment that didn't seem like it was getting smaller every time I took a breath. Unlike the kitchen, this room had a pretty bay window that had been built with the house and wasn't popping and creaking and dangerous seeming. The day we were there, the brightest yellow beam of sunlight cut through it, and Junie, face like she'd spotted an angel, told us that was a good sign. The place was meant for us. Bright light would make my mom feel better. I guess it was supposed to sizzle her sadness away.

"Well, what do you think, hon?" Junie asked me as we stood out on the spongy front porch. My mom was inside, upstairs, discussing the lease with the lanky landlord, a guy who pulled his pants nearly up to his chest, so it looked like the middle portion of his body had been chopped away.

"It's okay," I said. Even though I didn't really think so, I appreciated that Junie was helping us.

"Yeah, it's all right," she agreed. "It's as good a place to start as any. Your mom can't afford that house you guys was renting in Rodger's Forge. Hope you know that, Little Sam. She'd have stayed there if she could have."

I squinted over at her for a second, sat down on the top step, and watched a skinny white guy, a straightened coat hanger, stagger by. He gave me the chills. He had these smoldering eyes, two holes that were tucked under the hard, pale bumps of his bony head. "My mom doesn't call me Little Sam anymore," I mumbled.

Big fat Junie, wearing white cotton shorts, the kind with an elastic waistband, sat down beside me. Pale flesh, bread dough, dangled beneath her arms. "What's she call you now, hon?"

"Samuel," I informed her as I watched the man step behind a tree and start peeing. Somehow, we weren't all that far from our old neighborhood, but it was a whole new world.

Junie followed my gaze. "Hey you, git outta here!" she hollered when she spotted what the guy was doing. And to my surprise, the man hustled off to somewhere else.

Before moving, we had a huge yard sale to get rid of extra furniture. While it was going on, I had a great time. To me, it seemed like a carnival, with people barking out prices and my mom accepting them or calling back another price. But that night, when the frenzy was over, and I realized that a lot of my father's things were gone for good, I got queasy. My stomach churned for about an hour before I eventually spewed into the toilet. My mom sat on the dusty, cool bathroom floor, watching me as I hovered over the cold, slick white bowl. I could tell that she was sad, but I couldn't do anything about it. I was crippled by nausea. And that was just the beginning. For a time, my stomach got shifty and sore whenever I felt overwhelmed.

The next weekend, Junie and Ditch, who was tall and stretched out and constantly puffing on a cigarette, helped us move. And even though we used their delivery van to haul our stuff, it took us nearly six hours. We made three trips back and forth on Greenmount Avenue and York Road, and the whole time, my stomach gurgled. I hated the new place. It was so gloomy compared to our old home and dark as a crusty mayonnaise jar. It made me sad just to drop my stuff in it, to glance up at the seams of wallpaper on the ceiling, slathered with thick yellow paint, as I staggered in and out the crummy door.

When the last stick of furniture had been plopped down in the cramped hallway, Junie and Ditch went to get some beer. When they got back, they had three new houseplants with them, too. Each had a big gold ribbon, like a sunflower bloom, wrapped around the pot.

"Maxine, I knows you like the umbrella plants, hon, so I brought you two and a nice geranium to brighten up your winda, ta make it feel like home."

For some reason, my mother started crying, so Junie wrapped her lumpy arms around her and patted her spiny back. "Don't cry, hon," she whispered softly. "Don't you cry, Maxine. You watch, everything's going to straighten out. Give it some time."

Standing there, my head got woozy, and I snuck off, went and sat on the bathroom floor.

After a few minutes, my mother knocked, then came in, teary-eyed and sad. "You feeling sick again, sweetie?" She sniffled and shut the battered door behind her, walked over and scratched my back gently with her sharp fingernails, just the way I always liked.

"I don't know why," I gasped, starting to cry myself because I felt so crummy about everything. My tears dripped onto the floor tiles. "Maybe I ate something wrong."

[7]

"Oh, Samuel, it's all right to feel bad, you know. It's natural. As natural as laughing, sometimes."

But I didn't say I was sad. I didn't want her to think that I disliked the apartment she'd gotten for us. I worried about her.

Silent, we sat there for a while, hurt and weak in our hearts, then we stumbled to our feet. My mom gave me a hug, then I washed up in the sink, which sat on two chrome poles and was attached to the wall with what looked like Elmer's glue. We left the bathroom and weaved down the hall, around all the junk, and into the warm kitchen, where Junie and Ditch were drinking beer.

Junie got up and cracked one open for my mom, gave it to her.

Ditch smoked quietly at our enamel-topped table, crammed awkwardly into the bay window. He blew gray clouds through the red, rusty screen, which reminded me of a piece of farm equipment. Even though I'd known him forever, he'd always made me kind of nervous. To me, he was a little quiet, spooky. "Little Sam," he said, looking at me, "I could check with your neighbor downstairs, see if you could use the backyard. It don't look like she does. It's a mess. I could come over next week and we could clean it up if you want." He took a sip of beer, cheeks draping inward, then a drag on his smoldering cigarette.

"I guess," I mumbled, though I couldn't see what I'd do in the tiny yard. It was nothing but a completely cluttered plot of dirt surrounded by a wavy, crimped, two-foot wire fence. Weeds grew in the few spots where there was exposed ground, but nothing else. I spied a dirty shirt, like an old bandage. There were some cans and bottles and disintegrating boxes plus a broken piece of furniture piled up in the space. And believe it or not, it struck me as sparkling clean compared to the garbage can area just over the fence, in the alley. It seemed all sorts of nasty things were stacked around the stained plastic bins, atop small pools of sour water. The funny thing is, now I realize that my eyes saw more than was actually there.

"I'll check in with her 'fore Junie and I go home, Little Sam," Ditch told me.

I nodded nervously, waited till my mom and Junie started talking. "Ditch," I whispered, "I don't go by Little Sam anymore. It makes my mom feel bad. She calls me Samuel now."

He cast a glance over at my mother, drew his cracked lips against his wooden-looking teeth. Something bothered him about it, I could tell, but he didn't speak up. "Okay," he said, and took another drag on the smooshy filter of his Winston.

When they were gone and my mom and I were alone in our new place, we went our separate ways and started opening up some boxes. In my room, I tried to organize a little, but it seemed impossible. I pushed furniture around, but there was nowhere for it to go. After a few minutes, I gave up, sat on my cold metal desk, my legs dangling, and started reading comic books. I was halfway through one when my mom came to the door, leaned against the scarred frame. She held a ceramic cookie jar that was shaped like a mama bear in a dress and a checkered apron. I couldn't remember a time when it hadn't been on the kitchen counter, even though it'd never had cookies in it.

"There might not be enough room for her?" my mom told me, raising her eyebrows so that I knew she was asking a question.

"She doesn't have to be out," I said, sliding back into the plastic bag the shiny copy of the Thor comic I'd been reading. I imagined the narrow kitchen. "Maybe she'd fit on top of the refrigerator," I offered.

"Hm. Maybe," my mom said. She forced a smile. "I'll help you get your room straight, if you want?"

I looked around at the boxes and the furniture, gray and scratched in that rectangular cave. Like I said, it didn't seem like it could be organized. "Was this supposed to be the dining room?" I asked.

She thought about my question before answering. Her mouth moved back and forth as she considered. "I think it can be anything.

It's got a door on it, and that's unusual for a dining room. Most dining rooms don't have doors." She leaned in and opened the shrunken little closet. "They don't usually have closets, either."

I nodded and felt a little better. I hoped it really was a bedroom, that we weren't so poor I was about to live in the wrong room.

"It doesn't matter, anyway, because you know what I've been thinking? Me and you should be creative in here since it's just us."

I stared at her.

She swept her long straight hair, a brown scarf, over one shoulder. "Speaking of closets, I've been thinking about the one in the hall. I bet . . . ," she said, gears whirling as she spoke, "I bet it would make a cool television room."

"It's tiny," I said.

"Samuel," she chided me, "You're such a pessimist. Come on and look. " She placed the bear cookie jar on the floor, turned, stepped around a couple of boxes, and clomped down the hall. She opened the closet and looked in. "It's perfect," she declared.

"No it isn't," I said behind her. "You can't put two chairs in there."

"Not if you put them side by side. I was thinking about putting them in line, like a movie theater. We could fit three in here that way. We'd even have enough room left over to hang our coats. They'd keep it nice and toasty in the winter." She glanced over at me, eyebrows two tiny arches. "Don't be so negative, Samuel. It might be really neat."

I looked the space over, imagined watching a movie in the chair closest to the big black Magnavox television my dad had purchased a few years before to watch football on. I realized that it could be just like going to a small movie theater if we ever bought a VCR or got cable. Then I remembered how Junie'd told me the president had a private theater in his basement. "It's like the White House," I declared, imagining myself eating popcorn and drinking a soda in the little space.

"You'll see," my mom said. "It'll be your favorite place in the apartment by the time we're done with it."

[10]

But that comment sank my excitement, even though she'd meant it to do just the opposite. "Yeah," I admitted after a minute because I realized she was right. I knew it shouldn't be that way—a closet shouldn't be the best spot in a house. I turned away, lurched slowly down the hall into my mom's room. I wondered if she'd been standing in a sunbeam and that was why she was feeling better. I wondered if Junie was right about light being good for people who are sad. I looked out the window, made sure to place myself in the path of a bright ray. "Our street's pretty ugly," I mumbled when I could tell that my mom was behind me.

"No it isn't," she protested. "It's got a nice, old-fashioned character."

But I didn't notice that sort of thing, yet. "None of the trees have real limbs," I notified her. "Someone cut 'em all off." My arms fell to my sides. A knee unlocked.

"They're growing back," she said, and roughed up my hair, then placed a hand on my shoulder.

"The houses are terrible." I pointed toward one with a set of brick front steps that were crumbling gently, the ground in front of them speckled with pretty red gravel. There was a disintegrating mattress tossed onto the scrubby hedge beside it. It reminded me of the body of a big animal, flopped onto a bumpy side. I wondered if it'd been there long.

"That's the way it is in the city. You get mansions right beside places that need some care."

The street reminded me of my father's Baltimore Gas & Electric car with its cups and hamburger wrappers everywhere. But for some reason, it bothered me. Rodger's Forge had been spotless.

"Maybe you and I can clean the block up?"

Amazed, I looked over at her. "Why would we do that?" I asked.

"To make it look better," she said.

"Shouldn't someone else be doing it, since we just moved in? I mean, it's not our garbage."

"But it's our street," my mother pointed out. "Don't we want it to look nice?"

"Maybe," I muttered. But already I was scheduled to clean the back-yard with Ditch, and I didn't want to be stuck doing that sort of thing all the time. I didn't know what I wanted to do, but it wasn't that.

For dinner, we got a pizza around the block at Harry Little's. That's when I first noticed there was a Little Tavern on the corner of Thirty-second Street and Greenmount. I would have preferred grabbing a hamburger there, but I didn't say anything about it. I wanted my mother to be stronger before I started nagging her. Anyway, it was all-right-smelling pizza, and it tasted pretty good. Maybe it would have been better if my stomach hadn't been one giant knot, bubbling and burning, a bag of lava. It rained that night; it poured, and as we ate, water streamed down the inside of the sorry bay window in the kitchen, where our table was located. It looked like a fountain. Occasionally, I put a pale, clammy finger up and redirected the little rivers, but mostly, I just left them alone. Funny thing, the water didn't pool on the linoleum floor, either; it drained right through. Actually, I thought it was kind of nice the way it worked so cleanly. But I could tell that it both-ered my mom. She didn't eat but one greasy slice of Harry Little's pizza. She spent her time staring at the water as it trickled by.

"I'm going to get them to fix this," she declared, stood and went to the big ancient refrigerator to locate one of the National Premium beers Junie and Ditch had left. She sat back down, turned away. She gulped from the can and leaned onto one of her knobby hands, balled up, the mashed body of a bird against her forehead. "I hate this place," she muttered.

I didn't say anything, stared out the dusty window, chewed Harry Little's pizza, and worried, worried about what was going to happen to us.

when yer in the city, hon

when yer in the city, hon

Ditch and Junie came by the following Sunday. Ditch brought with him a brand-new box of plastic lawn bags, a rake, clippers, bug killer, and two pairs of old gloves. I tried to ignore the supplies at first, but I couldn't get away with it. After he swilled some coffee, I followed him down the stairs and out the front door, where the sky was a gray white tinged with the strangest golden highlights, and the air was heavy and warm. We walked around the block, past some of the pretty little patches and the places that were nothing but dirt spots. Halfway down the alley, we stepped over the wire fence and stood surveying the backyard.

It was as hard to imagine clean and nice as my sloppy room, so I didn't know where to begin. Ditch had worked at tough jobs all of his life, though, so he knew how to struggle through projects, get them going. He organized the cleanup.

We started by bagging all the junk lying around, the bottles and cans and stuff, a filtration mask, a pair of glasses, an old transistor radio, an easy chair, a broken plate, a couple of old eight-track tapes, and the door to a microwave oven. Somehow, it had all existed in the tiny space that was the backyard. It made my stomach roll, reinforced the feeling that I didn't want to be out there. I didn't see any purpose in it. If I had to walk around the block to get into my own backyard, I knew it would never happen. Not that I was lazy—the alley nearly scared me to death.

"Use the fire escape," Ditch said. "It goes right up to yer bedroom winda."

I looked at it. He was right. The black iron pieces clung to the side of the rowhouse like the dried-out body of a cicada. There was a little platform just beneath my sill. It looked like the last tenant had also used it to get outside. On it was an ancient rag mop, gray yarn hardened like curls of thick ox hair. There was also a half-finished quart of beer, label faded as an ancient dollar bill, and a plastic ashtray. It would be easy to climb out onto the landing. The thing is, my window had a big iron grate over it, a large padlock on the inside, and I didn't know where the key was. I hadn't seen one.

"You've got to have a key. What good's a fire escape if you can't get to it?"

I shrugged.

He lit a cigarette with a red Bic lighter, cupping a hard hand to shield the flame even though there wasn't any wind. "I'll find the key for you," he assured me. "Your mom probably knows where it is." His bony chest swelled as he sucked in a lungful of smoke. The buttons on his shirt pulled against the thin fabric, and I thought they might tear off.

I nodded, but I wasn't sure my mom would know. In the week since we'd moved in, she'd seemed more and more lost. A crummy key was such a minor thing that it must've slipped her mind, fallen through her loose fingers, gotten lost in some drawer or beneath a piece of furniture. Maybe it was under the mattress of my bed, which wasn't on its metal frame yet.

Ditch glanced up at the back of our apartment, appeared to examine the bricks. "Worried 'bout your mom?" he asked.

I looked at him, mumbled something, probably not even real words. Ditch was so tall and thin, tough, like a hunk of frayed cable sticking out of a wall.

"Junie will get her up and around. She's good at that kind of thing."

I leaned over and picked a white bottle cap from the black dirt and dropped it into the garbage bag that sagged against one of my legs.

Ditch bent and grabbed the mushy easy chair at the top of its back and around its side, grunted, and lifted the waterlogged hunk of furniture. He stumbled toward the alley and placed it over the fence, by the bashed and gnawed garbage cans. One cushioned arm drooped toward the ground, splintered and broken. Turning, Ditch swiped up the rake and started into a corner, cigarette pointing up, then down, locked between his lips as he panted.

I wended my way around the little yard, searching the grass and soil for foreign objects, placing the smaller items in my bag. I picked up a stick and used it to dig things up, played like it was a metal detector. The place wasn't such a mess. The yard had looked bad from above, but it was OK, not half as shot as the back part of our rowhouse. My eyes locked on that, and I saw all sorts of things I didn't want to. The mortar around the brick was stained and cracked. It looked as if one side of the building was going to fall away from the other. Above my head, the bay window, where my mother and I ate, appeared fragile, the wood beneath it unpainted and pale, misplaced nails poking like spikes between ragged floorboards. Getting a peek at the guts bothered me. I was sure it would come crashing down one day. The sides of it were all covered in pale, spongy shingles that didn't match the brick. Also, there were thick black wires drilled into it haphazardly. They swooped out to the bristling brown telephone poles in the alley. A couple of scraggly pigeons, thumbprints, sat on one. I studied them and listened to their swallowing noises.

Moving toward the steps, I realized that someone had recently painted them, though not very well. They'd slapped on a coat of purple paint, dripping it all over the concrete pad beneath, getting some on the brick wall, too. Instead of scraping, they'd just painted right over the crusty old layer. Big flakes, the size of potato chips, were frozen in place by a hardened coat of purple. It looked like pictures I'd seen of the slums, dark-skinned kids munching on ancient wafers from around a windowsill or a door frame.

Underneath the soft planks were two or three old paint cans, a dry stick pointing out of one. I squatted down and yanked the cans out. Spider webs made fiery crackles when they moved.

On my knees, scooping out layers of leaves from below the steps, I noticed the back door to our downstairs neighbor's apartment. It was bright red metal and in good condition, except that someone had written "honky" down the center of it with runny silver spray paint. I shivered and looked over at Ditch, who was halfway across the backyard, about six feet from me. "Mr. Gordon?" I called softly, voice raspy, scraping over my vocal chords like crunched gravel.

Ditch stopped raking and turned around. Perspiration ran down his face in fat drips, chips of glass.

I hesitated, gulped, and wished I hadn't called him. "Um," I said, "who do you think wrote this?" I pointed nervously up at the door, the heat of the sizzling sun pounding on my shoulders.

Ditch took the drippy word in and looked back at me. "I guess some nigger," he said. "Can't imagine a white person doing it. It wouldn't make sense, would it?"

"Someone walked into the yard?" I stammered.

"Walked into the yard?" he asked, rubbing a hand up and down the smooth old rake handle.

"You know, someone trespassed or something?" I stood up so I wouldn't feel so small.

He shrugged. "Guess someone just stepped over the fence and wrote it out of pure meanness or jealousy or something. Common round here, Little Sam. Lot of jealous people who wish they had what

[16]

you got. They're right over there." He pointed with a long, tough, gloved finger, the tip as smooth as slate, off toward Greenmount Avenue, or at least that's where I knew he'd meant to point. By mistake, he aimed off toward green Roland Park, where if someone was jealous about something, it probably wasn't money.

I nodded, even though I figured he was wrong about people wanting what I had. I didn't have anything, at least, not anything worth wanting. I barely even had a bedroom.

"Worried 'bout someone bothering you out here?"

I kicked at the pale and cracked cement landing. "Guess," I croaked, embarrassed.

Nodding, he dropped the rake, walked over, and sat on the rotten steps, keeping his runny eyes on me the whole time. The boards bent beneath his weight. Stripping off his gloves, he placed a giant scarred paw on my shoulder. I looked at it and realized that his fingernails were strange. They were wavy and stuck out above the last knuckle like broken shells, like they'd been embedded into his bones with a hammer. I wondered if they hurt, because it looked like they would.

"I got funny nails," he told me.

I couldn't look at him, he was so right.

"My dad had 'em, too."

I couldn't remember my father's fingernails.

"Know what? No one's going to hurt you round here if you just use yer head. See a mean-looking nigger in the alley, hop on up the fire escape and lock yer winda. Most of 'em'll just be mindin' their own business, though. They don't want no trouble, usually. They just want what you got, even the stuff you throw 'way." He looked over toward the garbage cans. "You'll know what's what soon enough. Don't go hanging out here after dark, that sort of thing. That's when they start trouble, if there's going to be any. After dark." He reached into his pocket with his free hand, withdrew a half-full pack of Winstons. He shook it to the side, and a filtered tip stuck out of the top, a white antenna. He poked it on his bottom lip and dropped the soft-pack back into his shirt pocket.

"Want a Coke?" Ditch asked, sliding his heavy hand off my shoulder so that he could cup his Bic lighter. The tip of his cigarette turned red as he sucked at it. "A 7-Eleven right round the corner," he said, smoke snaking from his mouth.

I looked at the ground, at Ditch's torn-up work boots, splats of white paint across the toes. "There's a 7-Eleven near here?" I asked, excited.

"A 7-Eleven," Ditch told me again.

"Sure," I said.

"Well, all right," Ditch replied, standing, unfolding like a horse getting its legs beneath it. He loomed over me the way trees loom in winter, leafless and bare.

Tired, I stepped over the fence and started down the asphalt-black alley after Ditch. We were going in the opposite direction from the way we'd entered that morning, and I looked into our other neighbors' yards. Some were messes, others weren't. Just like back in Rodger's Forge, a few of them had Formstone garages with large wooden doors, like castle gates. That was normal. The thing that I couldn't believe was that each took up every inch of ground from the back door of the house to the alley, and that a couple were in such rough shape. Windows, half-protected by big iron grates, were broken out. Graffiti and laundry-pen writing cluttered wood areas. There were holes close to the ground, in the Formstone or beneath rotting planks, where I imagined large rodents and insects wriggling around, waiting for night. But then, like a cave opening to daylight, a whole string of homes near the end of the alley was spotless, filled with grass and flowering plants, decorated with nice little items. The greenness lit up the air around these homes, glowed sweetly against the trimmed and tidy bricks. Little stone paths wended their way to the alley area, which just happened to be clean, too. They filled me with a glimmer of hope.

We turned down Thirty-second Street, passed by Harry Little's Pizza, and started across a large empty parking lot, plastic grocery bags blowing like tumbleweeds across it, getting stuck on battered parking meters. I saw the 7-Eleven up on the corner, less than a block off of Greenmount Avenue. After a minute, we tramped over a patch of brown grass and hopped off the curb, crossed this narrow street with about a thousand Coke bottle tops melted into the tarred surface. I stopped and looked, amazed, before we clomped up a flight of cement steps. Turning sideways, Ditch and I slid between two parked cars and made our way toward the door, where a couple of rough, moon-faced teenagers stood talking. They glowered at us with their chins tilted up, made me more and more nervous as we got closer to them.

"Hey, man, you got a quarter?" one of them said, and I nearly fell over Ditch's heels to get away, to get into the store. I heard them laugh at me as the door slowly closed.

Inside, it was like every other 7-Eleven I'd been in, maybe a little more worn, though. Ditch got a coffee, and he told me to go find myself a soda. Lost in the selection, I nearly bumped into this black lady shivering in front of the refrigerators, her arms wrapped tightly across her chest. I tried not to stare at her. I focused instead on finding myself a Dr Pepper.

"You likes Dr Pepper, too?" she croaked when I got my hands around a slick bottle.

I glanced her way anxiously, wondering why she was so cold. It was almost as stuffy inside the store as it was outside. "It's got a good flavor," I whispered.

"It really do." She groaned softly, like she was in pain. "It really do."

On my way to the counter, which was blocked off in a wall of thick Plexiglas, I stopped by the comic-book rack and gave it a quick scan. I didn't have the new X-Men or Fantastic Four, and I peered at their covers. The X-Men looked kind of boring. Cyclops and Storm were holding hands. But the Fantastic Four was a continuation of a story from the month before. They were still fighting Galactus for control of the universe. The Silver Surfer was even helping out. I gawked at the scene on the cover. The Flame appeared near death, and a stretched-out Mr. Fantastic was screaming in Galactus's giant hand. I swallowed, wishing that I had brought some money with me.

Ditch walked up beside me. "Want a couple comic books?"

I felt like telling him that I did, but I knew I shouldn't. "No, thanks," I mumbled halfheartedly.

"Yer sure?" he asked.

"I guess," I told him.

"Look, I'll let you pick two, and you can go by and take out the garbage for Junie or your mother at the store."

I glanced up at him.

"Go on," he prodded me.

Excited, I snatched up the two I'd been eyeing and followed him over to the counter, where he pulled out a ratty five, damp from sweat, and paid.

When I walked back outside, the same guy harassed me for a quarter, called me something, though I wasn't sure what. As we headed off, I was glad to put some distance between myself and the boy, his weasel eyes blotted red.

"Ya know, I've never asked ya if ya like playing any sports," Ditch said as we turned down Thirty-second Street.

"I guess I do," I told him cautiously. My bag of comic books slapped against my leg as it moved back and forth, made me feel good and calm.

"Bet yer too young ta remember how yer dad and me went ta every Colts game we could, even when they stunk. Ain't been the same round here since they pulled outta town." Ditch took a sip of his coffee, a puff on his cigarette, and walked quietly a few steps, then said softly, "You should get into organized sports, junior-high ball. Help build yer confidence up."

I nodded, but I didn't want to change. I'd already had too much of it. Anyway, organized sports meant large groups of kids my age, and I'd always been quiet around kids my age. Plus, a screaming coach would have nearly killed me. I liked sports but not under those circumstances.

"Who's yer favorite player?" he asked.

I thought for a minute. "Eric Dickerson, I guess."

Ditch nodded. "He's all right. Kind of greedy, though."

I didn't say anything, ashamed that I liked someone who was greedy.

"He's okay," Ditch said as we turned down the alley, ambled past those gleaming yards and homes. "Least ways he's playing for the Colts. He'd be a big star round here."

"That's why I like him," I said.

"Well, Sam, don't like him for that. The Colts been gone for years, and they ain't coming back."

I nodded, feeling stupid, and we stumbled silently through the alley, stepped over the fence and into the backyard. There was a blazing orange bird twittering away on the fence next door, and that made me feel light and floaty. Just staring at the little guy made me know that everything would get better, that Baltimore could open its arms and welcome people in.

I put my bag of comics and my Dr Pepper on the purple steps and started working again, cleaning up the small yard that mean people trespassed into without a thought. Then the bird flew away, and I missed him. As I put yellow plastic twist ties on the lumpy bags I'd filled, I wondered if I'd ever have the guts to do anything in that plot of land, even if it was spanking clean. I didn't tell Ditch, though. I kept it inside of me, a pound of stones.

[21]

My mom was napping in her room, something she'd been doing a lot of. Junie had left for the store, and Ditch headed out when we were done in the back. Exhausted, I watched television in our closet. The TV was on the floor, and I rested peacefully on top of a chair and a pile of coats.

Bonanza was blaring at me. Hoss and Little Joe were taking nitroglycerin up a mountain to stop a fire. I'd had no idea how unpredictable the stuff was until then. One good bump or jolt and the Cartwright brothers were dust. Funny thing, too; my mom had told me once that Ditch took nitro for his heart, and I wondered if the medication and the explosive were the same thing. I couldn't figure out how Ditch's throat hadn't burst or his stomach blown up. I figured saliva defused it or something.

When *Bonanza* was over, I watched a little of *The Big Valley* with Lee Majors, who was also the Six Million Dollar Man, but I got bored with it pretty fast and cut the Western off halfway through. I climbed over the coats and the chairs and stood out in the dim hallway, looking at my mom's closed bedroom door covered with a spray of thumbtack holes. I walked into my room and stared out my grated window at the backyard. It was nice-looking. It didn't seem nearly as threatening as it had before Ditch and I had cleaned it up. I even considered taking some G.I. Joe figures down there and playing. I didn't, though, mostly because I would've had to walk around the block, and my legs already ached from work. Plus, I was still a little nervous. The alley didn't look any better. Actually, it looked worse stacked with our bulky green garbage bags and that slumping easy chair and its floral pattern of soppy leaves.

I went into the kitchen and sat down at the table. I reached up and pushed some smelly beer cans out of the way and rested my head against the smooth enamel surface, shell-shocked that we'd sunk so low. I knew that was why my mother was sleeping so much, because she was surprised by everything, that my father was gone and we were completely poor. I shook my butt back and forth, and wondered if the bay window would suddenly flake off. I kind of hoped it would.

Outside, angular shadows covered the houses across the alley, hiding their flaws, the rusty downspouts and tar-covered roofs, the crackling paint. The way they were lit, they actually looked pretty. I heard a dog barking somewhere. I glanced down and searched around the gray garages, the bent wire fences and small trees. There were a couple of men—a white guy with a cap on, a black man with a beard—strolling along, bobbing on springy knees, shock absorbers. They went from garbage can to garbage can, then stopped when they got to the pile of crud Ditch and I'd stacked up. The window was open and their voices were clear in the heavy air. They yanked out the sagging easy chair, arm pointing at their shins. Then they tore open the plastic bags. I couldn't believe it. Rusty cans, hunks of glass, fabric, sticks, and other stuff formed a carpet in the alley. They rooted through it, then gave up and continued walking, looking into other backyards, searching through everything. By Thirty-second Street, I saw them pick up a new, baby blue garbage can. They wrestled with it, and it wrestled back, chained as it was to a dented post. But eventually, something broke, and they carried it off like it was theirs all along.

My stomach churned. I got up and walked back to my disorganized room. I flopped onto my bed and looked at the mess around me, the boxes that were open but not unpacked, the clumps of dust, and the blob of sheets at the end of my bare mattress. I looked up at the square glass light shade above, at the cobwebs that hung from it like strings of crystals. It made me feel alone, like the last person in Baltimore.

I rolled onto my side and propped my head up with an arm, settled a few scraps of paper in front of me, drew a small picture of Iron

Man. When I finished, I drew one of Wolverine, then pulled over the bag of comic books that Ditch had bought me, slid the Fantastic Four comic out, and opened it. For a few seconds, I was feeling so sorry for myself that I stared at the first page without reading, without even seeing the art. Finally, I forced my eyes to focus on the amazing opening panel—the Thing, the Silver Surfer, and the Invisible Girl dodging a meteor shower. It soothed my nerves just to see it. I began the story, breathed relief a few pages in: the Human Torch was still alive. Excited, I shot through it, and when I was done, I turned back to the first page and started all over again. But before I could finish a second time, I fell asleep.

When I woke up the next morning, there was a dull blade of light angling across my messy bedroom, dust swirling in it like tiny pale bugs. There were so many particles in the air, I was scared I might start choking. I stood and looked out on the day. The sky was white. It deflated me because I'd been hoping it would be sunny for my mother. I turned from the window and my shoes squeaked on the floor. Looking down, I realized that I still had them on, that I still had all of my clothes on from the day before. I tried to straighten out my crumpled shirt by rubbing my hands across it like a cold iron, but it was no use. I gave up and went into the kitchen to search for something to eat.

I was sitting at the table, crunching on Pringles, when I heard someone start up the creaky steps from downstairs. The footfalls stopped at the top, and a set of keys jangled. One slid into the lock. I watched as the glass knob, cut like a big diamond, turned and Junie's plump fingers, worn green polish on each nail, wrapped around the door. As she entered, I saw that she wore a creased pair of silver sandals that glistened in the half-light. The rubber soles were worn low beneath both of her big toes. Under a flabby arm, she carried a bag of groceries. She smiled at me as she gently shut the door, and her yellow sundress fluttered, an unstaked tent.

I smiled back. Junie could look sweet in her own way.

She made her way into the kitchen and set the bag down on the small counter. Before saying anything, she removed the red can of Pringles from my hands, located the plastic top.

"Your mom ever get up last night, hon?" she whispered.

I shook my head.

She pursed her lips. Dull wrinkles spread across her saggy features. She placed her hands on her giant hips, looked me over. "You're wearing the same thing you wore yesterday," she observed. "Why, I bet you didn't even wash your hands after working out back."

I looked at my palms; the creases were filled with dirt.

"I'm ashamed that Ditch let you go like this," she said. "You go wash. Go take a shower, hon. I'll cook you up some breakfast."

I just stared at her blankly, as if I didn't understand.

She unloaded a gray carton of eggs, a package of fatty bacon, and a tube of Pillsbury biscuits. She pulled out a can of V8, punctured the top with a rusty opener, then pulled a dusty glass out of the cupboard and filled it halfway. "Your mom's getting up today. Don't you worry."

I smiled again but just continued to look at her. For some reason, I didn't feel like I even had the strength to move. My butt felt like lead, weighed more than a sofa. My eyes stared out in the general direction of the cabinets.

Junie gently shooed me out of the chair and steered me into my room. She watched my progress as I unlaced my sneakers, stripped grimy socks from my moist, pale feet. "Shampoo yer hair," she instructed me, then turned and went down the hall to wake my mother. I could hear their voices as I shut the bathroom door.

[25]

Out of the shower, I brushed my teeth and parted my hair with my fingers. I couldn't see into the foggy, cracked mirror because it was too high, so I didn't know that I had a white blotch of toothpaste on my chin. Opening the door and creeping down the hall with a towel wrapped around me, I saw my mom sitting slumped in the kitchen, drinking her V8, talking to Junie, who was frying bacon. In my room, my whole body pounded with happiness. I got dressed as fast as I could and rushed out to see her.

"Honey." My mom forced herself to smile. She was dressed in a faded T-shirt and shorts. Her skin looked gooey, soft, her bare feet nearly skeletal. The wrinkles from her pillow had dented lines into one side of her face, so that around her nose it looked as if patches of pink material had been sewn together. Her eyes were deep and watery, lids pouchy as blood blisters. "You got toothpaste on your chin," she told me. She wiped it off with her shirt, then gently wrapped her chilly hands around me, dug her face into my hair.

My nose was buried near her underarms, and I couldn't help noticing she smelled bad, like sour onions. The odor made me feel kind of miserable. I mean, as far as I remembered she'd never stunk before.

She held me for a few minutes, then made a promise. "You watch. We're going to be all right. We're going to do fine."

"Mom," I mumbled, choked up.

"We're going to have fun here. You'll see. We're gonna like it." She pushed my stringy bangs away with her nose and kissed my head, let me go. Turning her weepy eyes from me, she looked outside. "You and Ditch did a wonderful job out back. Stuck it all in the alley, huh?"

I looked over the table and down toward the backyard. "Two guys tore open the trash bags. That's why it's like that."

Junie looked around, her dress swirling above her flat, bound feet, calluses nearly up to her anklebones, like the plates on a turtle shell. She poked at bacon strips with a fork. "That always happens round here. Ditch shoulda known." She shook her head, speared a slab of bacon, and flopped it onto a plate with a paper towel draped over it.

"They stole a garbage can, too. I watched them do it."

Junie sampled her cooking, munched on a cooled bacon strip. "That's why you got to chain 'em down."

"It was chained."

She shrugged, chewing. "Must have been plastic. Am I right? Well, see, they say buy metal when yer in the city, hon."

the biggest geek in history
the biggest geek in history

The next day, a Monday, my mom, still looking frail and sleepy, took me to register for class at Robert Poole Middle School. Because we didn't know any better, we took a boxy city bus up to the Rotunda, got off, and walked nearly a mile, which wouldn't have been so bad except my mother had had trouble keeping her balance for that whole week. She staggered about, and it didn't matter what kind of shoes she had on. It was terrible, because I knew it had to do with the way she felt inside. I'd never seen her so uncoordinated. Also, Hampden, the neighborhood that Robert Poole Middle School is located in, is kind of a tough place. The people have been there so long that it's become a little community separate from the rest of Baltimore. It's rundown, angry, and suspicious. Once, my mom and I watched a Tom Cruise movie about a steel town, and the place reminded me of Hampden. Generally, they don't like blacks there, and it's normal for some of the guys to harass women, especially women who don't look like they belong. So my mom must have made a perfect target, worn-out and off balance like she was. After we turned the corner at Roland Avenue and Thirty-sixth Street, our heads down, these three young guys started taunting her. They followed us from Roland Avenue all the way down past Falls Road till we were less than a block from the school. It was horrible.

"*I'll* help ya walk, baby."

"Ya just need to stretch them legs of yers."

"Looks like ya just rolled outta the sack. Ya enjoy the sack?"

"Look at her. She ain't listening to ya. She thinks she's too good for ya."

"No way."

"Look at her."

"That ain't true, is it? Ten minutes, I'd show ya who's too good. Don't even know what good is, I bet."

Humiliated, I just wanted them to stop, to leave us alone. I wished I could have pummeled them like Thor or the Hulk. I imagined doing it, turning, grabbing them by the front of their black T-shirts, and tossing them through a crummy brick wall. I felt like it was my job to protect my mom since my dad was gone, but I couldn't do anything but hunch my shoulders and walk faster. I couldn't even help my mom walk, and she really needed the help.

At the corner of Falls Road, we had to wait for the light to turn. All sorts of cars whizzed by, and the three guys milled about a few feet behind us, by a blue stone bench chipped in a million places, with "Baltimore, the City That Reads" written on it in yellow letters. Desperate for the light to change, I searched down the hill, waited for a break in traffic so that we could bolt across. That's when I saw a BG&E sedan cruise off the Jones Falls Expressway. As it approached, a thrill leaped into my heart. I was positive that my father had returned to save the day. I searched through the bent, rowhome reflections on the slanted windshield as the car got bigger. I imagined that my dad would get closer and closer, then just whip the steering wheel to one side and plow the three guys over, just like that, without even blinking. I would have been so proud. I waited, counted on the maneuver. I kept thinking, "Do it!" But the car passed straight by. From the side, I caught sight of the driver, a man I'd never seen before in my life, a flat-nosed Asian guy. I almost fainted on the sidewalk, I was so let down. And the whole time, the taunts continued.

Across the street, I tried to give my mother some help by steadying her with a hand. We stumbled and tripped our way down the walkway as fast as we could. Then, finally, the school rose up to the right, just beyond a short strip of wooden rowhouses, crimped and twisted silver fences surrounding tiny, clean front yards. As we neared the edge of the parking lot, the guys behind us got bored. I heard them discuss leaving, then they did, just turned and left, headed back up the street to give someone else a hard time. I was so relieved that a sleepiness swept through me. I wanted to lie down between cars and stare up at the blue sky, dotted with pretty cotton-ball clouds.

"I hope those guys get run over," I told my mom as we approached the school steps.

She looked down at me, licked her frail, dry lips, scaly as snakeskin even with her makeup on. "You shouldn't wish that on anyone," she told me, grabbing the cold black railing to brace herself.

I looked over my shoulder, across the parking lot, and down the road we had come from, giant old American cars lining both sides. I was nervous, thinking the guys were waiting for her to pass by again. "I know," I admitted softly, but I still hoped they'd get hit by a big fast-moving eighteen-wheeler. I worried that they'd made my mom feel even worse, saying all those mean things. She seemed so fragile, like I could have hurt her, and I only came up to her shoulder blades. I was worried that she'd go home, lie down, and never rise again. My dad was gone, and my mom would be gone, too. That thought horrified me. Taking the gray stone steps, I got dizzy, hot, could barely breathe. Suddenly, the steps were as slick as ice, stretching off in a strange direction, a big slide. I leaned forward and unexpectedly banged my knee.

"Ouch!" I howled, then sat down, gasping in pain even though it didn't really hurt that much.

"Oh, honey," my mom said, stooping down to check on me. "You okay?"

Eyes watery with fear, I looked up at her. "Mom," I whispered, thinking that maybe if she waited for me I could protect her better than I had. "Mom, can you stay till the end of school? I want you to stay. Please," I begged. "Please." To buy some time, I rubbed my knee like it was still hurting.

"I wish I could," she told me, wobbled, lost her balance, and sat down with a thud beside me. She kept her legs together, like she was trying to hold a penny between her knees. "I gotta go to work. I gotta make some money so we can live."

"No you don't. We could stay with Ditch and Junie," I informed her in a whisper.

"We can't," she told me. "I've got to go."

I swallowed. "No," I croaked.

"I've got to," she repeated.

I didn't know what to say. She was going to leave me. Thick, gummy tears came into my eyes. "Well, don't go home, okay?" I mumbled. "Don't go home, Mom. Go straight to work. But don't pass by those guys again. Go some other way." I put my hand out and touched her bony knee.

She laughed sweetly. "I'll go down Falls Road," she said, "and I'll go straight to work."

"Go into a store if anyone bothers you again," I instructed.

"I will," she said, smiling sadly, standing like she was on stilts.

"Don't go to sleep again," I pleaded.

Her mouth bent out of shape at the corner, tugged downward toward one side of her chin, a lipstick smear. "I'm not gonna do that. I'm not tired anymore." She stood up, grasping the rail so tightly that the skin stretched like rubber across her knuckles. I could see the skinny blue blood vessels in her fingers. They made me love her with all my heart. "Now, come on, Samuel. We got to get you signed in." She held out her other hand, and sheepishly I took it.

I didn't want to be there. I wanted to be, of all places, back home in my new room, door shut and locked, G.I. Joe figures and their assorted vehicles scattered across the gritty floor and mattress. The teacher, Mr. Belcher, looked ridiculous, nearly causing me to crack up. He wore this white dress shirt that was so tight it clung to his soft, flabby body like a superhero costume. The way his belt cut him in half reminded me of a squeezed water balloon. Big smooth tires of fat hung over the leather strip and lumped up around his narrow rib cage, swollen spots. Even his sleeves were tight. You could see where his undershirt stopped halfway down his arms. His vinyl pocket protector, bristling with pens, pencils, and a tiny protractor, was wedged halfway out of his shirt pocket by the hump of his soft chest. I imagined that when he took off his clothes at night he was twice as fat, that his body popped free like a spring.

Mr. Belcher was going over long division, which I didn't really know and had no desire to. I worried about whether my mom had made it to work, whether she'd gone back to bed, about the kids around me who looked like they hated that I was there. I felt crummy except for when my eyes caught sight of Mr. Belcher shimmying about up front. My stomach even started gurgling, and I got scared that I might get sick. I kept swallowing, hoping to prevent it. Lunch was getting close, and I worried that it might push me right over the edge. It didn't help that the tiled halls had smelled like smooshy green beans and detergent for the last hour and a half. It was hot, too. Mr. Belcher didn't like to keep the windows open. He liked it warm, so that sweat beaded on his upper lip and drenched the underarms of his tight shirts. That entire fall, my head swam in his class.

"A pop quiz," Mr. Belcher suddenly declared with about fifteen minutes to go before the bell.

Most everyone groaned, the way hot water boils out of a radiator. Some kids cussed under their bad breath, rolled their pink eyes, and pouted.

Mr. Belcher placed a hunk of chalk down on the little shelf below the big green board, numbers scrawled across it like Egyptian writing. He walked similar to a robot, arms just barely bent, back to his gray metal desk. He found a stack of papers and counted them, then handed a bunch to the first student in each row, who took one, then passed the rest back. It was too much. My stomach suddenly leaped, then spasmed uncontrollably.

I raised my hand.

Mr. Belcher, neck bulging at the collar of his shirt, lifted his eyes, lids thin slabs of clay, to see me. "Don't worry, Mr. Webber, I don't expect you to take this."

My stomach was too far gone to care. Saliva gushed into my mouth, flooding around my gums. "Can I go to the bathroom?" I asked in response.

He observed me, his thick mouth slack, like I'd insulted him. "I don't know," he replied.

I stared back, horrified, ready to lose it on my pale desktop and on the girl in front of me, whose long straight hair fell across the first few inches of the tattered math book I'd just been assigned.

"Can you?" he asked, studying me, papers tucked in the crook of an arm.

"Yeah," I mumbled thickly, answering his question.

"No," he said. "I realize that you can, but that's not the way one properly phrases a question, Mr. Webber."

I glanced around me, begging for an answer to Mr. Belcher's riddle. Then it came to me. It was the oldest trick in the book. "May I go?" I howled.

[33]

"The bathroom pass is on my desk, young man," he said patiently, and continued handing out the quizzes.

I rose from my chair slowly, trying to look calm. At Mr. Belcher's desk, I tucked the bathroom pass under one arm and headed out the door. In the hallway, away from watchful eyes, I broke into a jog, rounded the corner, and searched desperately for a boys' room. My vision was hazy. My feet felt distant and numb, like they'd both been asleep or submerged in a bucket of ice water. Panting, stomach pushing at the back of my throat, I became more and more desperate. Finally, after three long corridors, teachers grunting and groaning stuff in each class, I found the bathroom.

I hit the heavy wooden door with my hands extended, ran across the tiled floor, fell to my knees in front of a white commode, barfed into the clear water. A continuous flood erupted from me till I didn't have anything left in my stomach, till it tightened into a knot. Mouth open, yuck lacing my lips like milk, I slumped down, leaned against the partition, and closed my eyes to catch my breath. Then the janitor walked in, a large black man with a slow gait.

I stared at him in horror.

His big, bulging eyes, cue balls, took me in. "Y'all right?" he asked me after a moment, pulling a giant gray garbage can on wheels through the door. He let it go, and it rolled to a stop by the sinks.

I couldn't speak.

"Look like you got sick?" He sounded like he had cotton balls in his mouth forcing him to speak slowly.

I climbed from my knees, head still woozy, and grasped the toilet paper dispenser, this big silver box, so the room wouldn't start circling.

He tromped over and looked into the toilet. "You're sick," he said to me. A bunch of dark plastic bags stuck out of one of his back pockets. On his head was a Chevron gas station baseball cap. Beneath it, his kinky hair was black and gray, his craggy, brown skin dotted with thick whiskers and acne scars. "You want me to take you down to the nurse's office?" he asked.

I swallowed. "No," I muttered.

He wore a blue work shirt with a white oval on one side for his name. Nothing had been written in the space, though. "Yer sure?" he asked me.

"Yes, sir," I managed weakly.

He nodded, studied my face. "School started two weeks ago. Ain't seen you round here."

"I'm new, today," I mumbled, picked up the hall pass, and started for the door.

"Hey," he said.

I turned.

"You didn't flush the toilet. That ain't my job."

I breathed in, skirted around him, and pushed the cold, wet silver knob down. Water burst into the basin, swirled, a wave, then rushed down the hole in the bottom.

"All right," he said. He tilted his old head, scratched the bottom of his heavy chin. "You still don't look too good."

I nodded, turned, and started for the door again.

"You got throwup round your mouth," he called after me, but I just kept going, too embarrassed to wash my face in front of him. I did it at a water fountain, instead. I scrubbed it with my hands, wiped it dry with my forearm. Then, stomach like a fist, mouth sour, I stumbled down the foul-smelling hall, stopped, and studied the empty corridor. I turned around and looked in the other direction. Everything was exactly the same. I checked the big bathroom pass I was carrying, thinking that it might have a room number on it, but it didn't. On top of everything that had happened, I was lost. There wasn't even a teacher wandering around in search of delinquent kids.

I shuffled over to the gouged and bent lockers, looked at the rusty numbers hoping that they might tell me something. They didn't. I looked at the tiled floor in an effort to recall a landmark, something I could use to find my way back, but nothing came to me. I sighed weakly, turned a little, and rested my cheek on a cold locker door. I wondered where the one I'd been assigned that morning was. The number was written on one of the pieces of paper a lady in the office had given me to start school, and that was on my desk in flabby Mr. Belcher's class.

I twisted around and put my other cheek against the metal. It was a horrible day. To start, the guys in Hampden had taunted us. Then it had turned out that Robert Poole Middle School didn't have a bookstore, like my mom had thought they would, so I had to start class without note-books, pencils, binders, and other sorts of stuff. Standing in the office that morning, she'd been nearly as embarrassed as me. Eyes wide, she promised to fix the problem after work, but I was stuck carrying around a few scraps of yellow stationery that a secretary had given me, while everybody else had brand-new Mead organizers, book bags, and plastic rulers. It must have looked like we were so poor we couldn't afford any-thing. I shook my head. All of that was bad, but it wasn't as bad as getting sick in the bathroom, and that wasn't as outright horrible as getting lost. Getting lost was the worst. People would think I was the biggest geek in history, and they would be right. *I* even thought I was a geek.

Leaning against those lockers covered in bumpy blue paint, I slumped forward and stared down at my feet, at the sneakers I'd got-ten on a shopping trip with my father the previous winter. Whatever excitement I'd had about meeting new people, starting middle school, was completely gone.

"You lost now?"

I looked up, horrified, and gawked at the janitor, his Chevron cap with fingerprints across the bill.

"You can't just stand round in the hall. You got to go back to class if you ain't going to the nurse's office."

I couldn't speak. I tried to, but nothing came out of my mouth except a thin squeak of air.

"Where you s'posed to be?" He leaned down and picked up a wad of paper, squeezed it in his big hands, tossed it into his garbage can on wheels, which now had a big push broom jammed in it, black bristles up, a giraffe.

"Mr. Belcher's class," I barely managed.

"Mr. Belcher's class." He nodded, a blasé look on his face. "Come on. I'll show you where it is, 'fore you get into trouble."

I fell in beside him. He didn't walk fast like Ditch did. I actually had to slow down for him. After about ten feet, he pulled the garbage can around and pushed it in front of him, which allowed him to go a little faster, but not much. The little wheels beneath the bin spun quietly across the smooth floors.

"Feeling better?" he asked me, without looking down.

"I guess," I told him.

"You looking better. Don't look so green round the gills no more," he said, and his lids, like bat wings, pulled shut over his eyes, then rose gently as if he was peering around them.

One more turn and he stopped, brought his worn boots, brown and wrinkled as discarded paper bags, up under him, and rested a hand on the lip of the gray can. The other adjusted his hat. "Ain't supposed to wear a cap inside," he told me, like I'd said something about it. "I know that, but I don't have no one to impress. That's what I tell the teachers whenever they say they wished I'd take it off."

I nodded.

He pointed at a door down the hall. "That's it, the room you was looking for. Won't embarrass you. Go on. Maybe he didn't even know you was missing. He don't notice much sometimes, being a bit odd and all." He turned, drawing the wheeled garbage can around with him.

"Thanks," I murmured at his wide back.

*　*　*

A woman from the office found me at the end of the school day, escorted me up to the bus stop on the corner of Thirty-sixth Street and Falls Road. We stopped beside the bench with "Baltimore, the City That Reads" written on it, not two feet from where those guys had bothered my mom and me that morning.

"This is where you'll catch the bus in the afternoons. You'll ride the Forty-two Downtown. Any questions?"

I shook my head.

"You'll catch the Forty-two Falls Road on Charles Street in the mornings. Okay?"

I nodded.

"Good," she declared. "Well, it's nice to have you at Robert Poole Middle School, Mr. Webber. I'm sure you'll make friends before you know it." As she walked away, she waved, her hand flapping back and forth behind a clump of curly reddish hair and the pink shoulder of her coffee-stained blouse.

I stood a little apart from the other kids, held my plastic-coated bus pass in one hand, the blazing yellow sheets of paper in the other. We were there for about ten minutes before a big blue-and-white city bus pulled up.

The bus cruised about half a mile down Falls Road, made a slow wide turn onto Forty-first Street, creaking and groaning, tinted windows nearly popping from their frames, and started up the steep hill toward the Rotunda Shopping Center. I felt like a grownup, traveling alone like I was. I was momentarily thrilled to be making my own way, something my father had never let me do. At the top of the hill, where my mother and I had started our walk that morning, three hollering, excited kids, two girls and a boy with an eye patch, stumbled down the bus steps.

We drifted past the Rotunda, the Giant Supermarket stuck on the side, and rumbled down the long hill, through the southwestern edge of fancy Roland Park, onto University Parkway, up a hill, and past the Johns Hopkins lacrosse field. Kids hopped out at various stops, and eventually the bus turned south onto St. Paul. Along with four other Robert Poole Middle School students, I climbed off opposite the line of stores that included Junie's Florist. The other kids didn't even look at me before running across the road, disappearing into the broad blocks of Charles Village. Like an old man, I stood there and watched as my new neighborhood, glowing a delicate reddish brown, appeared to gather them in and guard them with the hunched shoulders of old rowhomes, so many eyes. Then I turned and saw the back of the bus just as it disappeared over the hill, on its way downtown.

I waited for a wave of traffic to whistle by, then shuffled across the street, along the sidewalk, and up the steps to Junie's Florist. My mom was cleaning out the big glass refrigerators with flowers in them, wiping them down with a peanut-shaped yellow sponge that was twice as big as her hand. Junie was on the phone, talking to a friend about a television show. She smiled at me. The older man, Mr. Oritz, who worked when Ditch did other things, was outside, in the little garage where they sold shrubs and bedding plants, like petunias and stuff. It had once been a little driveway between buildings, but Junie'd gotten permission to put a roof on it and close it off. Ditch had welded together the sign above the gate. It was made out of old pipes, but you couldn't tell because it looked so good. It said JUNIE'S GARDEN SUPPLIES and had big bags of dirt and pine bark stacked beneath it, against the inside of the fence. Mr. Oritz, with his little shrunken face and hands like frying pans, watered and arranged the plants while my mom and Junie held down the fort inside.

"Mom," I said.

She looked over her shoulder at me, then stood. "How was your day, sweetheart?" The skin around her eyes was crinkled, puffy. Her bright red smock sagged over her like a wet pillowcase.

I swallowed. "It was okay," I told her.

She wobbled, leaned against the glass refrigerator door with a thin shoulder. "Just okay?" she asked, trying to sound worried instead of tired.

I nodded, looking at the papers in my hand. I decided not to tell her that I'd been embarrassed about not having any supplies. "I got sick," I explained to her, cupping my hand so that Junie couldn't hear what I said. "Then I got lost in the hallway, and the janitor had to show me back to class."

She gnawed on her bottom lip. "You got sick again?" she said.

"Uh-huh."

"What got you sick, do you think?" She pushed some hair off of her face.

"I thought I was going to have to take a pop quiz in math, even though I didn't know anything. Also, the halls stunk."

She smiled, mouth pulling back, lighting up her face, which had been pretty before my dad disappeared. "The halls stunk?"

I dropped my hand, couldn't help grinning back. "Like mushy food. It was from the cafeteria."

"Well, no wonder you got sick, Samuel." She touched a palm against one of my cheeks. It was cold and damp from the sponge, clammy.

I looked at the floor, decided not to say that no one else had thrown up, at least as far as I knew.

"You want to get a Coke at the Waverly Deli?" she asked me.

Sometimes she knew just how to make me feel better. I nodded, backbone tingling.

"You could get your school supplies, too, at the Dime Store, if you want."

I shot a look up at her, stunned that she expected me to get them there. I'd been hoping that we'd take the bus up to the Rotunda and buy them at the Rite Aid, where I knew they'd have everything I wanted. The Dime Store down the street didn't sell name brands, so they wouldn't stock Mead organizers, which was the binder I'd wanted.

"Here's ten dollars," my mom said, reaching into a pants pocket and finding a crumpled bill. "Get whatever you need, and a Coke at the deli, too."

I nodded, but I knew ten dollars wouldn't put a dent in the number of supplies I'd been hoping to buy. My father had always given me twenty dollars to start the year.

"Something wrong?" she asked me.

I shook my head, pivoted, and started for the door.

My mom called to me, "Can you get me and Junie a Coke, too?"

"Okay," I told her, even more depressed.

I got home about an hour later. My hands were so full that I stabbed the frame twice before hitting the keyhole. I stepped in and stood quiet and surprised in the hallway with its high ceiling and old rectangular windows directly above the tall doorways. It was kind of nice and comfortable, aglow and silent in the dwindling golden light from my mom's room to the left. To the right, the kitchen and my room were soaked in a soft blue gray, the closet and bathroom straight ahead dark and hazy, almost swirling. Slowly, I looked down at the bag in one of my hands. I'd been able to get three folders, a package of pencils, two hundred pages of looseleaf paper, and a big spiral notebook with a blue cloth cover and a tiny pocket on the inside. In that store of dustiness and cobwebs, I'd done better than I thought I would, worse than years past.

I stood in our hallway for more than ten minutes. It was so soothing and peaceful I didn't want to move, cause it to go away. It was the first time I felt good about our apartment, felt like it could be OK. The colors slowly tinted darker, shifting in silent, steady change.

Eventually, I turned and walked into my small room, kneeled, and settled onto my mattress, twisted so that I could stare at the shadowy walls. Lying there, I began to wonder about all the people before me who'd witnessed dusk come to that house, and something inside me shook. I felt like one small bit of a living neighborhood, a part of something that could feel hard or welcoming, like a person.

drowning
drowning

Catching the bus after school started getting me down. I'd never taken one with any consistency before because, like I said, my dad had always picked me up when the day was over. So, rambling for home on the floaty, moaning city bus began to remind me that he was gone, that I'd become responsible for my own well-being. Staggering off onto the sidewalk along St. Paul Street, I sometimes felt like my head had been pushed into a muddy bog. I didn't want to go home, and I didn't want to hang out around Junie's. I really didn't know what I wanted to do. I missed my father so much sometimes that it confused me.

After school, when I felt all right, I spent time in the rectangular dirt patch out behind our apartment, playing with my G.I. Joe figures, kicking around among the tufts of grass that looked like sprigs of blond hair, like scalps scattered about. I lugged aircraft, a few land vehicles, and a handful of tiny men down the fire escape in a beige plastic grocery bag from the Giant, sides bulging like a potato sack. Then I removed my toys, careful not to snap off a plastic missile or a brittle gun barrel. I never had to think of a scenario. Wild stories just

[43]

fell together. From week to week, month to month, only one thing remained the same, my character. Whichever tiny figure I chose to be me—the frogman, the Army Ranger, the fighter pilot—he was always fearless, strong, and intelligent, a natural leader, a hero. He was different from the real me in every way, but I never thought about that.

When it rained, I drew intricate pictures of superheroes or sword fighters, read comic books and stories. When I felt bad, a zombie, I watched television, sat in the warm woolly-smelling hall closet, let shows pour over me. I didn't care what was on as long as there was something: Oprah yammering to someone about a sex problem, the early news live at the site of a shooting spree across town. It was like I wasn't there.

Two afternoons a week, no matter what kind of mood I was in, I helped out at Junie's Florist. I worked outside in the garden center. I straightened things, watered, and at first, pulled weeds from around plants. I wasn't very good at that, though. I had trouble identifying the plants and the weeds. Even still, my mom or Ditch or Mr. Oritz found me things to do, and I kind of liked doing them, getting tired and dirty. I even thought I amazed people with my strength, my ability to lug a bag of lime ten feet. Also, Junie paid me pretty generously, fifteen dollars a week. I stowed the cash in a drawer in my room, bought comic books and new G.I. Joe action figures with it.

On Saturdays, when I was home and my mother was at Junie's, I met her for lunch at the Waverly Deli. My favorite thing to eat there was a St. Pauly, this English muffin sandwich with egg, ham, and a bright yellow square of American cheese hung over the top, similar to a stiff blanket. Grease usually puddled around it like gooey engine fluid, soaking into the bottom of the muffin so that it was soggy in my hands. As we ate, we talked. Sometimes my mother actually seemed normal again.

"What should we do tonight?" she'd usually ask me, teeth working over a rubbery slice of corned beef, made from big hunks that floated in warm brown water for what seemed like days. You could look in at them from behind a steamy glass window along the counter, like they were supposed to be appetizing. They didn't do anything for me, bobbing up and down like logs. They must have excited my mom, though, because she always ordered the corned beef sandwich.

"We could go to a mall or something," was my usual answer. We'd done that every so often when my father was around. We'd drive out to Security Square Mall and eat at the Wendy's or the Roy Rogers, then just walk around, soaking up the thrill. My mom and I had gone out that way a few times, but I could tell that she never really loved doing it. I couldn't understand why, because to me there was a magnetism to malls, even a sort of excitement in the creepy nighttime bus rides back to Charles Village, Baltimoreans gently swaying as if they were glued to their plastic seats, as if their spines were made of Jell-O.

"Yeah, I guess we could," she'd mumble, almost sleepy. "You know, we could just rent a movie and VCR, make popcorn or something?"

"Mom," I'd sputter. "No, please. Let's just go somewhere," I'd beg. "Anywhere."

Around the third week in October, when Baltimore was going bald, the few trees in Charles Village losing their leaves, exposing limbs that appeared to be a tangle of barbed wire and browned laundry cord, my mom didn't get up. It was on a school day, and I begged her to crawl from the snarl of her floral bed sheets, but she wouldn't budge. Lids heavy, lips the color of orange china, thin as nails, she instructed me to fix myself breakfast, then if she still wasn't up, to head off for the bus stop.

I ate a bowl of cereal in the kitchen, stomach leaping, burping, and squawking like my heart. I stared at the walls of the bay window, damp paint curling away from the wavy sheets of plywood. Outside, litter skipped down the blowing alleyway; small leaves, yellow and red, twisted in wind devils. Oily water, slicks of blue, dribbled

[45]

beneath the garbage cans, gurgled around the bottoms. The sky was dark and moving fast. The pigeons on the arching wires leading to the bottom of the bay window were hunched up, reminding me of used Brillo pads.

Before leaving, I begged my mom to rise, but she wouldn't. She said she was exhausted, more worn-out than she'd ever been in her whole life.

"I'm tired, too," I said.

"I know, honey," she moaned, lifting a limp arm to touch my cheek. "Go on. You'll miss the bus."

Leaving, I slammed the door to our apartment as hard as I could, making the patchy walls shake. I practically hated her for falling apart again. Stumbling down the steps, into the hallway, then out the front door, my head swirled, my legs and feet felt awkward and unsure, my stomach ached painfully. A few heavy globs of rain pelted me as I made my way toward Charles Street. Then tears started down my face, opaque and thick with salt.

In English, my first class, Mrs. Sporely, a tiny black woman with a crippled hand, read S. E. Hinton's *The Outsiders* at the front of the room. She leaned against her large metal desk, one of her fragile legs thrown over a corner. She had a pretty voice, deep and strong despite her little body. Normally, I loved to hear her read, especially from that book, so suspenseful and tough I borrowed it from the library, burning through it twice, wishing I could be good, brave Pony Boy—the guy it was about. But I was in another world that day, feeling sorry for myself. Waves of sadness, like warm air, beat softly against my brain, drowning me slowly but sweetly. It almost felt nice.

When the bell rang, I was the last person out the door. Moving slowly, I moped down the hallway, a half-slouch arching my narrow back like an old person's. As I walked, books on my hips, I kept close to the lockers. Halfway down the corridor, I turned and shoved open the bathroom door with a slumped shoulder.

Plopping my books on a sink, I scooted up to a urinal. Behind me, a toilet flushed and a skinny black kid banged open a stall, walked over, and grabbed his stuff. He turned, headed for the exit, pushed the door open with a thump. For a moment, noises from the hallway ricocheted off the bathroom's hard walls, fading as the door closed on squeaking hinges. Someone else entered, crossed the smelly room on rubbery soles, slapped a worn, wire-bound notebook next to my stuff.

I looked over and quickly turned away. I stared blankly a foot or two in front of me, at the grungy wall, at the graffiti written with blunt pencils. It was Newt Novacek. He terrified me. He wasn't the worst bully in school by a long shot, but he was probably the ugliest. At thirteen, two years older than most sixth graders, he wasn't exactly small, either. He even had body hair. Short, wilted curls sagged out of the top of his oil-stained heavy-metal T-shirts, continued up his neck to the first fold of his double chin. Standing in the lunch line with Newt, even if five or six kids separated us, had always scared me. I'd made a point of staying as far away from him as I could.

I listened as he struck a match and ignited a cigarette.

"Ya going to tell on me?" Newt slurred, then drew in on his Winston.

Zipping up as fast as I could, I stammered, "N . . . no."

"Ya seem like the type ta squeal." He leaned casually against a sink, jiggly stomach pushing at his already stretched shirt like he'd swallowed a load of gerbils. On the front of it was a screen print of a screaming skeleton with a long wispy ponytail.

I flushed the commode.

"Bet yer gonna tell," he said, voice choppy, body nearly as wide as high.

I didn't reply.

He looked down, by his blobby hip, past the flaring top of his jeans. "These yers?" he asked, pointing at my books, delicately balanced on the lip of the sink.

I nodded weakly.

[47]

He pushed them onto the floor, gave the pile a kick.

"Runt," he said, frowning, wispy, pale mustache above a wide mouth, like a pushed-in roll of clay. His teeth were as square as Chiclets, stained brown. He blew smoke out of his flaring nostrils. "Yer trying ta git me suspended, ain't ya?"

I stared at my stuff on the floor.

"Pick it up," he said, waving a plump hand in front of him. An ash fluttered from the tip of his cigarette.

Nervous, I dropped to my knees, pulled my scattered books toward me, the rumpled sheets of lined paper with superhero drawings scrawled across them, some class notes, and half-completed homework.

Newt bent and scooted the pile I was putting together around with a square foot, leaving wet impressions on my cheap school supplies. "Whatcha gonna do 'bout it?" he asked me.

I was so humiliated, I felt like dying. "I'm not going to tell," I swore to him, wishing more than anything he'd stop. As embarrassing as my no-name school supplies were, I felt ashamed that I couldn't protect the stuff from the big clod.

The sole of his black tennis shoe brushed the top of my hand and left a sticky splotch across my knuckles. "Ha," he huffed, a leering smile on his pale, zit-covered face.

Behind me, the bathroom door creaked open.

Newt's foot stopped.

"What's going on in here?"

I closed my eyes, humiliation beating across my shoulders. I felt like such a wimp.

"Helping 'im pick up his stuff," Newt said. "Fell offa the sink."

"Don't look like you helping to me."

I peered over my shoulder, took in the Chevron cap, the work shirt with its blank white oval over a breast pocket, the brown face.

"Maybe it don't," Newt said.

"It don't."

"Nope. Maybe I ain't."

"I bet." The janitor rubbed his face with his hand. "That a cigarette between your fingers?"

"Whatcha think it is?"

The bell rang out in the hallway. On top of everything, I was late for class.

"Against the rules to smoke in school."

"So?" the bully said, backing up a little.

"We going to hafta head down to the office, you don't put that thing out."

"You ain't taking me down there," Newt told him, drawing in on the Winston, ash glowing a defiant fire orange.

The janitor stepped forward, wrapping callused fingers around one of Newt's arms.

Newt struggled, his soft muscles mashed like a squeezed pillow by the janitor's grip. By mistake, he dropped his cigarette to the floor, and one of the janitor's feet stretched out and crushed it.

The janitor effortlessly pulled fat Newt forward, next to him, where he towered over the pudgy boy. "We going to the office," he said.

"What's yer problem?" Newt howled.

"I'm the one has to fish cigarette butts outta the toilet. I been fishing butts for years, and I'm tired of it. Show me some respect." He gave Newt a tug toward the door.

Newt bucked back and forth, but he couldn't break the old man's grip. His sneakers wouldn't hold on the gritty floor tiles, either. He looked over a round shoulder, eyes like knife slits, lips curled back, exposing blackened, sore gums. "You're dead," he spat at me. "You're dead," he hollered as the bathroom door shut behind him and the janitor escorted him down the hall to the office.

[49]

Shaking, I gathered my scattered books and stuff, papers wrinkling from shallow lakes of water. I couldn't believe he blamed me for getting dragged off to see the principal. I hadn't done anything. I was the victim. My head whirled. In all likelihood, Newt was going to pound me to death. Maybe he'd burn my eyes out with the tip of a smoldering cigarette. I started hyperventilating. The world was filled with injustice, stuffed like a scorched Thanksgiving turkey. The ones against me were the worst of all, though. Since the day my dad was gone, I saw my life rolling down one of those corkscrew slides in a public park, like a leaf twisting down slowly from a high branch.

Lightheaded, sorry for myself, I clambered to my feet, wet books soaking into my shirt. I tried to pull myself together. There was a *plop plop plop* sound as tears landed on the wrinkled, white leather of one of my dirty sneakers. I wiped at my face, my nose. "Ah, ah," I clucked like a baby, wondering what would happen when I got to class late. I'd probably get in-school suspension, get tossed into the same room with Newt.

After a few sorry minutes, I banged through the heavy bathroom door, lurched into the empty hall, my lids puffy and tight. The first nauseating smells from the cafeteria were filling the school, and they took my breath away. I cupped a hand over my nose till I could get used to them, bent forward, legs stiff, knees wet from kneeling in front of Newt. I rounded a corner, tripped, and stumbled over my own feet. I turned another, and there, in front of the dark, stained cement steps, was a teacher doing hall duty. She was sitting at a miniature desk, grading papers.

She looked at me, cold and irate like a rabid raccoon I once saw with my dad out at Loch Raven Reservoir. A bunch of animal-control officers had jammed the raccoon into a cage, and he'd somehow squeezed a clawed arm through the grillwork so as to take swipes at their hands. He even gnawed at the metal mesh with his needle teeth. "I hope you got a pass," she said.

I stared at her, dumb. I'd been thinking that I'd get in trouble when I got to class, not before.

She smiled wickedly. "Didn't think you did. What's your name?" Her spinsterly blond hair was tied up in a bun, a crash helmet if there'd been a stripe down the middle. Her back was as stiff as a pole.

"Uh." I balked, clearing my tight throat. "Little Sam Webber," I rasped, sputtering like a voice coming through one of those old, hand-held radios. "Sam, I mean."

As she rose, I imagined a long skinny bug. "Come on," she muttered. "We're going to take a little trip to the office."

"But," I said, "I didn't do anything."

"Is that what you think walking the hallway without a pass is? Well, it *is* something, I'll tell you that." Her heavy, faded skirt was covered with white fuzz. It bumped the back of her meatless calves, tendons sharp as cuts. She tucked her papers in her arms and started down the hall.

For a fleeting second, I considered running.

She turned. "Don't you dare," she hissed.

I weaved after her like a prisoner of war, a boy heading for the gas chamber.

She held the office door open for me, yellowed eyes wide, whirling. Entering, I almost bumped into the janitor.

He was on his way out. He stopped. He looked at me, looked at the teacher. "Whatcha doing with him?" he asked.

"This young man was walking the halls without a pass, Mr. Clemons." The polished wood door closed behind her, framed her scary face.

He nodded, twisted his mouth around so that it didn't look like a mouth anymore. His lips sprang back to normal. "Well, Mrs. Worlach, I don't usually butt into this kind of affair, but I got an explanation for that. He was gettin' roughed up in the boy's room." Mr. Clemons adjusted his Chevron cap. "That's what I'm doing here. Boy nearly twice his size'd kicked his books across the floor." He pointed at me with a finger that looked like a bent twig. "I come into the bathroom and this guy's on his knees trying to collect his things. Bell rung while I was sorting it all out. I meant to take him to class, but I forgot in all the excitement. Had to drag the other kid down here." He looked at the teacher to see if she understood.

"I only know that he was wandering the halls without permission."

"That's what I'm saying. He's late 'cause he was getting picked on."

I dropped my head.

Aggravated, the teacher sucked on her tongue.

"Come on. It ain't his fault."

The office workers were watching us from behind their desks. The pale old woman whose job it was to punish disorderly kids stood with her pencil and pad watching the whole affair. The assistant principal came out of his frosted-glass office to see what was going on. Door open, I spotted Newt's big, gnarled head, his sides that looked like soft mounds of mashed potatoes. I worried that he'd turn and see me, think that I was squealing on him. I put Mr. Clemons between us by moving sideways a little.

Mrs. Worlach's mouth puckered in anger. Her fingers fluttered. She rolled her eyes. "People wonder why discipline is so bad in schools. It's because we don't enforce anything. We're always making exceptions. All right, fine. Then, take him, Mr. Clemons." She peered down at me, her nose watering with hatefulness. She slashed at it with an arm of her blue sweater.

In the hallway, Mr. Clemons asked me where I was supposed to be.

"History," I said quietly, looking at the pits in his face. "Mrs. Jackson's class on the third floor."

We walked slowly side by side down the hall. Just like before, I had to concentrate to not leave him behind. He was so slow. Looking over at him, I noticed that he had a slight limp.

He glanced at me, raised his funny eyebrows, rubbed his prickly, unshaven face. "She nearly scared you to death, didn't she?" He laughed.

"Yeah," I whispered, a smile starting to light my face.

"She's a scary woman," he said.

My day kept getting worse. I ran into Mrs. Worlach on my way to the cafeteria after math, and she stopped me, put both hands on my shoulders, and gave me this look like she wanted to skin me alive. I couldn't even eat after that, and one of the things they were serving was bad hamburgers, practically the only meal they made that I could actually stomach. By the time gym class arrived, I heard that Newt was looking for me. Somehow, a rumor had gotten around that I'd kicked him in the balls, and infuriated, he was going to do the same thing to me, only worse.

"I didn't kick him," I told a couple of kids, but they didn't care. They wanted to see blood. Obviously, they didn't know me very well, because I wasn't about to give them anything to watch. I was nearly positive that Newt Novacek would crush me if I let him.

By the time classes were finally over, I was exhausted, sick of Robert Poole Middle School in every way, but I didn't want to go home. Even though the school day had been terrible, it hadn't been bad enough to make me forget how it had started, my mom moping in bed, unable to climb from her sheets.

Staggering up to the bus stop, past the different rowhouses of Hampden, by the community center where the young unemployed boys in the area played basketball in the afternoons, crowds of kids moved past me. Some of them cattle-called about a fight between me and Newt, but I tried to close my ears. I held my chin against my skinny chest, watched my shoes as they swung in and out of my vision, as other shoes strode past. I wondered where I'd go, what I could do for the rest of the day. If I hadn't left all my money at home, I could have bought a few comic books and hung out at the Waverly Deli till dark, drunk their syrupy Coke till my bladder nearly exploded. But I didn't have any cash. I was stuck.

At Falls Road, I stopped for the light, waited for cars to scoot by, examined the filling between the cement segments in the sidewalk. I was thinking that it looked like cardboard when someone behind me said, "Newt's waiting for you across the street." Immediately, my head popped up. My eyes beaded in on his face leering like a giant Pac-Man beside the bus stop bench. Without giving it a second thought, I took off running. My books bounced at my side as I passed other students on their way home. Glancing across the street, I saw Newt parallel to me, pounding along the sidewalk. I knew he couldn't keep up. If there was one thing I was, it was fast. He started falling back, and I wasn't going as fast as I could. My small legs skittered quicker than his shaky ham bones could dream of going. I put some distance between us, ran clear up to Forty-first Street, turned, and gasped up the hill, past the Royal Farms and the old shutdown dairy till I was at the Rotunda. I ran in, stood around in the ancient halls and caught my breath. Then a security man walked by a few times before asking me to leave.

It took me nearly an hour to walk to Charles Village, but I wasn't moving fast. I passed by Junie's close to four, tramped into the neighborhood, by ritzy, beautiful places without a single bent board and their trim painted bright colors. I passed some plain rowhouses that Johns Hopkins students rented, and a terrible one, too. It was dilapidated, like the crushed husk of a peanut shell, bedroom walls smudged with handprints, empty windowpanes stuffed closed with discolored fabric, old plaid curtains. I passed a tidy Formstone garage, brushed a hand against the sculpted concrete.

On Abel Avenue, I decided I didn't want to go inside. I plopped myself down on the high curb across the street, gazing at the front of our building, which I realized was in a lot better shape than the back, almost handsome. The wood was kind of a bizarre color, an old-fashioned—or what looked old-fashioned—tint, the same brown as antique photographs. It wasn't pretty, but it wasn't altogether ugly, either. It was sad, a quiet, relaxing type of sad, a sad that draws people out for soothing conversations. Not a real sad, but a good one. My mom and I never did that sort of thing anymore, though, talked. I wished that wasn't the case. I wished that we would sit outside together, drinking Coke or Kool-Aid, and talk about everything like we had before.

Above the porch roof, like a flat forehead, was the bay window. It was actually three windows that spanned nearly the entire width of the second floor. At the top of each was a stained glass design, a colorful flower with skinny petals. It seemed homely but nice to me, reassuring. Also, all the houses down the street had the same bay window, all with the same design at the top. I wondered if the people who had built the row had thought that all the residents would be exactly alike, have identical tastes. If they had, they were wrong. As a matter of fact, our old neighbors in Rodger's Forge, where all the homes were unique, had much more in common with one another. In Charles Village, the residents were all kind of peculiar. Hairstyles were different. Clothing was different. Everyone did something weird for a living. I ached for our old neighbors, people who had enough time on their hands to meddle in our business, to ask if we'd gotten any news about my father.

Staring down the street, what bothered me was that there were so many people, all of us unimportant. I hated that, that we were all unknown, that even our homes were alike. I worried that my mom might never get out of bed, and that no one cared because people had their own lives on their minds, maybe their own mothers who wouldn't rise, fathers who had disappeared. I wasn't sure I could take that kind of thing for too long. I wanted everyone to know how bad things were for us, for me, and to sympathize, to rally to help like they had when a baby had been whisked down Jones Falls on an inner tube. A three-year-old floating under the city had stirred everyone, but my situation didn't cause anybody to even bat an eye. It didn't seem right.

A fine sprinkle fell from the sky, but I stayed where I was, books beside me, let the misty drops coat my hair, soak into my jacket. Off in the distance, I heard the familiar rumble and clank of our neighbor's van. It sounded like a tank rattling along, but it was really just an old mail truck he sold snowballs and hot dogs from. I'd never had one of his treats, and I never wanted one. The slogan on the white, scratched, and rusty sides was DOGS KIDS LOVE TO BITE. Painted below it was a crummy cartoon of a smiling black kid, mouth open, a dachshund ready to slide in, head, legs, and all. The thing is, the neighbor was an ugly man, not the type of guy you wanted to buy food from. He gave me the creeps. He was big and tall with red frizzy hair and crimson canker sores across his chin. He made me wish that everyone who handled food looked like those actors in McDonald's ads, clean and happy. But when I first got to Charles Village, no one seemed that way.

Above the grumbling engine, I heard a door slam. I glanced toward our apartment, and there was my mom, tall and lean, with a nice white shirt on, clean jeans, her hair brushed. She walked down the steps, across the sidewalk, and onto the leaf-strewn road. She got up to me, turned, and sat down just as the neighbor with the mail truck pulled slowly around the corner of Thirty-second Street. She didn't say anything until he cut the noisy engine, until he'd drifted into a spot down the block, between two total jalopies.

"What're you doing out here?" she asked me softly.

I had to try not to smile, I was so glad to see her awake. "Looking," I said.

She wrapped an arm around me. "It's raining, you know?"

I glanced at her, her soft face. I squinted and realized that she was a pretty lady. "I know," I mumbled, turned, and gazed down at the asphalt.

"I told you I wouldn't leave you again. You should trust me. I wouldn't do it."

I nodded without looking. "Didn't seem that way this morning."

She tightened her grip around me, squeezed me nicely. "I really was tired, though. I've been going and going and going, nonstop, all fall."

I guess her pace had seemed normal to me, but I didn't say that. I was forgetting how things had been, how much slower we had moved. "Are you feeling better?" I mumbled.

"Yeah," she said, "except for worrying about you."

I was quiet for a minute or two. Then I asked, "You worried about me?" just to hear her say it again.

"Of course," she said. "You nerd; you're the most important thing in the world to me."

Smiling, I told her, "School was terrible today."

"Was it?" She laughed, wrapping a bony hand in one of mine. She stood, drew me after her. "What happened?" she inquired as we started across Abel Avenue, headed for our apartment. Before going through the front door, though, I got her to sit on the porch and listen to my stories. I told her everything—about Newt, the horrible teacher, and the janitor who had saved me. Sitting there, swaying back and forth in those half-rusted, forest green metal chairs that no one ever used, I thought it was wonderful—one of the best hours of my entire life. My mom was back to normal, back to being pretty and interested again. The long row across the street gleamed as if scrubbed and reorganized by professional cleaners, lacquered pleasantly by the gentle rain. I even ignored my wet butt and the cool air that made me shiver, made my skin look like the pink belly of a saltwater fish. I felt awfully lucky to be her son.

a plane could fall

a plane could fall

When I told my mom that Newt Novacek reminded me of my father, she couldn't figure out why.

"I don't know," I said, shrugging. I was sitting across from her in the kitchen. It was raining. Thick, acid drops beat against the tarred tin roof, the brick exterior, the thin layer of shingles over the frail niche. Water streaked the glass on both sides, searched the wavy, warped wood wall beside our elbows. By our toes, it drained like magic through the kitchen floor. "He doesn't look like Dad. He's fat," I told her.

She nodded.

"You should see the rolls under his chin. It's so gross."

"You know, being fat doesn't make a person bad. Look at Junie. She's a little heavy."

"Yeah, I know," I told her, and waved off her comment by looking at the flowing water on the wall. "What I mean is, Dad was a bully. Remember how he used to say he was? That's why I think Newt reminds me of him."

She took a sip of her beer. Swallowing, she put the can down and studied the logo. "I told him not to tell you that kind of thing. Why would a father tell his son that?" She focused on me again, rolled her eyes back a little so that her irises looked like tiny dinner plates broken in half. "Anyway, I don't think he was quite the bully he made it sound."

"Well, that's still why Newt reminds me of him."

"Yeah," she said, scratching an itch on her birdlike neck. "Then, maybe Newt will grow out of it, too."

I shook my head. "He's practically an adult right now, and he still acts like a kid, except for he smokes. Somebody said that he's even already a father, but I don't know for sure. He wouldn't be a very good one."

"A father?" my mom said. She pushed her lasagna tin away from her with an elbow. The fork fell down into the glop of tomato sauce and ricotta at the bottom. "How old is he?"

"Thirteen. But he's got hair all over him already. It goes right up his neck. He even has a little mustache. You can't see it very good, though."

"He's a baby," my mother said.

"You wouldn't think so if you saw him."

"What I mean is, he's too young."

I looked over at the wall again. I was absolutely amazed that water could run down the inside of a building. It was like we had a trick apartment or something. "How old were you when you had me?" I asked, too lazy to figure it out in my head.

"Twenty. And that was too young, too."

"Twenty?" I balked, thinking that that wasn't young at all.

My mom took another slurp of her beer. "Twenty's too young when you don't have any help from your family, when it's just you and your husband, who's just a kid, too." She looked out the angled window behind my head. I think she was remembering how she'd lost her parents because she'd married my father. They disowned her because he was from West Baltimore, from Pig Town. It must have been a terrible feeling, especially after my dad disappeared, when she knew he had given up on her, too.

My dad's parents were just the opposite. They were happy he got married so young. The thing is, his mom was a little crazy. She never really knew what was going on. But my dad's father supposedly liked my mom a lot. He called her Max instead of Maxine. He died of a heart attack when I was too small to remember. After that, my Grandma Webber was committed to a state mental hospital in Gaithersburg, Maryland.

"If Newt's got a baby," my mother mumbled, eyes unfocused, "I hope the Novaceks are a good family. I hope he has somewhere to go, people to help."

I took my fork and scraped it across the tin where my potpie had bubbled and cooled. "How could his family be any good?" I asked. "He's so gross. He's the worst person I've ever met."

The following Sunday my mom surprised me by coming home from work after only about an hour. Like a wild boar, she clopped up the stairs. Popping through the door, she spotted me in the kitchen and smiled. In return, I smiled back, thinking that we were going to do something fun, like go to a mall. I was in absolute shock when she told me she was going to go out with someone. I actually didn't think that she could. I thought that it was against the law or something. I mean, she was still married as far as I knew. Even still, just six months after my dad had disappeared, she was getting ready to go see a Sylvester Stallone movie with some guy I didn't even know. It made me crazy. I got angry at her. I wondered what my dad would say if he finally fought his way back from wherever he was and my mom was off with someone else.

Smoldering at the edge of her lumpy bed, I ground my teeth till my gums ached, till it felt like the roots might pop through the way a tree tears out of the ground. My mom was sitting in the soft, baby blue chair that Junie had slid into the corner of her gleaming bay window. Normally, she sat in it when she looked like a ghost, when she needed the sunlight to warm the top of her head and give her a little hope, but that day she was fine. She actually looked better than I'd seen her look in ages. Her eyelids were shaded, her lips bright red. She looked so much like a movie star that I couldn't look at her straight on. I almost wished she wasn't pretty. I wished she looked like Junie. I was scared the big clod coming to take her out would try to sweep her off her feet, take her away from me.

"Wha . . . what if Dad comes back today?" I stammered. "What do you want me to tell him?"

She adjusted in the chair. She wore a skirt that was so short she had to keep her legs together so you wouldn't see the diamond-shaped part of her underwear. "I don't think he's coming back, Samuel. I wouldn't go if I thought he might."

"You don't know, though," I told her.

She got up. The hard plastic soles of her fancy shoes clicked across the dusty floorboards. She sat down beside me. Springs deep inside the bed, covered in layers of thick fabric, creaked and sank. She placed a skinny arm across my shoulders, elbow bulging like a knuckle. She'd lost so much weight in the last few months, and she'd been thin already.

"I'm sorry, Samuel," she said, "but I don't think he will. I hoped that he would come back, for a while, but I don't think he will any-more."

"You're giving up," I told her, trying to remember my father's face. I was shocked to realize that it was gone. All I could get was a flesh-tone blank spot. It made me want to cry.

"I hope your father's okay, wherever he is, whatever happened to him, but you and me, we've got to go on, you know. We can't wait forever." She took a pointer finger, nail painted red, and brushed my face. She smelled pretty, which reminded me of the time when we'd first moved, when she'd slept days in a row and had gotten to stink a bit. "We just got to keep going. That's what Junie says."

I ground my achy teeth again, the way my father had when he worried. "Junie should mind her own business."

My mom shook me gently in her arms, like the way she adjusted our television to get a better picture. She said softly, "She and Ditch are the closest thing to family you and I've got."

I shook my head. "How about Grandma Webber?" I asked.

My mom took a breath beside me. "Grandma Webber's here but not here."

"She's crazy, huh?" I muttered.

"She's kind of out of it," my mom replied.

I tried to picture Grandma Webber, but I couldn't see her, either. I couldn't even remember if she'd rolled around in a shiny wheelchair or staggered about with an aluminum walker.

"By the way, Nerd, this isn't really a date."

"It's not?" I looked at all of my mom for the first time since she'd told me where she was going for the afternoon.

"No, of course not. You're going to crack up when you see him. He's got an overbite and glasses with tape on them, by one of the earpieces."

I imagined this cartoon character of a man, front teeth the size of Bugs Bunny's, a huge roll of tape wrapped around his glasses, like a dirty cast.

"He's the guy who delivers clay pots to us at work. I've known him for years. We're friends because he's always got something nice to say, but he's not my type."

I turned my head away and stared down at the floor, at this gray clump of dust and hair that wiggled back and forth. "But if it's not a date," I asked, "then why're you so dressed up?"

She let me go, shrugged, wrapped her hands together in her lap. "Because I haven't dressed up in so long, I guess."

I nodded, gave her a minute before I got annoying, then asked, "Well, what am I supposed to do all afternoon?"

She looked at me, nudged me with an elbow. "Play with your action figures?" She paused, put an index finger to her lip in thought. "You could figure out how you want your room to be laid out. We can finally put it all together when I get home."

"That's boring," I announced, kicked my legs, and jumped off the bed.

She chewed on the side of her mouth. "Well, you'll find something to do. You always do."

"No I don't," I informed her, then shuffled out into the dark hallway, hands plunged deep into my pockets, fingers fiddling with hunks of lint. Entering my room, I shut the door behind me, flopped onto my bed like a seal, like I didn't have any arms. After a while, I freed them, slipped over to my box of comics and pulled out a handful. I'd been reading for about a half hour when someone rang the front doorbell downstairs.

My mom clomped down the hall and stuck her head into my room. "He's here, sweetheart. I'm going. I'll be back before seven. Now remember, if you have any problems, go to a pay phone and call Junie, okay? You got a quarter?"

I looked up at her pathetically, nodded. "This is going to be the worst Sunday I've ever had."

"I know," she said, and clomped back down the hall, opened the door, and left.

I was in disbelief for a few minutes. I waited for her to come back, to return for something, but it didn't happen. Eventually, I dropped onto my back and stared at the ceiling, legs spread across the bed, arms open as if I'd been dumped from high in the sky, through the roof, and onto my mattress. Lying there, I listened to the shower drip into the tub. *Tut tut tut,* it went. It wasn't so bad, either. I wondered how the Chinese had turned it into a torture. I figured that a lot of things could get under my skin faster than that sound.

When I was sure my mom was gone and I was over the shock, I climbed off the bed and staggered down the hall and into the closet, turned on the television, and watched football. The 49ers were playing the Rams, but I didn't care, since my favorite player had been traded to the Indianapolis Colts. I watched, anyway. The closet was warm, and the smell of mothballs was comfortable. I liked sitting among them, even though sometimes they gave me headaches. I also liked the way the glow from the television lit up the little space. For some reason, the bluish cast reminded me of Christmas.

In less than an hour, though, I totally lost interest in television, especially football. Cutting it off, I scurried over the tattered chairs and back into the hallway. I wandered into the kitchen and examined the bay window. The wall part had warped so badly in the last storm that the wind whistled in around the molding. I found it kind of neat, but my mom didn't. In a tirade, she'd called our yellow-haired landlord out to look at it. He'd declared that it was fine. "Good as the day I built it," he'd actually said. I guess we should have figured *he'd* pounded the ugly thing together.

I went back into my sloppy room and kicked at the tangled pile of blankets on the floor. I felt pretty sorry for myself. I looked out my window, through the grates, cold and hard, at the chilly ground I'd played on for months. For some reason, it looked completely uninteresting. I hadn't cleaned it out in a few days, and there were four scraps of white paper, like cigarette wrappers, shifting inside the little fence.

Frustrated, I turned and went over to the dresser drawer with my money in it. There, from the bottom of an athletic sock with black and yellow stripes, I carefully removed a few bucks. I stuffed the wadded-up bills, the size and shape of a cracked golf ball, into a pocket, grabbed a sweatshirt from off the floor, and left the apartment.

All the windows in our place, except for the ones in my mother's room, were so filmy that they were practically tinted. For that reason, unless the windows were open, I never could gauge how nice it was outside. So, stumbling down the steps from off the front porch, I was absolutely amazed: the sky was bright blue. It soared above like it never ended, like it went all the way to the sun. Deep shadows and sparkling sunlight splashed across everything. I'd never seen Charles Village look so nice. Even Abel Avenue seemed okay, despite the leaf-less trees trimmed back by the city so that they reminded me of stone sculptures. It was cold out, breezy, but it wasn't a biting chill. It made me feel so much better than I had. I ran down the sidewalk, jumped, and brushed my fingertips across the hard limb of a tree. Leaning back, I looked up at it, crouched and sprang with my bouncy legs. Hands wrapped around the rough top, scratchy as a file, I clung there for a few good minutes, as if I was trying to stretch myself. Then I let go and dropped to the pavement. Excited, I ran down the uneven sidewalk, jumping at other trees, though there weren't many, and swinging from the stubby branches I could reach. The whole neigh-borhood felt like one big park: people waving from their porches, call-ing hello, and me waving back, dogs yipping kindly, and all the trees trimmed perfectly for dangling, for a skinny kid like me to howl beneath, imagining I was raised by apes.

I whirled and wended my way around the neighborhood for an hour, my heart knocking in my chest, shuddering in my ears. Then I was standing across the street from that wide, barren parking lot in front of the 7-Eleven. A single piece of trash skipped across the wavy asphalt, past the bent parking meters, like someone was chasing after it. Behind the lot were the backsides of stores along Greenmount Avenue, wires and pipes and two-tone paint jobs warming in the sun.

It wasn't so pretty, but it drew me in, thrilled my eyes. Gazing at it all, I was sure that no one could think up something so intricate, more detailed than all of my old neighborhood combined. My stare froze on the buildings, traced some of the lines, caught on the glints of color. I felt surrounded by a strange history. I wondered about the people who'd worked on that block, and I was sure there'd been millions of hands, all with their own story. It made me think about where I was, at the center of a spot on the ground where so much had happened, where so many had made their lives, and I was a part of all that.

Thoughtful and slow, I started walking, saw people in my head, pictures in black-and-white-and-brown tones. I shuffled down the sidewalk toward Thirty-second Street. At the corner, I stopped. My head cleared, and I looked up at Harry Little's Pizza. My eyes tumbled down past the abandoned buildings and the feminist bookstore, fell against the Little Tavern, a thin plume of bluish smoke rising from a tiny silver chimney on the flat roof. That's when I noticed that my stomach felt hollow and hungry.

At night sometimes when my window was open, I could hear guns going off on Greenmount. Also, police helicopters circling up and down it, searchlights sharp as laser beams, poking at the hard concrete buildings and curbs like someone digging at mud with a shovel. I was scared of Greenmount. I was sure that all of the cruel-looking black guys who passed through Charles Village lived and shopped on that road, and robbed, mugged, murdered, and sold drugs there. I knew that Waverly, a kind of nice neighborhood, was just a block or so east of Greenmount toward Memorial Stadium, but to me it seemed like a distant, glinting star.

Wild and jittery, I slipped down Thirty-second Street, past Harry Little's. There was a man inside rolling pizza dough. Down beyond the boarded-up buildings, by the feminist bookstore, window cracked, a crystal spider web, I gazed onto Greenmount. There were Burrell's Pharmacy and Liquor Store, Milt's Newsstand, and Economy Shoes,

[67]

white basketball sneakers glowing in front of a black wall, a life-size cutout of Michael Jordan in the window. There were a lot of people strolling along the sidewalk, staring into windows, shuffling into Mike's Grill and the Blue Horseshoe Bar. There were actually a few white people, though they weren't the kind of folks I felt comfortable around; it seemed like all of them had sores on their faces or hands, a gray-and-yellow bandage hanging on by the very last patches of adhesive, flopping, a wafer-thin fish.

I looked across the street at the steamy Little Tavern, the slick white exterior nearly blinding in the sun, the dents and scratches black as laundry marker strokes. I could see an older white lady behind the counter, bleached blond hair tied up in a bun, serving a line of black men, their shoulders hunched, at the counter. There were two open stools, orange cushions still compressed by now-departed customers. I took a deep, ecstatic breath and ran across the street, around to the Greenmount side, grabbed the door handle, and pulled until I realized that it said PUSH, then stumbled in. I slid a little on the greasy tile floor.

A couple of big guys turned around, looked at me, then pivoted, unconcerned, back to their food, coffee, and conversation. Nervously, I made my way down to the end of the counter and climbed onto the last stool. It let out a puff of air when I adjusted myself on top of it. Self-conscious, I tried not to make eye contact with anyone. Instead, I tried to appear adult, looking over the grill area. It wasn't so clean. Oily fingers had smeared a lot of surfaces, covered handles and knobs with a murky haze. Crumbs, like caked dirt, surrounded the big square toaster, ten scorched slots in the top. The refrigerator doors were splattered irregularly with dry shreds of lettuce and onion, a splash of pancake batter, pale as wet plaster. The accumulated grime made my stomach gurgle uncomfortably. At the same time, though, the hamburgers smelled perfect, thin, frozen and sizzling into pure-beef patties. It wasn't any worse than the Waverly Deli, I told myself

as the waitress, leaving a hunk of bologna and two giant pale pancakes sputtering on the grease-stained grill, brought her wet pad over
and looked at me.

I tried to smile, but I couldn't. My lips stretched flat instead.

She eyeballed me curiously from beneath chalky flaking eyeliner
as she withdrew a pencil from behind an ear the size of a half dollar,
big gold hoops dangling from painful-looking holes, stretched slits.
"Ain't you a little young to be in here by yerself?" she asked me. The
hairy brown mole on one side of her lip reminded me of a fat tick.

I nodded to her because I couldn't speak, not immediately. My
voice snagged on something deep in my throat, a sharp hook.

"Don't matter to me, hon." She scratched at the mole with a yellowed fingernail, sharp cracks down the center of it. "Whatcha
want?"

I licked my lips. She reminded me of our neighbor, the man who
sold snowballs and hot dogs from the old mail truck. I wasn't sure that
I wanted to eat her cooking, but I wasn't about to tell her that I'd
changed my mind. I looked at my hands, squirming on the Formica
counter, and rasped almost inaudibly. "Hamburgers. Two, please. And
a Coke."

"That it?"

"Yes, ma'am."

"Fine," she declared, returning to the grill before the bottom of the
pancakes turned black, before the bologna curled and burned.

After flipping and moving the sputtering food, she went to the
freezer and yanked out two tiny pink frozen disks, an off-white piece
of paper separating them. She slapped the burgers next to the cakes
and tossed the paper into an orange garbage can. She poked at the patties once or twice with her cracked fingernail, then pushed them down
with a big metal spatula, so that water sizzled around their sides.

I leaned atop the counter, over my cold hands, tiny, spike-sharp
elbows, fiddled with the sugar dispenser, tried to imitate the confident

actions of a relaxed man, at least the way my father'd done things. Making my way like I was, I thought about my mom, hoped she was having fun, hoped I hadn't ruined anything for her. A few minutes passed. Then amid other garbled conversations—comments about punks and idiots and women who weren't friendly or faithful, and the loudmouthed waitress telling everyone and no one about her sister who'd had a stroke and couldn't say anything but cuss words—someone to my right said, "So, that big kid ain't picked on you again, has he?"

I didn't glance over because I didn't think the person was talking to me. I picked up a saltshaker with a dented silver top, studied the salt. For some reason, there were rice kernels in it. I wondered if someone had dropped them in there by mistake.

"Hey, that fat boy ain't stirring up trouble for you, is he?" the person to my right muttered again.

The hairs on my neck stood up, rising against my collar like there was a huge bug walking down the center of my back. This time, I knew the guy was talking to me. Terrified, I risked a quick glance, spotted the Chevron cap, the face that was pocked by acne scars and textured with hard black whiskers, tough, a dirty woven basket.

The school janitor laughed to himself like he'd played a good joke, bulging eyes closing, flaps of rubber pulling tight over slick cue balls. "You remember me," he said. The sour smell of liquor burned the inside of my nostrils like a hot poker. "I'm the janitor at school."

I nodded my head. I'd fallen into a bad habit of not being able to talk when people I didn't know very well spoke to me. It was actually a fairly new thing, something that had happened since my father had vanished.

"You always so nervous?" the janitor asked me in that thick, sluggish voice of his, bad breath rolling from between his crooked teeth like steam. He drank some coffee, brown streaks, trails, streaming down the side of the thick china cup.

[70]

"Yeah," I said, the word barely escaping.

"How in the world you get along in that school? That ain't a sympathetic bunch of kids."

I shook my head. I didn't know.

The waitress stuck a plate of pancakes in front of him. He smothered them in syrup from a squeeze bottle, then stabbed one with a bent fork, tearing off a ragged, crunchy piece. "It ain't good to be that way, you know," he said gently before jamming the food into his mouth.

I nodded my head in agreement.

After chewing, he said, "No reason to be scared of anything, if you think about it. You take the fact we're sitting here. There could be a jetliner out of control, heading straight for this building, but if you worry 'bout that kind of thing, it don't get you nothing. You got the same chance everywhere. Plane could fall anytime, anyplace."

I glanced over my shoulder, out the big window, and into the brilliant blue sky. A bunch of seagulls swarmed in the distance, and two contrails were drifting apart in the high winds, but nothing like a fiery plane zeroing in.

The janitor shook his head. "Now you worried 'bout that, ain't you?"

"Kind of," I confessed.

"Well, that ain't the point. The point is, it ain't worth being nervous 'bout everything. You got no control."

I looked at his black features, his wide nose, nostrils curled back like the inside of a pretty seashell. "What if you can't help it?"

He winced. "These cakes is like glass the way she cooked 'em. Got a little chip stabbing me in the gums. Feels like a tack."

I looked down at the discolored plate, then to the side of it, at a red plastic cup, water beading around the bottom. "Gargle with some water."

He dumped some liquid into his mouth, sloshed it around like it was a capful of Scope. His cheeks swelled from side to side, acne scars expanding the same way a picture or a word does on a blown-up balloon. He swallowed, squinted. "Got it," he said after a moment. He looked down at me, tongue still working the wound. "You a dentist?"

I shook my head to tell him I wasn't.

He squeezed my shoulder. "That was a joke."

"I know," I said softly, embarrassed.

The waitress came over and plopped my two bad hamburgers in front of me, adjusted a cup of Coke to the side of my tiny plate, by a black-and-chrome napkin dispenser that had a dried smudge of ketchup on the side.

"Those things'll turn your arteries to stone," the janitor said, using his fork to point at my late-afternoon snack.

I reached down and pinched off a piece of a patty, brought it to my mouth, chewed, and swallowed. It was perfect. I looked at the janitor. "They're good, though," I told him.

"You know what," he said, cutting a big triangular piece of pancake, then stabbing it with wavy prongs, "my cholesterol is so high, I'd probably have a heart attack if I ate one. Believe me, them things is deadly."

I jammed a curve of the burger against my mouth. The bun bent back a little, and a couple of minced onions fell to the counter.

"What's your name?" he asked.

I looked over at him, didn't talk until the good-tasting mush in my mouth had cleared my throat. Tentatively, I rasped, "Sam."

"Sam," he nodded. "I've known a lotta Sams in my life. I knew one died in North Africa—Algeria, to be exact. Died from exposure, they said." He lifted his Chevron cap and rubbed ferociously at his nubby head as if a mosquito had just gotten him. "Knew this other Sam down in Atlanta, guy I went to elementary school with a long time ago. Had two thumbs on one hand, if you can believe it. When I was a kid, it was just about the strangest thing I'd ever seen. He couldn't wiggle it or nothing, though, 'cause it was just the tip, just the part with the fingernail." He shook his head, pulling his cap back on. "There's a Sam lives in my neighborhood now. Got the scraggliest dog you ever want to see. That mutt looks like he's made-a dirty strings, like he's a puppet or something, and Sam don't like no one. Sam Jones is the man's name, and he thinks all of us is stupid, 'cause he ain't happy." He shook the hunk of pancake on the end of his fork. "I think he's blaming the wrong folks. I tell him that when I see him, too. He once sicced his mutt on me for saying it, but that dog didn't even get up. That dog is a joke." The janitor's big eyes studied me, moved about like ball joints in rounded sockets. "If you're wondering, my name's Greely, Greely Clemons, but you can just call me Greely."

I was finished with one hamburger and staring at the other. I took a sip from my Coke, and the greasy cup nearly slipped from my hand and banged to the floor, throwing cola everywhere. Taking a breath, I looked at Greely.

"Cups in here is all slick," he said.

I nodded, was quiet for a moment before asking, "What's *exposure*?"

"You mean the guy in Algeria?" Greely had the fork in one hand, and with the other, he tapped on the counter. Each brown nail fell one after another against the Formica, starting with the pinkie and ending with the thumb. Then, as soon as the thumb touched down, he started back with the pinkie. It made me notice the skin on his fingers. It was wrinkled like flattened canvas. "That boy got lost on a patrol and didn't have no water or food or nothing when they found him wandering round in the dunes. Got fried in the sun during the day, then froze at night till his body couldn't take it no more. That's exposure. Exposure to the elements is what they meant." He checked with me to be sure I understood. "They said he went AWOL, but if you knew him, you knew he didn't. He was just a stupid nigger who didn't have the sense to follow no one. The Army saw it different than his friends, though. They always did when it came to niggers."

[73]

I couldn't take my eyes off Greely. I was shocked that he was call-ing black people niggers, especially because he was black. I nodded a little, gnawing at the inside of a cheek, pulling on it till there was a little hunk of soft skin floating around on my tongue. My mom had always told me never to call blacks that, even though Ditch used the term kind of loosely. I leaned toward him, caught a whiff of his harsh breath again. "Ah," I mumbled as delicately as I could, "why, uh, why are you calling him that?"

"Who?" Greely said.

"That guy who got lost."

"What am I calling him?" he asked, lifting his huge hands off the counter.

"You know," I whispered, leaning closer, till my nose was only a few inches from one of his soft sleeves. "Why did you call him a . . . you know?"

"A nigger?"

"Yeah," I rasped.

"'Cause," he explained, shrugging.

"My mom says it's wrong," I informed him.

He nodded. "It is," he told me, "for you. If a white person says it, it's wrong."

I didn't understand. I looked at the waitress as she poured a guy coffee and jabbered about her faucets at home, which were spewing reddish brown water. She'd even brushed her teeth with it that morn-ing, she said.

"It's like when you're mad at your mom or dad. You can say things about them no one else can. You can do it 'cause they's yours, but if I did it you'd get mad at me 'cause it ain't my place, I don't have the personal knowledge of them, and I don't care for them like you do."

I looked at his funny face as he took a glug of water. "You can say it because you're black?"

He shrugged. "It's true, Sam," he said. "It's a complicated thing, something almost no one understands." He flagged for some more coffee.

I waited a minute, then I asked, "What were you doing in Africa?"

"Fighting," he said. "It was during World War II, and we was fighting Germans in the desert." He mashed his lips together. "I fought in Italy, too. Fought all through Europe. Saw some things you wouldn't believe—horrible things and nice things." He rubbed across the counter gently. "One that I'll never forget is Florence. You heard of Florence?"

I nodded, but I hadn't.

"Well, you know how pretty Florence is supposed to be. They say it's one of the world's most beautiful cities. There's a big river to the south of it, and when we were moving north through Italy, we had to cross it. So guess how we did it? The whole division drove across and up and into the city on bridges that were made of floating barrels and piled up junk." He laughed. "It wasn't funny, but I'll tell you, driving into one of the prettiest cities in the world on a bridge made of junk just seems peculiar, don't it? It's comical, because when you go to Florence, you expect to see the best. That's what I expected, anyway. That's what we'd heard, that it'd done all right all through the war."

I swallowed. "That's the way their bridges were?"

He shook his head and looked into his coffee cup. "Naw. See, the Nazis had blown all the nice bridges up but one, and that one wouldn't of held any trucks or nothing. It was old, one of the oldest bridges in Europe, so we had to build new ones just to get across."

I studied the grease on my plate, shy about asking him anything else.

"The city was a wreck," Greely continued in his thick, cottony voice. "But you could tell it'd been nice. You could see it. Those Italians, they didn't want to fight. They know how to live, and they didn't

[75]

want any more of it. They just wanted Florence back the way it was. That's what I remember."

He talked some more about the war, and eventually I finished off my second hamburger. I liked listening to him. He had an easy, kind way, and he was filled with strange stories—memories and people so bright they moved inside my head. He talked to me as if I was a grownup, too, not a kid. I was split between wanting to stay to hear more and feeling like I should go. Finally, I told him, "I need to leave or I'll get in trouble." My mother would have killed me if she knew I was on Greenmount Avenue alone.

He nodded. "Not me." He slurped at the side of his thick, white mug, fat lips puckered as if he were planting a kiss.

I fished through my pockets and dropped my money and a tip on the counter. "Is that enough?" I asked him.

He examined the two balled-up bills and the coins. "Generous for this place," he told me.

I climbed down from the stool, stood beside it as the sagging orange pad expanded with air till it was the shape of the collapsed cakes my mom made. "I, ah, like your stories." I turned red.

He smiled. "Don't let that fat kid pick on you," he said.

"Yes, sir," I replied.

He stuck a big hand out. "Gimme five."

Grinning, I gave it to him, good and hard, then peered up, muttering, "See ya in school." I made my way to the end of the Little Tavern, struggled to pull the thousand-pound door open, and left. In the cool, shivery air, sun warming the top of my head the way it did my mother's when she sat in her room in her baby blue chair, I waved to Greely, a dark ghost in the steamy window. Then, I took off running for home, nervous about exposing my back to gunfire. I felt light and quick because of my afternoon, my day, my new neighborhood's strange heart hidden beneath a thin layer of roughness, the pretty rows of warm red brick, of wide wooden porches and bay windows throwing frames of deep yellow light across the sidewalks.

Seven o'clock came and went, and my mother didn't arrive home like she had promised. At seven-thirty, I stood looking out the blurry glass of her bay window, down on the dusky night of Abel Avenue, on the cars and the former mail truck with the painting of the black kid eating the wiener dog on the side. I bunched her curtains up in my hands and stared. I didn't even know what kind of car the clay-pot man drove. I wouldn't be able to tell the police anything except that his glasses had tape on one earpiece and that he had an overbite. It made me sick, standing there, streetlights twinkling like fiery stars on the cold glass by my cheek. Sylvester Stallone movies were never very long.

Finally, around fifteen till eight, a small car pulled up out front and my mom got out. She walked around the back, by the dented bumper, and leaned down to look into the driver's-side window, said something, turned, and disappeared under the broad porch roof of the rowhouse.

As soon as I heard her enter downstairs, I took off down the hallway, dove onto my mattress, grabbed a comic book, picked it up, and started reading, or pretended to, at least. I listened to her shoes click on the wood steps, imagined her shadow falling across the plaster walls. When the apartment door opened, I pretended I didn't even hear it. Shutting the door, she checked for me in the closet, then walked straight down the hallway to my room, where she stood silently looking in.

"I'm sorry," she said after she'd been there for a while.

I turned my head, frowned as well as I could, so that I felt the muscles tremble in my forehead. "Forty-five minutes is nearly an hour."

[77]

"I know," she said. "If we owned a phone, I would have called."

"Well," I hesitated, "may . . . maybe we should get one if . . . if you're gonna start going out."

"And who's going to pay for it?" she snapped at me. "We can't afford it." She turned around and slowly wobbled off to her room.

Worried, I jumped up and followed after her. From the hallway, I watched her fall into her blue chair, pull off one earring and study it. I went in quietly and leaned against the side of her bed. The shiny black shoes she had on reflected the bare bulb screwed into the round brass plate on her ceiling.

"Your father gave me these," she said after a few minutes of dangling the earring, a big puffy silver heart on a long hook, in front of her. She looked over at me. "I'm sorry for snapping at you, Samuel. It's just that I miss him sometimes," she said. "I wish he hadn't gone away." She ran a hand through her hair. "He hurt us both forever."

I bit at my cheek, at the raw area I'd gnawed while talking to Greely. I didn't know what to say, so I said the first thing that came to my mind. "It's not his fault."

"Yeah," she replied, "I know." She dragged a hand through her hair again, then gingerly took off her other earring, got up, and placed them both on her dresser.

"I need to do something tonight, occupy my head for a while till I stop feeling sorry for myself." She turned around and kicked her shoes off. "You want to go organize your room?"

I pushed away from her bed with my hands, palms sore from swinging on stumpy tree limbs, from grinding across dusty bark. I examined my hands, then looked up. "I guess," I said, feeling better, the way I had when I'd left the Little Tavern, shot home, a bottle rocket in sneakers, head filled with wild pictures Greely had inserted. I didn't really want to straighten my room, but I hoped it would make my mom feel better, carry her thoughts away.

wrestling with everything
wrestling with everything

For me, the nervous type, Robert Poole Middle School could seem overwhelming. During one stretch in the late fall, at the end of October and into the start of November, I went to the nurse's office at least twice a week. That's where my trouble with queasiness was labeled "hyperventilating." For no reason, I took such deep gulps of air that my stomach rumbled and my head spun. The worst thing was that I didn't even know I was doing it till the room started to roll, till it was too late.

Even still, I tried hard not to draw any attention to myself. The thing is, it was kind of difficult to go unnoticed. At the sight of me wobbling back and forth, face a pasty white, teachers would halt class and send someone scurrying for the school nurse, a middle-aged black woman with the prettiest almond-shaped eyes, dark as a tunnel, and the thoughtful, delicate hands of a person on a soap commercial. I'm sure Nurse Jones got tired of fetching me, of escorting me, dazed, from the classroom. She'd hold my elbow as if I were an old lady, take those perfect fingers and squeeze my funny bone so that it buzzed, and I'd stagger out of the class like my feet had turned into

[79]

long metal points. Everyone got sick of me being sick, including me. Classmates pestered me as I tottered away. It got so that people I didn't even know held a grudge against me. A handful of students I'd never said a word to drilled me in the head with pointy paper planes, lobbed spitballs into my hair, or popped the back of my locked knees while I was standing in the lunch line, nearly collapsing me to the floor.

The first couple of times I got ill, Nurse Jones gave me some medicine and let me sit around till I was calm and back to normal. It wasn't until the third visit that she started asking me questions about school and my family. She tried to act like she was just making conversation, like we'd become friends since I'd been in there so much, but I knew what she was doing. My mom and I had just gotten a phone installed, and Nurse Jones worked at coaxing the number out of me by swearing that she wouldn't use it, by telling me that she needed it for her records. She'd been sweet and I didn't want to get her in trouble, so I gave it to her on around my eighth visit, but I knew that I shouldn't have.

The night she called, I was sitting in my room, on my bed, which was finally off the floor, playing with a couple of G.I. Joe action figures. I was pretending my white sheet was a mound of shifting snow that would unexpectedly buckle and roll over me and my troops. My mom answered, and I paid no attention to the conversation, figuring it was probably Junie, since she was about the only person with our phone number aside from the clay-pot man, and he was down in North Carolina somewhere, rumbling through the countryside in an eighteen-wheeler with a big green tree drawn on the side. My mom jabbered for a while, then hung up the phone. She paced in the kitchen, then walked into the hall and knocked on the frame of my open door.

I looked across the narrow room at her. If we'd both stuck out our arms, we could have touched puffy fingertips, soft as pincushions.

"That was the school nurse, Mrs. Jones," she told me.

My chest tightened.

"She says you've been into her office eight times in the last three weeks, that you were in there this morning, hyperventilating so hard that she thought you might black out." My mom unwrapped her arms, which had been in a knot on her chest, and entered my room, sat on my bed so that the box spring groaned.

Unintentionally, she collapsed my snowbank. "She's worried about you. And now I'm worried about you."

Embarrassed, I focused on the knob of one knee, the fabric of my jeans rolling over it.

"You need to tell me these things. You got to tell me when you've been sick," she said, reaching down and squeezing my hands, which were sitting in a tangle on my lap, a web of loose shoestrings.

I didn't reply.

"Why didn't you tell me?"

I shook my head because I didn't know.

"She says that you're very sensitive, that she worries you might be too sensitive to handle some of what's going on."

My face got warm, as if a thumping radiator was on beneath my skin.

"She thinks that the situation might be overwhelming. She said that maybe I should take you to see someone so that you can talk about it."

A horrified look crossed my face.

"She's worried about you, that's all." My mom snarled my hair with one hand, dropped it to my back, and ran her sharp nails up and down the dull bumps of my spine. "It's not natural for you to get queasy and hyperventilate all the time, you know. It means there's either something wrong in here"—she gently touched my flat stomach—"or here," she said, reaching with her other hand and placing a finger against the plate in front of my heart.

I shrugged. "It's not dad," I blurted weakly after a moment. "I don't know what it is. I just get sick." I shrugged again, lifted my head, and looked right at her. "It's school, I guess. I don't have any friends." A tear escaped from the corner of an eyeball, and I smeared it across my cheek so that it probably looked like a slug trail.

"It's okay to cry," she told me, hugging me gently. She kissed my temple, the very spot a paper plane had hit me that morning. "You think we should invite some of your old friends over? Would that help?"

I shook my head to tell her that it wouldn't. I didn't want them to see where we lived, our skinny rowhouse apartment with the dark alley out back. Anyway, I'd never had close friends in Rodger's Forge, or in my old school, for that matter. I'd been more accepted, but I always enjoyed my parents' company more than anyone else's. I'd reserved space to do stuff with them, for special rides downtown, for swatting a softball with my mom.

"Why not? I bet Joey misses you."

Joey Jenta was the kid who'd lived across the street from us. We'd collected comic books together, but I'd never done too much with him because he had a big head that always bothered me for some reason, and he smelled like cologne. Joey liked to wear his father's Stetson aftershave. The problem was, he wore a little too much of it, so that when he was around, my nose always ran like I had hay fever or something. Also, I knew for sure that he'd stolen one of my Captain America comic books. When we were moving, he'd helped me pack, and suddenly it was missing. He'd always liked the cover. He'd pulled it out whenever he came over.

"Well," my mother said to me, still squeezing me like I was a pillow, "we should do something, make some changes and see if you still get sick."

I shook her off me by wiggling.

"I want you to tell me if it happens again. I don't want Nurse Jones to have to call a second time."

I nodded, picked up the action figure I'd been pretending was me, and pushed his arms up over his head, the way I made him react whenever something was about to hit him square in the chest, like a car or a bullet or a boot. "I'm getting better right now," I told her.

The following day, I monitored my breathing as well as I could. The last thing I wanted to do was hyperventilate again. I knew exactly what my mother would do. She believed in psychology and all of that, so I knew that I'd end up in some doctor's office discussing things. She'd done the same thing to my father a few years before, when he'd gone into one of his long funks. She'd sent him to this man out in the Mount Washington area to talk. I remember my parents arguing over that one, and that hadn't been about money. That was, my father had said, about his pride. Anyway, I knew that I didn't have too many episodes left before we'd climb into a cab and head out to that same doctor's office. I'd discovered that my mom was secretly seeing him. I'd spotted the bill on her bedside table one night while I was waiting for her to get home.

At lunch, I slurped on some chow mein at a table by the cafeteria door. I always sat alone, away from everyone else, gagging down whatever the kitchen staff had stirred together in those giant metal pots with black bottoms. From a distance, I watched the other students in the middle of the room horse around, laugh, and talk. Since I'd started at Robert Poole Middle School, I'd seen a lot from my table. I'd witnessed blowout fights erupt—big fiberglass trays hurled to the scuffed linoleum floor—people kissing, and guys and girls screaming at each other like hand puppets with giant mouths.

I was pushing around a scoop of mashed potatoes, plopped out of place beside my chow mein, when I looked up to see Greely wander into the cafeteria. We always said hello to each other since that day in the Little Tavern, but I didn't call out to him. I didn't want everyone, along with Greely, to look at me. I watched him walk across the dining room and get a tray, then step around the thick wall that separated the kitchen from the dining room to choose his food. When he was gone, I looked down at my potatoes again, mashed them with the prongs of my fork, so that skinny mounds rose between the tooth-dented tines. I took a gulp of my milk and looked over toward where Greely had disappeared. I guess I must have started staring at the Thanksgiving decorations, construction paper cutouts of a turkey, a pilgrim, and a giant ear of corn, because I was still looking in that general direction when he hobbled out, came toward me, tray heaped high with the day's other selection, Salisbury steak. When he got to the table, he looked down. "You mind?" he asked.

I shook my head.

He yanked a chair out and sat down with a grunt. "Oh, man, my knee is so stiff it ain't funny," he said scowling, rubbing at the gnarled joint beneath the thin dirty fabric of his blue work pants. "So," he lifted his big eyes at me, "how you been doing, Sam?"

I mumbled, "All right," nervously, then glanced at the tiled wall a few feet away, at the poster of McGruff the Crime Dog that was taped to it. Someone had drawn a pair of glasses on him with a red pen.

Greely nodded. "You still buying burgers up at the Little Tavern?" he asked, tearing open a bag of sugar and dumping it into his nearly clear iced tea.

I shook my head again.

He chopped a hunk of Salisbury steak and paused, held his fork loosely between the tan pads of his fingers. "You been sick, Sam?" he asked. "I seen you going to Nurse Jones's office a lot lately."

Fidgeting, I tugged on a thumb. "I've been hyperventilating," I told him. "It makes me dizzy."

"Hyperventilating. That's breathing really hard, right? That what you were doing the day I saw you sick in the bathroom?"

"Maybe," I told him.

He touched the side of his dirty Chevron cap, perched on his round head, to indicate how smart he was. "So what's causing it?"

I shrugged.

He nodded, shrugged back. "So, where you live, Sam?" He stuffed the Salisbury steak into his big mouth, didn't chew, but pushed it around with his tongue, then swallowed.

"Charles Village," I replied.

"Guess I shoulda figured that out, since you was at the Tavern," he said. "That's a nice neighborhood."

I made a funny face.

"You don't like it?"

"Not like where we used to live."

"So where was that?" He raised his fuzzy set of eyebrows.

"Rodger's Forge," I said, and dropped my cheek to a balled-up fist, so that I didn't have to use my neck muscles as we talked.

"Wow," he muttered. "Parents must have some money." He wiped his reddish lips with one of the small, rectangular paper napkins on his tray.

"They don't."

"I know," he mumbled. "Just joking round," he confessed to me. "I'll be honest with you, Sam, Nurse Jones told me you've been having some rough times, that something's going on with your father."

I lifted my head and looked at him, "She can't tell you that."

"Maybe she shouldn't have, you're right. But I asked her; she told me 'cause we's friends. I seen her dragging you down the hall five times 'fore I even did. I was worried 'bout you, thought you might have food poisoning from them burgers I saw you eat." He smiled kindly.

I dropped my head again.

"Come on, Sam. I was worried 'bout you."

I swallowed.

"What's going on to make you sick?"

[85]

I swallowed again, lifted my eyes. "Someone kidnapped my dad."

Greely stared right at me, shook his shoulders, and said softly, "God, Sam. When?"

"In the summer," I choked.

"My Lord, I'm sorry. I really am. Must be horrible."

"Yeah," I whispered.

"Must make you feel crazy sometimes."

I didn't even lift my head to him, just kept my temple against my sharp fist and knuckles.

"Look," he said, "we don't know each other from Adam, and I ain't much, just a janitor, but if you ever wanta talk or something, you just ask. I could even meet you at the Little Tavern. Nurse Jones's got my phone number, so she can get in touch with me." He tapped one of my hands with a fingernail so that I would look at him. "Okay. We don't have to talk 'bout your father, either. We can do what you want." He picked over the remains of his Salisbury steak, smeared a piece through gravy that was as thick as ketchup. "Sam," he said again after a minute, "sound like you starting to breathe heavy. You better watch it."

I was doing all right when I shuffled into the musty boys' locker room for physical education, sixth bell. I worried, though, because it was a class I'd begun to hate. Twice I'd left there on the nurse's hip, feet dragging and stumbling beneath me, a Raggedy Ann doll. I knew that I wasn't a very good athlete, except for my fast legs. There were others as weak as me, but I think it was the fact that no one wanted me on their team that was causing my problems. Without fail, I was always the last person chosen. It bothered me so much that I usually thought about it halfway into the next bell.

After changing, nearly forty of us shuffled through a big metal door and into the gym. We lined up along a wall that was covered with red, white, and blue vinyl padding. We stood there until the late bell rang and Coach Murtleson made his entertaining exit from his office across the gym. He waddled out as if he was playing in the Super Bowl, except he didn't look like he could play anything. He was in awful shape for a man who taught fitness. He had a huge round gut, a soft chest, and big muscleless arms, sandwich bags with beans in them. Starting from behind the bleachers, it took him all of the way to the top of the basketball key before he was able to run smoothly, and that was only because he was coming to a stop. His clothes showed off how spongy he was, too. He always wore these colorful polyester coaching shorts that squeezed his body like a tight rubber diaper. He also liked giant pressed Polo shirts that he'd tilt the collars up on. In his big hands, he'd clutch a clipboard with a pencil swinging from it, and a silver stopwatch. Both were dwarfed by thick eel fingers. While he caught his breath, he called the roll, mounds of sweat streaming down his face.

That week, we were learning to wrestle, a sport that I wasn't very good at because it didn't have anything to do with running. Coach Murtleson showed us some basic offensive and defensive moves while standing up, told us to imagine that he was down on the big red mat as he swung his hands about in front of him. I couldn't imagine anything, though. I knew that he couldn't get down on the floor. He'd sink in on himself like a half-deflated medicine ball.

"Wrestling's easy," he said. "A little history here: It's a real old sport. It was either the Egyptians or the Greeks who wrestled all of the time. I think it was the Greeks. And they always preached the same thing, that it's all about leverage. Leverage is the key. With the few moves that I know, believe it or not, I could take a man twice my size."

We started out with some floor drills, where we got on our hands and knees and someone got on top of us, wrapped an arm around our stomachs, and fastened their fingers around one of our wrists. When Coach Murtleson blew the little whistle, we all rolled and struggled, and eventually, I was pinned. For an entire bell, I was bent into funny positions, stretched across knees, and pushed into the springy red mat. By the end of class, my skinny arms and legs were achy with useless effort.

Back in the smelly locker room, most of the class pulled out old torn towels and headed for the showers. Part of our grade was based on hygiene, so after whatever game or skill we learned, we were supposed to hose down in front of each other and get dressed. The thing is, I didn't do it. I hated the idea of exposing myself to all of those guys, even though, as Coach Murtleson said, it was supposed to make me feel more natural about my body. I could only imagine that it would make me feel a lot more unnatural. Others must have thought the same thing, too, because they never showered, either. We were able to get away with it because the coach didn't come into the locker room all that much. Instead, he inspected us as we left, and since I didn't sweat a whole lot yet, I never stank or looked all that much more messy than anyone else.

Unfortunately, Coach Murtleson swept through the locker room that day, gathering all of the unhygienic students together in a clump.

"I could fail you, boys," Coach Murtleson told about seven of us. "Hygiene may be the most important thing you learn in physical education." He shook his head and rubbed one of his hands across an oily sideburn.

Stricken with fear, I kept tabs on my breathing, filled my lungs part way, released the air after a moment. I swayed a little back and forth, barefoot, as if a breeze rocked me.

Coach Murtleson looked over at me. "How many friends you got?" he snapped.

I was too busy to speak, so I just shrugged self-consciously.

"Not too many, huh? Well, you ever considered that your body odor might offend people?"

I opened my mouth to tell him that I hadn't, but he didn't wait for a response. Instead, he spun around and asked another kid the same question. When he'd hassled about four guys that way, some who did have friends, he boomed, "I want all you boys in the shower. I want you to scrub behind your ears and wash your hair, and when you're done, towel off and dress. I'm going to inspect you all before you go. You can bet that."

A black kid raised his hand.

"What?"

"What you gonna do if we's late to our next class?"

"I'll write you notes," Coach Murtleson shot back, aggravated. "Hygiene's important. It might help you get a job one day." He rested a knotted fist against a bulge on his soft waist. "Go. Get going." He shooed at us.

As I was showering, the bell rang. I heard it from behind the water as it drummed loud and distant on my head, an oil can. I washed with my eyes squeezed shut, facing the tiled, mildew-covered wall so that all anyone could see of my private parts was my bony bottom, small as a scrunched baby pillow. I got out and self-consciously scampered back to my rusty blue locker. I was dripping wet, whipped my hair around, a soaked dog. Other unhygienic boys did the same thing, covering their personals with their hands or a knot of clothes. I didn't have a towel, so I had to dry off with my stale gym shirt. I scrubbed at my head with the thin fabric and straightened my hair with my fingers. Then I slipped on my underpants and yanked on my pants. People from the next class started filing in. As I started tugging on my socks, this big kid I'd never seen before kicked one of my shoes across the room.

I rose onto my toes and jumped across the wet floor, snatched it up. Spinning around, I nearly ran into Newt.

His eyes narrowed, and a smile shot across his big bent face, exposing those perfectly square teeth, harsh as a picket fence.

"Look who's here," he said.

I swallowed.

[89]

"Been lookin' all over for ya," he informed me. His cigarette breath and the sour gym uniform he had stuffed under one of his stinky underarms turned my stomach. "Ya still think you're so smart?" he asked me.

I promised him that I didn't.

"Got three days in-school suspension thanks to you."

I took a step back. "But—I didn't do anything. I promise."

He lifted a fist like he was going to punch me across an eye.

I cringed to take it.

"You're dead," he told me, dropping his arm slightly. "I'll get ya after school. Ya can bet on that. Ya catch the Forty-two, don't ya?"

"Um, no," I lied.

He raised his big fist again, just as Coach Murtleson lumbered into the locker room, hall passes in his hands—flapping cards made of tissue. For the first time ever, the coach looked good to me, even the lines of anger that creased his soft face.

He stared at us. "We got a problem here?"

Newt didn't budge.

"Is there a problem?" the coach repeated louder.

Newt grunted, "Nope."

Coach Murtleson glared at me. "Finish getting dressed," he said, like I'd been wasting my time hanging out.

At my locker, I pulled on my shirt and slid into my damp sneakers as fast as I could. Newt sat down beside me, whispering taunts, "This afternoon. Today. Meet ya at the bus stop."

I was breathing calmly, but my fingers trembled as I took the hall pass from the coach and I entered the long empty hallway by the stairwell. I wasn't scared, though. Instead, I was filled with ticking blue flames that rose so high they caused me to vibrate. I didn't know how, but I wasn't going to let Newt pound me into dust. I was going to think of something. Climbing the cement steps on my way to government class, I actually felt confident, determined to take charge of my life, to give up waiting for my father.

By the time seventh bell was over, I knew what to do. As fast as I could, I skittered through the bustling hallways, searching for Greely. I hunted for him in deodorized and sanitized bathrooms and in messy, jumbled utility closets, and finally located him putting away paint brushes in a big storage room down in the basement. He'd just finished washing the bristles, and his big tan palms were an unhealthy yellow, the color of our chalky classroom walls.

The scarred wooden door was open just a crack, wide enough for me to fit my head in. That's how I spotted him. "Greely?" I said to his back, and he kicked over a push broom and nearly tripped on a dented galvanized bucket by one of his feet.

"Sam," he muttered, when he'd regrouped, "don't do that to an old man. You'll put me in my grave."

I nodded nervously.

He studied me as his heartbeat slowed. "What can I do for you?" he finally asked.

My mind whirled with images of Newt, but nothing came out of my mouth. Foam stuck like glue in the corners.

Greely turned and wrapped damp paper towels around the clean brown bristles of his brushes. "Being nervous again, ain't you?" he said as he worked.

"Yes, sir," I admitted.

"What'd I say about that? It don't get you nowhere."

"I know," I managed, followed by a shaky, "Greely?"

"Sam?" he said as he placed the brushes up on an old shelf, a splintery plank so dusty it was gray.

"Remember that fat kid who was picking on me?" I asked him.

"Sure," he said, turning around completely and leaning against the deep sink he'd been working over.

"He's going to kill me," I mumbled. "He's going to beat my brains out at the bus stop. That's what he told me." I entered the dark storage room and pulled the door closed behind me.

"He told you that?"

"He told me," I whispered.

"Well, I'll tell you something. That kid's a bully. You know what a real bully is? It's a person who thinks he can get away with something 'cause all the cards are stacked in their favor. I seen it a hundred times growing up in the South." He pulled on the bill of his Chevron cap. "How can I help you, Sam?"

"Just follow me up past the bus stop," I whispered, relieved.

"Gimme a minute," he said, and disappeared into a back room.

Among crowds of students, we made our way up to Falls Road. We didn't say much. Greely tossed around a few comments about his sore knee and the fact that painting didn't do anything to help it. My mind was busy, spinning with thoughts of Newt, who was probably waiting for me like a gunfighter, standing by the bench that had THE CITY THAT READS written on it, his caved-in face angry.

Sure enough, Newt was there. I stared across the street at him, at his thug friends who'd come to watch him batter me. He smoked a cigarette, studied Greely and me as we turned down Falls Road toward Forty-first Street. Newt didn't even move or yell something after us. He just inhaled and exhaled the smoke of his Winston. I thought about what Greely had said: a bully is a person who thinks he can get away with something. Well, that afternoon, Newt couldn't get away with anything, and that made me feel all right, talkative, and cunning. He knew Greely wasn't a pushover and could have torn him in two homely parts.

Twenty minutes later, at the top of Forty-first Street and across Roland Avenue, we stopped. Greely smiled. "That kid's gonna get his one day. You just wait, Sam."

I nodded, looked at his funny face, those big eyes. "Thanks, Greely," I said.

"No reason to thank me," he replied. "I got this thing in my heart against bullies. Seen them lynch men who ain't done nothing and couldn't do nothing. Bullies of all sorts leave a bad taste in my mouth."

I hunkered my shoulders under my old nylon coat. "What's lynching?" I asked, squinting in the November sun, blazing hard and yellow just to the right of a tall, blackened, and rusty apartment building down Roland Avenue, toward the heart of Hampden.

Greely jostled his head a little, stuck his big bottom lip out in thought. "It just means stringing someone up without figuring out whether they's even guilty or not. Happened in the South a lot when I was a young man. Some white guys—not all of them, but some— would grab a nigger and hang 'em for no reason except maybe they wanted to set an example, wanted to make it clear that we had better stay in our place."

I reached up and rubbed at the side of my nose, pushed at a nostril so that it squeaked. "Where was your place?" I asked, remembered how Greely could use the word nigger, but I couldn't.

"Poor and weak and intimidated, that's where it was."

I looked over my shoulder at the Rotunda, at the Giant Supermarket, stuck on the side as if it had spun out of control and crashed into the older building. I felt a little guilty.

"Come on," Greely said, thumping my back. He started walking again. "I'll go with you all the way down to St. Paul Street. That's where we head in different directions." He looked over his broad shoulder at me. "Getting cold out here, Sam," he explained.

I scampered after him, caught up. I wanted to do something, show him I appreciated his help and what he knew about bullies. "Hey, Greely," I said, scooting all about, "you wanta see me jump up and touch that sign?"

He nodded. "Been waiting to see a kid do that."

So I took off, thumped it with two fingers, felt like I was gliding above the ground, scooting through the sky low and fast.

the heimlich maneuver
the heimlich maneuver

We ate Thanksgiving dinner at Junie and Ditch's place in Hamilton, this neighborhood across town from ours. They lived in a big old house that they'd owned for about thirty years. It was a nice place, but it always seemed a little rundown, from the patchy brown yard to the arching roof over the front porch. Even still, it wasn't anything like our apartment. It was huge, the way most of the homes in Hamilton are. It had three stories to it, and a tall steep roof with two gables in the front. The sides were flat and straight, covered with slightly faded boards that Ditch sometimes replaced but didn't paint for a while. The windows were also tall, so tall that Ditch had to stand on a ladder just to clean the uppermost rectangles of wavy glass.

The inside wasn't bad, just a little dark and kind of stuffy feeling downstairs. It seemed like the sort of place where germs swirled around forever. The Gordons never opened a window on the first floor, even in the middle of summer. They didn't pull back the curtains, either, which I found strange because Junie had told us that sunlight made people feel better. Every window was nailed shut and shielded by a thick, golden fabric that was as coarse as wool. Also, for

[95]

people who made a living selling plants, there weren't too many around, about one in each room, dried up leaves surrounding them. What they had instead of fresh air and such was a collection of Oriental rugs. On the floors downstairs, in every room but the kitchen, there were big colorful wool carpets, all overlapping, like papers stuffed in a tiny drawer. I don't know why they kept them that way, because it didn't show them off or anything. All that was visible of some were the corners. Walking around, you could tell there was a lot of padding beneath your feet because the carpet was so spongy. Also, the heavy furniture looked like it was sinking into the floor, including Ditch's fake-leather easy chair, located in the corner where Sylvester, their tabby cat, always peed. When I was a lot younger, I did forward rolls all around their downstairs, just ducked my head and went, because it was hard to hurt myself in there, except when my heels or legs hit furniture or something.

Upstairs, their house had a completely different feel. The curtains were pulled back, and on nice days, the windows were even open. White wall-to-wall carpeting covered every room and stretched down the hallway. It was so white that, before you trudged up the steps, you were supposed to kick your shoes off, so as not to soil the brilliance. See, the second floor is where Junie displayed her Hummel figurine collection, so she liked to keep it neat. There were porcelain kids everywhere, on practically every table, doing things like fishing, selling lemonade, and potty training. In one bedroom, she had an entire case devoted to them. My mom used to go up there and stare at it, because she loved Hummel figures, too.

On the third floor, they just stored old junk. That's where Ditch kept his *National Geographic* magazines and a baseball glove that an Orioles player had signed for him years before, after a game. He also rode a stationary bike up there. When he was doing it, you could hear one of the pedals squeaking all the way downstairs, a cat's whine.

It was cold out, wispy snow flurries occasionally fluttering to the ground. The sun was behind a layer of deep gray clouds, thick as a hunk of lint, low in the air, moving slowly. In the living room, Ditch and the clay-pot man, whose real name was Howard, sat slumped over National Premium beers, watching football. My mom, Junie, and I were in the kitchen, next to the old gas stove, where a massive Butterball turkey gurgled away. My mom was working on her specialty, cheese-filled mashed potatoes, as Junie dumped watery cans of creamed corn and spinach into a large aluminum saucepan with a half-melted plastic handle. I sat at the kitchen table, stirring a bowl of pumpkin-pie mix. I could have done it faster with a blender, but I didn't mind taking the time. I didn't want to go out and talk to Howard. From the two minutes I'd spent with him, I didn't like him all that much. On top of that, he didn't look all that ridiculous. As a matter of fact, he looked closer to normal. My mom had exaggerated his features to make me feel better.

Junie stopped what she was doing and turned her big back to the old puckered and scorched Formica counter. A beautician had convinced her to get a perm-and-bleach job for the holidays, so her wide, sagging features glowed beneath a halo of tight curls. Also, she'd tucked her embroidered denim shirt into her stretchy blue pants, bunching up wads of extra fabric at her hips.

"So, Samuel, hon, whatcha want for Christmas this year?" Junie asked me as she took a breather from opening cans and sipped on a beer.

"Don't know," I told her as I worked.

"Your mom says you want clothes."

I didn't want clothes at all, but I knew I needed them. One of the sneakers that my dad had bought me nearly a year before had two holes in the rubbery toe, and my winter boots no longer fit.

"Yeah, I guess," I lied.

"Anything else?"

I couldn't think of anything. "Not right now."

"Whatcha think of that, Maxine?" Junie practically yelled. "Your son don't want anything for Christmas but a new wardrobe."

"Don't believe it for an instant," my mom told her from across the kitchen as she grated cheddar cheese onto one of the Gordons' red dinner plates.

"He looks pretty serious to me."

My mom glanced over at me. "He always thinks of something."

"Course he will. He's just like Ditch," Junie replied. "Just like Ditch. Why, last year we was nearly two weeks away from Christmas before he comes up with this idea that he wants a snow blower. You remember? Got his heart set on it. We don't get enough snow to use one around here, I tell him. You remember? Still he wanted it." Junie shook her curly, platinum head. "Men always think of something. That's the truth."

I continued stirring the pie mix.

Junie lifted her chin and peered into the bowl. She clicked her tongue. "God, hon, how long you gonna do that for? It's got to be smooth by now."

"I guess it is," I said.

"Well, let's pour it." She put her beer can down and grabbed the pie crust on the counter behind her and brought it over to me.

I pulled off the stiff plastic cover and turned the mixing bowl up on its side, so that pumpkin sauce dumped slowly, like lava, onto the graham cracker crust.

"That's a nice looking pie, hon," Junie commented.

My mom turned around, bent at the waist so that her skinny body got even more pinched. "Samuel, if I'd known you could cook, I'd have had you prepare dinner for me a few times." She smiled, her pretty made-up face wrinkling around the eyes.

"This isn't really cooking," I told her seriously.

My mom laughed, something that she'd been doing a lot more of since her second date with Howard. That bothered me a little. She swore that they were just close friends, but I knew my mom liked him, and I had no idea why. He wasn't quite as bad as she'd said, but he still wasn't great. My dad could have snapped him in half. Not that Howard was small; it was just that my dad had been so big that normal-sized people appeared to shrink around him.

"Samuel, you're getting a little too serious for your own good," Junie told me, knotty fingers squeezing the edge of the silver pie tray, shaking it back and forth to get rid of air bubbles. "Why don't you go see if the boys'd like another beer, watch some football, or somethin', instead of hanging out in this old kitchen."

Reluctantly, I got up from the table and handed Junie the spoon. I walked into the living room, across springy layers of Oriental carpet, toward the loud television, crowd noise blaring like a heavy rain.

I walked in behind the couch where Howard was sitting, stumbled across the room, and stood by the television. I watched the Lions run a bad play. The quarterback got crushed by a Viking defensive lineman. "Junie wants to know if you guys want another beer," I said.

Howard smiled at me. "Well, thanks, Samuel. I could use one, and I bet your uncle Ditch could, too."

Ditch lifted his can and shook it so that I could hear it was nearly empty. He didn't glance over, though. He was too focused on an instant replay.

I stared at Howard's weird face, searched for an overbite that wasn't really there. His front teeth were pointy, but that was it. Sadly, he didn't resemble Bugs Bunny in any way. He looked more like a vampire. "Ditch isn't my uncle," I informed him.

Ditch turned around. "Come on, Sam," he said. "Neither of us needs ta hear that kinda talk on Thanksgiving."

I looked down at my feet. "You aren't, though," I said weakly.

Ditch rocked his long body from off the squishy cushion of his fake-leather easy chair, watched the end of a play, and walked past the television. He ignited a cigarette with his Bic lighter, cupping the flame with a hand the way he always did, then crimped the filter between two yellowed teeth. He hunched down in front of me, narrow knees snapping and popping, jutting out beneath him like steel rods, feet similar to the wheels on an office chair. "Feel like I'm your uncle," he said.

I couldn't look him in the eye.

He roughed up my hair, blew a cloud of smoke over a narrow shoulder that was covered in flannel. He stood back up, took another draw on his Winston, said, "You watch the game, Sam; I'll go fetch us some beers. Talk ta Howard some." He scraggled my hair again and drifted off toward the back of the house and the kitchen.

Howard bit at the inside of his cheek, adjusted on the couch, elbows on the hard lumps of his thighs. "So," he said, after a minute, "who you want to win?"

I shrugged. "The Lions."

"Me, too, I guess," he said.

I turned slowly and walked over to one of the Gordons' large wing chairs, deposited myself amid the flower pattern, and stared at the television, which was built into a huge wood cabinet along with an old record player and a radio. Each could be hidden by a sliding door, but Ditch and Junie never pulled them shut.

"How do you like your new neighborhood?" Howard asked.

I shrugged, because I felt all sorts of ways about it, none of them the same from day to day.

"It's not so bad," he said.

I didn't reply.

"I always liked Charles Village. I like the Waverly Deli. You like the Deli?"

"My mom likes the corned beef."

"Me, too," Howard said. "Me, too." He smiled, looking around. "How about yourself?"

I pulled up one side of my upper lip, the area below a nostril. "I don't like it."

He nodded his head gently, wiped across his sharp widow's peak, his short black hair that he wore spiked up like the bristles of a brush. "Some don't," he admitted.

Ditch tottered in with their beers, two cold cans of National Premium. "You guys talk any?" he asked, tossing one to Howard, then settling back into his chair.

Howard nodded. "Sam's a nice guy," he said.

"Sure is," Ditch replied, eyes fastened on the television screen again, a thin stream of air whistling from the cushions he was sinking into. "He's my pal, even if I ain't his uncle. Right, Sam?"

I nodded. "Yes, sir."

He cracked open his beer. "Why'd you call me 'sir,' Sam?"

I wasn't sure myself, so I told him, "For Thanksgiving."

He shook his head. "You're a handful. You know that?"

I smiled, got comfortable.

"Look at that crap," Ditch exclaimed, shaking his head about a play.

"Their coaching staff sucks," Howard offered.

"You're right about that."

I listened to them watch the game for a while. They carried on about the players, the cheerleaders, and even John Madden's voice. Then, on a long bomb, a perfectly thrown pass that a wide receiver let trickle through his hands at the goal line, Ditch pounded the wide arm of his chair and said, "Look at that nigger. He can't catch anything. He can run, but his hands aren't worth a damn."

"Dropped two against the Redskins," Howard recalled sadly.

"Should be looking for other work, 'cept he's fast."

They continued fuming, but I no longer listened to them. I sat back in that big wing chair and thought about the way Ditch had called the man a nigger. It shocked me, even though he'd used the word as long as I could remember. It was just that I hadn't heard him do it since I'd made friends with Greely. I slid from the soft chair, turned, and headed off toward the kitchen.

Pushing the squeaky swinging door open, I stood by the shiny table, near the warm oven. The pie I'd made was on the counter, behind my mom and Junie, who were talking over beers.

"You looking for Coke or something, hon?" Junie asked me.

I shook my head self-consciously. "I just wanted to talk to my mom for a minute," I told her.

Junie raised her patchy eyebrows and pushed herself away from the counter. She set her beer down. "Alone, hon?"

I nodded.

"Well, you two go ahead and talk in here. I gotta go to the bathroom anyway."

My mom squeezed her lips together. "Thanks, Junie."

Junie untangled the tight knot on her frilly white apron. Before leaving, she stuck out a big hand, orange polish shimmering on each nail, and cupped my cheek gently. "I'll knock before I come back in," she told me. "Just go ahead and talk."

When I was sure she was out of earshot, I asked my mom why Ditch used the word *nigger* so much.

She pulled the oven door open and looked at the big turkey, then shut it. "Because he doesn't know any better," she finally told me.

"He must," I said.

"He knows he shouldn't," she agreed. "The thing is, Ditch grew up at a different time, when everyone called blacks that."

"People shouldn't, though."

"You're right, sweetheart."

"Ditch shouldn't."

She shrugged, stroked a bony hand sharply through her shiny brown hair, the way she did when she was getting frustrated. "I agree."

I looked over at the thick golden curtain above the kitchen sink, drawn shut in front of a blurry window. "Will you tell him not to?"

"Oh, honey, I can't," she said.

"Why not?" I asked.

She shook her head, looked embarrassed. "I just can't."

"What if he says it to Greely one day?"

She smiled a little. "I don't think he'll ever meet Greely."

"But what if he does?"

"He won't," she said. "Ditch wouldn't be mean to one of your friends."

I yanked out a chair and sat slumped at the kitchen table, staring glumly down at my dim reflection, floating atop the brown grain.

My mom took a deep breath. "Maybe I'll talk to him the next time I hear him say it."

I lifted my eyes so that I could see her frail ankles.

"Ditch is a nice man."

"I know that," I said.

"You shouldn't hold it against him." She stepped over and ran a finger down my back. "Where'd you get your social conscience? Your dad never had one."

I shrugged. "What's a social conscience?" I asked, hoping it was good.

We sat down for Thanksgiving dinner after the end of the first football game and before the start of the second. My mom and Howard were located across the table from Junie and me, while Ditch sat at the head, sucking down gobs of turkey and stuffing and cheese potatoes and yams and cranberry sauce and Junie's spinach-and-corn concoction and slices of ham from the deli counter at the Giant. He always ate like he was starving to death. My dad had kidded him about that. Since he wasn't there, though, Junie was the one to give him a hard time. She told him to slow down, which he didn't do.

Straight in front of me, Howard ate at regular speed, but he slurped sometimes. He did it when he sipped at his beer. Nobody seemed to notice, or at least they acted as if they didn't. But I shot my eyes at him whenever he picked up his can, just so he'd know that someone heard him. Not that it stopped him from doing it.

"Wish we could always eat this well," Junie said. "Ditch, how're the yams?"

"Jus' righ'," he told her.

"Is the turkey overcooked?"

"Perfect," he assured her without looking up.

"If I do say so myself, this is the best dinner I ever cooked," she declared.

"It's wonderful," my mom said.

"It's really good," Howard crowed beside her, glasses magnifying the weathered wrinkles around his eyes.

Junie looked at me. "Hon?"

"It's good," I told her.

"Well, it's unanimous," she said, and scooped up a hunk of chewy stuffing with the prongs of her glimmering metal fork.

After a few minutes of silence, my mom asked Howard what the tradition was at his house. Embarrassed, he told us that they really didn't have one, that his mother liked to be spontaneous. The year before, she'd made a pot of spaghetti instead of a turkey.

"Spaghetti?" I laughed.

He nodded, slurped his beer. "I told her it was strange."

"Never heard of anything like that," I said.

My mom caught my eye by moving her finger up and down.

I avoided her gaze.

"It's all right," Howard mumbled. "You'll like this, Sam. You know what she's making for dinner today?"

I shook my head, jammed some potatoes into my mouth.

"Tuna casserole."

I nearly spit. "For Thanksgiving?"

He lifted his scarred hands to show me he couldn't do anything about it.

"That's nothing," Junie chimed. "I once knew a woman who cooked creole every single night, even on holidays. I don't know what she put in it, but it was always creole. I could tell."

"Something Torbois was her name," Ditch said.

"Whatever it was, she was strange," Junie told us.

"She used ta live two houses down," Ditch explained. "She was part French or something. From Louisiana. Looked nearly black. She was some kinda writer, and her husband was some kinda fish scientist, who worked on the Bay. You couldn't talk to him at all, he was so boring. You remember that, Junie?"

"He was boring," she agreed.

"Anyway, they was both strange, and they lived right down the street. The whole neighborhood hated that, 'cause she was so dark and he was so boring. They lived here less than two years, but it seemed like ten. We was all glad they left. You could smell her creole cooking every night in the summer. By August, it was turning your stomach."

"Were they Cajun?" my mom asked.

Ditch and Junie shrugged.

Howard put his hand up against his throat, his blackened, busted thumbnail swollen like an eye.

My mom glanced over at him, dropped her fork to her plate with a clank. "Howard's choking!" she shouted.

My eyes locked on him, and sure enough, she was right. Howard couldn't breathe. His angular face was red as a fire hydrant, and his eyes were wide and panicked behind the thick scratched lenses of his glasses.

My mom gave Howard a wicked thump on his back, but it didn't help. He continued to clutch at his neck and make awful wheezing sounds.

Junie squirmed from her chair and rushed about the oval table. She yanked Howard out of his seat and spun him around. Wrapping her smooshy arms across his chest, she gave him a quick, sharp squeeze.

Howard grunted, and his wire-rimmed glasses popped off, but nothing else happened.

Junie grit her teeth, gave him another hard, quick jolt, and a hunk of white turkey meat shot out of his mouth, careened through the air, and landed right on his plate.

Howard fell to his knees.

Junie stumbled backward and leaned against the wall-papered wall, breathing hard. "Lord!" she exclaimed.

"Howard," my mom pleaded, "can you talk?"

He put one hand in the seat of his chair and the other on the table. "Yeah." He coughed, locating his glasses on the carpet.

"Don't try to get up," she told him.

He took some deep breaths and stood, anyway. He looked embarrassed. "Tha . . . that's ne . . . never happened before," he swore to us, sucking wind. "Never."

Ditch tried to calm him by giving him a pat on one shoulder. "Don't worry about it. Consider yerself lucky," he said, taking a smooth draw on his cigarette.

"Howard," Junie croaked behind him.

He turned and peered at her.

She held out her arms and stepped away from the wall, gave him a big hug.

"Thanks," he told her.

"It was my cooking, wasn't it?" she joked.

"You're cooking's wonderful," he mumbled. "I just ate too fast."

She smiled, winking at me over his shoulder. "Well, hon," she said, "I'm glad you're all right."

In my chair, I rose to my knees and pointed at his plate. "Did you see where it landed?"

"What?" Ditch asked.

"The piece of turkey."

Everyone looked at me.

"It landed on his plate." Amazed and fascinated, I showed them, shaking my head.

Ditch nodded, but I could tell he didn't care.

Junie looked down at the hunk of turkey nestled in the middle of Howard's corn and spinach. "Well, no wonder you choked, Howard; you didn't hardly chew."

After supper, I helped my mom and Junie clear the dishes, while Ditch and Howard, who was no worse for the wear, got comfortable in front of the game. I scraped all the glop into the Gordons' big plastic garbage can, and my mom ran the plates and pots under a clear stream of hot water before dumping them into the dishwasher. Junie filled the Mr. Coffee and wiped down the counters. "God," she said after a few minutes, "I was worried that boy was going to die." She scratched a spot on the rough tip of her nose.

My mom nodded, resting a wet plate against her thigh. "I can't believe it happened," she murmured.

Junie tramped over to the loud refrigerator, fan chugging. She pulled the door open. "He needs to chew more. You saw that piece of turkey." She pushed at the condiments and the bowls with crinkled Saran Wrap across their tops. "Maxine, guess what?"

"What?" my mom asked, depositing the plate she'd been holding into a slot on the dishwasher rack.

"We don't have no more milk. What I gave you for the potatoes was it. Ditch must have forgotten it last night." She shut the refrigerator door. "And he takes more in his coffee than anyone else."

I handed my mom the last plate, slid behind her, and washed off my hands.

"Samuel," Junie asked me, "You mind running down to the 7-Eleven?"

It was cold out and I was feeling stuffed, but I knew I didn't have a choice. I shrugged.

Junie went over to the counter and pulled the top off a ceramic mushroom. She stuck her hand into the pink stem part and located a five-dollar bill between rubber bands and matchbooks.

"A gallon of whole," she instructed.

"Thanks," my mom called to me as I shuffled through the swinging kitchen door and into the living room. I walked past Ditch and Howard and unhooked my puffy coat from the rack in the foyer. As I pulled it on, Howard asked where I was going.

"The 7-Eleven," I mumbled.

"You want company?" he asked.

I didn't want his, but didn't say anything.

He stood up. "I could use the air."

Ditch started snoring as Howard slid into his dirty jacket. I turned, opened the storm door, and walked out onto the front porch. I ambled over to a car battery, gave it a shove with my foot, but it didn't budge. I went back to the door, looked in on Howard, who was wrapping a scarf around his neck. I staggered down the springy front steps, walked onto the lawn, where I waited, breathing steam from my mouth and watching tiny flakes of snow drop silently to the ground.

When Howard came out, he shook his arms and jumped up and down to get his blood going. "Cold," he said.

Instead of saying anything, I started for the sidewalk. Trudging along, I stared straight ahead. At busy Harford Road, two blocks away, big rusty American cars buzzed past, and a television repair shop and a used-lighting store were visible in a low line of rowhouses across the thoroughfare.

"Hard to believe I nearly choked to death."

I was a little curious about that. "Did it hurt?" I asked him.

"No. I just couldn't breathe."

We passed a monstrous house that had caught fire a few weeks before. Ditch had told my mom about it the day after it had happened. The pale shingles on the roof were charred and the broad windows on the second and third floors were scorched. It was dark inside, and the big front door under the porch roof was clamped shut with wide, pale boards that someone had spray-painted red swastikas all over. The same person had probably broken out the windows. As bad as it was, though, I was sure that it was better than our place on Abel Avenue. I wondered where the family who lived there had gone and if they were planning on salvaging their home. I didn't like the Hamilton area all that much, but if they were just going to tear the house down, I wished that they would give it to my mom and me.

"Sam, do you dislike me because I'm younger than your mother?"

I stopped dead in my tracks. "You're younger than my mom?"

"You knew that," he said.

"Nobody tells me anything."

"Well, it shouldn't matter," he declared, face pale, flat as a marble step.

"How old are you?" I asked desperately.

"Old enough," he said. "Twenty-seven."

I was horrified. "My mom's thirty-two!"

"See, there's only five years between us."

I didn't want to hear it. I spun around and walked as fast as I could, stumbling toward the 7-Eleven. My worn sneakers thudded dully on the coarse cement. Finding out that my mom was dating a younger man made everything seem so much worse. There was something awful about it, like she was desperate, like our whole situation was desperate.

Howard caught up to me. "Come on, Sam," he said. "At our age, five years is nothing."

I jutted out my bottom lip and kept going.

"Come on," he said again.

I turned the corner and stared ahead at the big plastic 7-Eleven sign, glowing. I focused on the glass storefront and the tall white steeple on the pitched roof. There was a jacked-up black van with a bad muffler parked in the handicapped space. It rumbled like a loud race car. As I got closer, I noticed the dirty green shag carpet on the dashboard and ceiling. It reminded me of dying grass.

Inside the store, I slowly walked by the comic-book rack so that I could see the titles and covers. Then I picked up speed and walked straight back to the humming refrigerators, grabbed a cold plastic jug of milk, and headed for the Plexiglas-encased counter.

At the register, I stood behind this burly guy in a wheelchair. He was one of the ugliest people I'd ever seen. I felt sorry that he was crippled and all, but he was filthy, and he stunk. He had a grimy bandanna wrapped across his lumpy forehead, long stringy hair, and a greasy leather motorcycle jacket on. His face was pudgy and scarred and droopy like it had been smashed and patted back together. As I paid for the milk, I watched him roll out to his van, open the door, and pull himself up into the driver's seat. The way he reached down and folded his wheelchair flat in one quick motion, you could tell he was mad about something.

Heading back, Howard followed a few steps behind me. "So, Sam," he said as we rounded the corner onto the Gordons' street, "saw you looking at the comic books. You like to read them?"

"Yeah," I grumbled.

"Me, too," he said. He caught up to me, jammed his hands in his pants pockets. "I like Iron Fist more than anyone else. You?"

"The Beast and Wolverine."

"I prefer the Beast to Wolverine. He's got a sense of humor."

I slowed down, adjusted the cold 7-Eleven bag in my hands.

"I'm a fan of the Avengers, so I like the Beast a lot." He rubbed his narrow chin. "I guess my second-favorite superhero is Dare Devil."

I stopped. "Are you lying?"

"About what?"

"That you like comic books?"

"Sam, I collect them, or I used to. I must have five hundred in some boxes at my mom's place."

My eyes darted around self-consciously. "You think you want 'em?"

The snow started falling harder, dozens of tiny flakes spinning in tiny tornadoes to the frozen ground. Some of them stuck in Howard's hair, on the tip of his widow's peak, like dull gray fireplace ashes. "I want 'em," he told me, "but you're welcome to take them home. Maybe we can even trade a few."

I smiled suspiciously.

"Who else do you like on the X-Men?" he asked.

I started walking again. "Cyclops and Colossus."

"Colossus is Russian, right?"

"Yeah."

"I like Alpha Flight. You read Alpha Flight?"

"Guess what? That's my third-favorite comic," I told him.

"Mine, too," he said.

That's when I started to like Howard.

everyone's scared, some

everyone's scared, some

Greely lifted his coat from a worn metal hook in a series of similar worn metal hooks that were draped with ratty sweaters and wrinkled shirts, and we left the downstairs storage room. It was still cold and damp out, causing his bad knee to tighten around the joint like it was squeezed by a thick belt. As he climbed up the worn cement steps to the first floor, he wore a grimace on his face and kept a hand on the slick wood rail covered with little dents, bolted loosely to the tiled wall, shaky as a busted chair.

"Some fool needs to tighten this thing," he told me, rattling the banister.

"Who's supposed to do that?" I asked.

"Me," he said.

Outside, despite the cold temperature, there were still a few kids milling about Robert Poole Middle School, smoking cigarettes, talking trash by the street, leaning against neighborhood cars, some pitted and crunched from accidents and gnarled by rust, others kept spotless, buffed even on the strips. Greely and I made our way slowly past them, up the sidewalk, toward Falls Road, leaning rowhomes on the left and the recreation center on the right. On the basketball court, a skinny dropout wearing a torn blue parka took a shot over a tall boy with an orange stocking cap pulled down over his ears.

"You don't play nothing, do you?" Greely asked me.

I lifted my shoulders, let them drop. "Not anymore. My dad and I used to throw the football sometimes."

"You should do something, Sam. Growing boy like you should do something."

I didn't reply, because I didn't think the same way. I didn't feel that I needed to do much of anything.

"You still got a football?" Greely asked me as we turned the corner at breezy, cold Falls Road, then headed slowly north toward Thirty-sixth Street.

I bit my lip. I'd always kept my ball in the trunk of my father's car, but I hadn't seen it when my mother and I had cleaned the car out before the sale. The ball hadn't been there. It made me mad to think that the kidnappers had taken it, too.

"It disappeared with my father," I whispered softly to Greely, feeling kind of down. It had been a gift from my dad, and I hadn't even realized that it was missing.

"Your father took the ball with him?" Greely dug his monster hands deep into the sandy pockets of his coat.

"No. My dad didn't have a chance to take anything. He kept the ball in his trunk, and when he was kidnapped, the police found his car, but the ball wasn't in it anymore."

"Was it a nice one?"

"It was small, so that it fit my hand."

Greely shook his head, bulging eyes rocking in his skull like a floating compass. "Bet you wish you could get it back."

I was too embarrassed to tell him that I hadn't even noticed that it had been gone till that moment.

"Reason I ask is I figure since I see you most every afternoon, it's my job to make sure you get some exercise. Little exercise would take away some of your nervousness. We could toss a football or something. I don't like baseball. Don't like the game. Never have. Don't want to toss a baseball around, but a football, well, I like football. I wouldn't mind doing that."

"Can you?"

"What, with my leg, you mean? Don't have to run to throw something. Heck, I'd make you run; that's what I'd do. Then you could go home and feel tired from activity, not from just sitting around all day."

We passed by the shabby EZ Market, specials taped to the window out front. A block down the sidewalk, pounding music seeped through the brown stucco walls of Batman's Lounge. It sounded like an erratic heartbeat.

"What'd you do to your knee?" I asked Greely as a huge truck barreled by. The suck of wind yanked on my clothes.

"Didn't hear you, Sam."

"How'd you hurt your knee?"

"My knee. Busted it during the war, in a small town outside Berlin. Germans surrendered something like nine days later. *Pow*, I get shot walking over to trade my cigarettes for this guy's peach cobbler. Bullet went right through the cap like someone took a drill and cut a hole in it. Doctor said I was lucky it didn't explode into a thousand pieces. I was on crutches for around four months. Then I walked with a cane for a year and a half. Believe it or not, it didn't start bothering me again till about eight years ago. 1980, I think. Got arthritic and tight. Guess God's telling me I'm getting old."

We turned and started up Forty-first Street, past the pale brick dairy, shut down and dark behind the panes of dusty frosted glass.

"So, you never did tell me how your Thanksgiving was, Sam. Last I heard it was going to be the worst you ever had." Steam from Greely's big nostrils bellowed out in front of him, disappearing before he walked into it.

"It was okay," I admitted, embarrassed. "Howard's okay." I looked at Greely. "You want to know something that happened?"

"Sure," Greely said, thick voice muffled.

"Howard almost choked to death. He got a piece of turkey caught in his throat, and Junie had to squeeze his stomach to get it out." Thinking about the incident got me excited.

"She gave him the Heimlich," he said.

"She squeezed his stomach." I adjusted my books in a freezing hand. "It took her two tries."

He laughed, a smile pulling across his face, exposing a bottom tooth that stuck out in front of all of the others. "What she did is called the Heimlich. She gave him the Heimlich maneuver."

"The turkey flew out of his mouth."

"That's what happens sometimes," Greely said. "I once took a class on it."

When my mom got home from work, I scampered out of the hall closet, where I'd been watching *Donahue,* and followed her into the kitchen. I tailed her as she filled a stained metal pot with water, then placed it on the stove, over a sputtering, loud blue flame.

"Something I can do for you, Samuel?" she asked me as she twisted open the top on a jar of Ragu.

"I have a question about Christmas," I said, and took a seat at our cold table. A breeze blew right through the warped wall.

She dumped the Ragu into a pan and plopped that on the stove, next to the water. "I knew you'd think of something you wanted," she teased me on her way to the closet to get a can of vegetables.

"What I was wondering is, can Greely come for Christmas dinner?"

My mom slowed, opened a drawer, and withdrew a skinny metal can opener. "You know, I'd say fine except that we're going to eat at Ditch and Junie's." Puncturing the top of the can, she cranked the big flat handle shaped like a bow tie. "They might not like us inviting extra people."

"But I don't think he has anywhere to go."

My mom placed the opener in the sink. "How about the school nurse? She told me that she thinks an awful lot of him. Maybe she's going to invite him to her place for dinner." She stuck the can of corn in the middle of the oven and turned up the heat, got herself a beer from the refrigerator, and sat at the table across from me.

"I want him to come to our Christmas dinner. That's what I want."

She pulled the tab on the top of her beer. She took a swig. "I hate to admit it," she said, "but I just don't know how much Ditch or Junie would like Greely."

"'Cause he's black?"

She shrugged, pulled her hands tight around her, rubbed opposite arms to keep off the chill that crept through the wall. "This place is ridiculous," she said, breathing out. She smiled, reached over, and touched one of my arms. "I don't condone their attitudes; it's just the way they are. I wish it wasn't."

"But Greely's nice. He's really nice. He can practically get along with anyone. He jokes around and everything. And he knows a lot about history. He was in World War II, you know. That's why he walks so slow, 'cause someone shot his knee."

She adjusted in her seat, chewed on the skin at the tip of a finger. "You know what? You should bring him by the store. At least introduce him around."

I sat up. "When?"

"Whenever he doesn't mind the extra walk."

* * *

[116]

The following afternoon, Greely and I made our way to Junie's Florist, past the WaWa convenience store and the Laundromat, groggy-looking people watching their fading clothes through the round glass doors on the washers and dryers. Newspapers rolled and tumbled on the uneven sidewalks and streets, skittered like dead birds, as if they were twirling down from the clouds. Storm drains were packed with bright leaves. There was the bank, the video store, and the speed-reading school, where out front a scraggly white guy huddled, shivering like a cold dog. He asked Greely for change. The man's butt bones were as sharp as two shovel blades, and there was a brown cast deteriorating on one of his knotty wrists. His face was sunken, cheeks chewed as toffee.

Greely felt in the patched pockets of his baggy blue work pants, bent down, and gave him a few coins.

"What I need is ten bucks," the guy told him thickly.

Greely shook his head, eyes flashing dangerously, as they could at times.

"That kind of man scares me," I said as we approached the sign that Ditch had welded out of old pipes. Mr. Oritz was outside, smoking a slim brown cigarette and poking at a muddy white bag of pine bark mulch with one of his tiny feet.

"People can be scary," Greely admitted.

"You never seem scared."

"Don't be crazy, Sam," he said. "Everyone's scared. I work through it. That's what you gotta do after a while."

I waved to Mr. Oritz and opened the door to the floral shop. Two cowbells bonked together. My mom and Junie stood in the back of the room, behind the long counter, by the softly humming electric cash register. My mom was putting together a flower arrangement in a green glass container that was supposed to look like a cowboy boot. It was the arrangement of the month. I knew because I'd helped her make one the week before. Junie was talking to her, twisting a piece of floral wire around one of her stubby fingers. As Greely and I tramped slowly toward them, my mom smiled anxiously. Junie's face, glowing slightly in the gleam from her new ball of blond curly hair, went kind of expressionless.

"This is my friend Greely," I said.

My mom made an effort to seem relaxed. She wiped one of her cold hands off on her smock and stuck it out so that they could shake. "I'm Samuel's mom, Maxine Webber."

"Nice to meet you," Greely said, his strange, sluggish voice crawling from between those thick pink lips of his. He yanked off his Chevron cap, stuffed it in a big coat pocket.

My mom motioned toward me. "Samuel's told me a lot about you."

"He's a nice kid. Got a good heart."

"Only sometimes," she joked.

Greely let out a laugh that sounded like a snort.

My mom's mouth flattened into a lumpy line. "The school nurse says good things about you." She shifted her eyes. "I had to call her, Mr. Clemons. I hope you don't mind."

"Mrs. Webber, I got no problem with you watching out for your boy. You gotta do it. I could be a pervert, far as you know." The bumps on Greely's head caught in the bright lights above the counter. They looked like holes in his skull, like his brain was lit up.

My mom smiled, swept a slab of hair back, and turned toward Junie. "Mr. Clemons, this is my boss and friend, practically my mother, Junie Gordon."

"Mrs. Gordon?" Greely said, offering her his callused hand, scratchy as the surface of a brick.

Junie crammed a set of pale fingers into his, held on for two quick quivers, then let go.

"Greely's the maintenance man at Robert Poole Middle School," my mom told her. "He's been watching out for Samuel."

Greely shifted from one gigantic foot to the other. I could see the rubber soles of his scuffed boots flatten and expand. "Try to keep this mean kid from bothering him," he told her.

"Newt Novacek," my mom said.

Junie squished her nose around with a couple fingers. "That fat kid you told me about?"

I nodded.

Junie studied Greely's bizarre face, the eyes that resembled two oily golf balls with black dots on them. "Well, it's nice of you to look out for Samuel, Mr. Clemons."

His head lulled to one side. "I don't take to bullies. Seen enough of 'em in my life." He pushed back his stiff coat and dug his hands into his pants pockets.

"This world's filled with 'em," Junie said.

My mother bent forward and tapped one of Greely's thick arms, swaddled in layers of musty-smelling fabric. "I hope you don't walk too far out of your way in the afternoons."

"Naw, Mrs. Webber. I live right down the road, the thirty-nine-hundred block off Greenmount. It ain't far."

She nodded.

"Listen, you folks gotta call me Greely. I ain't used to anyone but school kids calling me mister." He adjusted his weight again.

"Everyone calls me Maxine," my mom said.

Junie didn't say anything.

"Had a friend who was named Maxine," Greely mumbled. "Didn't move with much speed, but she was nice. Met her nearly thirty years ago." He paused. "Guess how?"

"How?" I asked softly, leaning against a dull metal card rack.

Greely smiled down at me, lifted eyebrows that resembled two charcoal smears. "Believe it or not, I met her two days after the Little Tavern on Greenmount started serving blacks at the counter. Think it was the summer of 1960. I went in and this woman I was sure wouldn't want nothing to do with me, Maxine, treated me like I'd been eating there all my life. Went to her funeral when she died a few years ago. That's how friendly we got. Always liked the name Maxine 'cause the only Maxine I ever really knew was so nice. Always wanted to meet another, find out if it was that name." He smiled again.

"It's not the name," I informed him.

"Why not?" he said.

"Because names don't matter."

Greely lifted his shoulders, looked across the peeling countertop at my mom, then back at me. "Sam, you're too serious for a kid, you know that?"

Junie snorted, rubbed her nose again. "That's the same thing I tell him, Mr. Clemons. He's too serious. He's a serious boy."

"Worries too much is what I think. I told him to try and not be so nervous, that it don't get you anything but a sore stomach." Greely withdrew a hand from his pocket, gripped one of my shoulders, and gave me a shake.

Wobbling in place, I felt my face heat up.

"He's always been serious," my mom said. "He's been intense since the day he was born."

"Take after his father?" Greely asked.

My mom bobbed her bony head, muscles in her neck yanking and releasing like big rubber bands. "Yeah, his dad was a worrier. He let things he couldn't control bother him."

"That's the way it can get," Greely said. "I'll be honest, I was a worrier once. Understand what it's like to see just the problems and nothing else. Can turn you inside out. Ain't a good thing to be. Little seriousness ain't bad, but too much makes a person crazy. That's what I figured out." He shrugged. "If I figured out anything."

A customer came in and the cowbells banged and clanked together.

Greely took a moment to look around the cluttered shop, the row of chrome-trimmed refrigerators, their steamy windows, the dried flowers with their petals as delicate as paper, the cards and ribbons and theme vases and little statuettes. "Don't believe I ever shopped here," he said.

"Neighborhood store," Junie told him, reaching under the counter and withdrawing a half-finished Pepsi. She unscrewed the top and took a few glugs.

Greely reached into his coat pocket, withdrew his mashed baseball cap, wrapped a hand across the bill, and tugged it onto his head. "Should get going. Got to check on a neighbor. Fell down and broke her hip, and she ain't got no one." He looked at my mom. "I been meaning to ask you. You think it'd be all right if I tossed a football around with Sam once or twice a week? Wouldn't get him home too much later than right now. I think a boy his age needs to run round some."

My mom glanced at me, smiled. "I don't see why not."

I protested. "I can't throw worth anything."

Greely snickered. "I ain't exactly Lynn Swann, Sam. You ain't got to toss it very well to get it to me."

I rubbed a sneaker across the thin carpet. "I don't know where my ball is."

"You know what? I might just go buy me one tonight."

The customer, this nerdy looking college student, walked nervously up to the counter and asked Junie how much the roses cost.

"Just one?"

"Um, yeah," he answered.

"Three dollars, but we wrap 'em in nice paper and put some baby's breath in with 'em."

"Can I get three?" he asked.

"Sure," she said, crawling from her creaky stool and walking around the counter.

Greely tipped his hat toward my mom. "It's been nice to meet you."

My mom tightened her lips together again. "I'm glad you came by," she said. "I appreciate what you've done for Samuel."

"Been good for me. I ain't had a kid friend since last time I saw my own."

"When was that?" she asked.

"Good while ago," he muttered, reached down, and touched my shoulder. "See you tomorrow, Sam."

"Bye, Greely. Thanks for coming with me."

"My pleasure. Watch out for falling rocks."

I smiled wide.

Greely moved slowly, the way he always did, toward the front door, between a rack of overgrown houseplants and a table with ceramic sombreros on it.

Junie pulled her glowing head from one of the refrigerators and called to him. "Nice to meet you, Mr. Clemons."

He spun about more gracefully than I thought he could, lifted his Chevron hat. "The same, Mrs. Gordon," he said, then waved and pushed the door open with his big square behind. The cowbells bonked, and he was down the steps and on the sidewalk.

"He's nice, huh?" I said to my mom.

"He seems like a sweet man."

"You think he can come for Christmas dinner?"

She bit her lip. "Let me talk to Junie," she said, pulling the glass cowboy boot back in front of her. "Now you get to work. Mr. Oritz and you have to move all those mulch bags away from the fence. Last night somebody reached through and tore some open."

In back, I exchanged my good coat for one of my father's heavy old sweatshirts. I always wore it when I worked, even though it hung down to my knees. The dark fabric was splotched with dirt and grime and paint flecks. I rolled the baggy sleeves up and headed out the side door.

Wyman Park was damp and cold, the ground squishy with water. Greely and I stumbled down to the field between tall slick brown trees. Our heels carved up curls of brown mud. It was quiet. Sounds were muffled in the clear hollow. Assorted cars rumbling around the dense, clean neighborhood behind us passed by before we even heard them. On the Johns Hopkins side of the field, a creek in a rut of mud and roots lapped softly against graffiti-covered rocks. The white stone bridge above it made a whirling windy sound when trucks bounced across, moving fast and heavy on University Parkway.

The sky was a greenish yellow, thick and slow-moving as oil, heavy as ten wet blankets. It looked as if it could fall and suffocate all of Baltimore, plaster everyone's lungs like thick custard. Planes were barely visible, lurching above, like fish in a pond.

I put my books down on a Domino's Pizza box that sat crumpled and discarded by a garbage can.

Greely wore his same old work boots, cracked and wrinkled, every seam dusty with indoor dirt, sprinkled into place from mops and brooms and saw blades. The acrylic weave of his navy blue work pants looked metallic where it bunched up around his calves. He wore layers of ratty sweaters under his thin blue work coat. Another white oval above the breast pocket didn't have his name scrawled on it. His dry, thick fingers were exposed, pale palms tan, like the skin on my stomach. On his head, he wore a fraying yellow-and-black Steelers' stocking cap. He'd pulled it down over his ears, tugged it low on his brow, so that it looked as if his eyes were about to explode out of his face.

"You ready?" he called, squeezing the small rubber football he'd bought the night before at a G. C. Murphy's on Greenmount. He raised it to a powerful shoulder.

Unenthusiastically, I mumbled, "Sure." We stood about twenty feet apart. I told myself to keep my legs apart, to watch the ball into my hands, just as my father had instructed me on Saturdays and Sundays during halftimes.

Greely tossed it awkwardly, feet turned in toward each other, fingers straight as writing pens, a big ugly grimace on his already funny face. The ball wobbled end over end.

It splattered into the mud. "You're a terrible quarterback." I laughed.

"Harder than it looks on television."

I heaved the ball back to him with a grunt. "My dad could throw a spiral. He tossed them perfect."

"Your dad was a good athlete?"

"Yeah." I grunted, slogging a few feet to try to make a catch that bounced out of my hands. I thought back to similar times with my father, his Colts jersey flapping loosely around him. He'd always gotten frustrated with me when I didn't listen to his instructions. He'd tell my mom that I was uncoachable, which made me feel like an idiot. "I always told him I liked them soft, but he still threw 'em hard. He was trying to train me. He couldn't help it, either," I added.

"He was that strong, huh?"

Greely's question seemed to echo in my ears, amplify and bang about. I picked up the muddy rubber ball, looked at the bumps, scraped some dirt and tan stalks of grass away with a fingernail. Around that time, whenever I was just on the verge of having absolute fun with someone, I started feeling sunk in and knotted by guilt. I felt like I was mistreating my father, even though he wasn't even around. After Howard and I had talked about comic books on Thanksgiving, my insides had bound up like a tight, twisted rag. Somehow, it seemed like it would never go away, like I would always feel terrible and sad and disturbed till I was old. Standing there, dampness seeping in around my toes, I knew that if my dad were to walk up, spot me tossing the football with Greely, he'd think that I'd forgotten about him, that I didn't care anymore. Before he was gone, he'd worried constantly about that, that he was out of my thoughts. He'd get depressed if I confirmed that he had been.

I lifted my eyes and looked toward the windy bridge, along the fancy stone rail, to make sure he wasn't around. Pivoting, I peered into the thin woods in front of the neighborhood. I searched behind leafless wet trees, trunks fat and wrinkled, like pounded steel rods. He wasn't standing in them. I turned back to Greely and said, "He could lift up the back of a car with one hand." Then I tossed him the ball.

"Wheels off the ground and everything?"

"Like two feet."

Greely's black eyebrows rose and disappeared under the yellow roll of his hat. "That's pretty good," he said, studying how he held the ball. He tossed it gently.

Jumping up to make the catch, I let it plop off my shoulder, and it fluttered dead into the spongy turf. Voices rolled down from the rowhouse neighborhood. My head was filled with memories of my father playfully rocking his car up and down by jumping on the bumper. I'd been sitting in the driver's seat, laughing. As far as I knew, he'd never really lifted one, but I also kind of wondered if maybe he had at some point. He'd been so big that it didn't seem impossible. I'd seen him scoot the refrigerator in our old house away from the wall.

"Once, he picked up a refrigerator so that my mom could get an earring."

Greely shook his head. "Your dad must've been nearly the strongest man in the world."

"I guess he was," I said.

Greely flung an ugly pass. "You think you'll get that strong?"

Embarrassed that I'd lied, I mumbled, "No," made the catch, and tossed the ball back. It slipped from my hand, though, and landed ten feet from Greely.

He walked over and retrieved it. Cocking his arm, he said, "Run that way," flagging me to my right.

I started trotting.

"Faster, Sam," he called, then put the ball into the air.

Greely's pass looked more like a punt. It flapped about in a lop-sided spin, descended slow and clumsy. Running as fast as I could, kicking up the ground like a racehorse, I didn't think I'd even come close to getting beneath it. The ball grew in size, seemed to accelerate past me. At full stride, I extended my hands. Just as it whizzed over my shoulder, I lunged. It slapped loudly against my soft palms, rose a few inches, fell into the crook of my arms. For about a second, I felt elated. Then I slid to a knee, came to a stop, and glanced at the mushy ground.

"Sam, my man!" Greely called from across the field, voice as distant as the *shoosh* of wind from under the bridge.

I kept my head down, gulping back hunks of cold air. Washed over with guilt, my strength seemed to suck toward my chest, clutter the area around my lungs and heart.

After a minute or two, Greely plodded over. "That was great," he said.

I wiped limply at my face. I couldn't talk.

"What's wrong?" Greely asked after a minute.

If I'd said something, I'd have started to cry.

"Get the air knocked out of you?"

I shook my head.

"What?"

"My dad," I confessed.

Greely studied me. "What about him?" he asked delicately.

"I . . . I guess I wonder where he's buried at."

Greely took a moment before he spoke. "A lot of people probably wonder the same thing, Sam."

"He never lifted a car," I admitted sadly.

Greely squatted over me, knobby hands on his wide knees, spotlight eyes fastened on my bony face. "I know," he said softly. "It don't matter. You miss him, that's all."

"I really do," I told him.

Strength began pouring cautiously back into my paper-thin muscles, my greyhound legs. "Sorry I lied," I whispered, dragging my coat sleeves across my face to wipe it clean.

"Lie? That wasn't a lie. It wasn't good enough to be one. Fact is, Sam, no one can lift a car with one hand, not even Mike Tyson, I bet."

I drew my bottom lip up under my teeth and held it there.

"That it?" he asked me.

I took a deep breath, opened my mouth. "He didn't lift a refrigerator, either."

"I figured that, too." Greely reached under an arm and helped me up. "You're a mess, Sam," he teased me.

I nodded my head because I knew I was.

"You want to keep throwing?"

I shrugged, but I really wanted to. I enjoyed doing it. I felt I'd get better, start to calculate how a pass would come at me, slide into my hands. I wasn't so uncoordinated. The problem was my arms. They were quick, but not all that strong.

"If it's up to me, we'd be out here another twenty minutes."

"That'd be okay," I said.

"You keep catching like that, speed stays like it is, and every college coach in the country'll want you."

The ache inside began draining away. "I'm too small," I informed him.

"Small is only in the head, Sam."

I smiled, hoping that was actually the case.

[127]

"You ever heard of Gerald McNeil?"

I shook my head.

"Nickname was the Ice Cube. Shrimpiest man in the NFL for a while. He was tiny, like a kid's tiny. But he could catch and do some damage just 'cause he was quick, move about like a cat. That's how you are."

"You think!" I said, excited.

"Maybe we oughta call you Ice Flake, 'cause there's no denying you're small, but there's also no denying you're a bit of a kook. Sometimes." He grinned.

I glowed. "Ice Flake," I repeated. "That's kind of a cool name."

"Got a good ring," Greely agreed.

We threw for thirty more minutes, but I never snared anything nearly as spectacular as that long bomb. I actually dropped a lot more than I caught. Greely's passing didn't get much better, either. He did something funny with the ball right before it left his hand so that it nearly always fluttered instead of spiraled. Even still, I scudded about with new self-respect, enjoyed myself as if I'd never seen a football before. And I didn't feel uncoachable. I actually felt like I was bursting with all sorts of untapped skill.

When we were done, we climbed up the muddy hill between the trees and walked down the lumpy asphalt road, through the clean little neighborhood, and onto University Parkway, with its tall apartment buildings, all of them old except one. The modern-looking high-rise was covered in some kind of white stone, streaked with rust from the metal bolts that secured the aluminum rails to the balconies. Thick greenish yellow clouds were still passing by above, giving the building a funny cast, like it was painted with slippery soap.

Cars shot by, heading up past the Johns Hopkins lacrosse field or in the opposite direction, north through fancy Roland Park. I looked back over a shoulder, past the bridge we'd been playing beneath, to the gentle left turn onto Forty-first Street, the road that passed by the

Rotunda. A thick cement median that organized the street reminded me of pictures I'd seen of a sleeping walrus, stomach flat and still from the tug of gravity, clunky cars beside it, jittering atop their black tires.

"Sam," Greely said a few minutes later as we kicked along the pale sidewalk, by the fence in front of the lacrosse field, "I can't walk home with you every afternoon. It ain't right. I think two, three times a week wouldn't be bad, but not every day."

Newspapers and crunched wax cups flapped and clicked along the bottom links of the fence like squirming fish in a long flat net. I jerked to a stop and glared at Greely. "What?"

"It ain't right," he repeated. "You're a young kid. Boy your age needs to be with a bunch of different people to grow up right. Anyway, you don't want to hang out with an old man all the time. Who would? You'd get sick of me 'fore I know it."

"I don't get sick of people," I told him, feeling a little desperate. "My mom and I eat together every night, and I don't get sick of her."

He laughed softly. "Maybe you don't," he said, "but that's just one of the things I'm talking about. You might not understand it, but you need your space. That don't mean that we aren't friends. We're real good friends. Really good, Sam. What I'm doing is trying to make sure we stay that way."

"But you're the only person I talk to," I told him.

He reached down and shook me gently back and forth by a shoulder. "Shoot, Sam, who talks when we're together? I'm the conversation hog. 'Side from that, your mom and Mrs. Gordon are always round."

"But they aren't the same."

"Sure they are."

"They won't throw the ball with me or tell me about stuff that I don't already know. I've heard it all from them."

Greely rolled his eyes. "You didn't even want to toss the ball till I dragged you out. And I bet you ain't ever asked your mom or Mrs.

Gordon about what it was like when they were younger." He shook me again. "Some people need prompting. Come on. It ain't like I'll never see you. Two, three times a week, like I said."

I lowered my head, sure that he didn't like me anymore.

That night, when my mom got home, I was sitting in my favorite room, the closet, watching a *Cheers* rerun. I hadn't turned on the light bulb above, and the room was dark, hanging coats throwing flickering shadows into the hallway. With my back turned, eyes on the big screen, I mumbled to her what Greely had said, thinking, of course, that she'd be sympathetic.

She stood in the doorway. I heard her plop down her plastic bag of groceries, take out a beer and open it. "You probably don't understand, but he's right."

I spun around in a huff, knees on the ratty cushion of the upholstered chair. "No, he's not," I told her sharply.

Her face was blue from the television, eyes deep and tired. "He is, Samuel. I'm sorry. You're just a boy, and he's in his seventies." Something adjusted in the grocery bag, thumped against the wooden floor.

"What does that mean?" I asked, hanging over the fraying back of the chair.

She took a sip on her beer, placed it by the wall, took off her puffy coat, and hung it. "It means he's right," she said. "You'll understand and forgive us both when you're older."

I slithered around and stared at the screen.

"By the way," she spoke to the back of my head, "I asked Junie about Greely eating Christmas dinner with us, and she said she'd feel Ditch out. She thinks it'll be okay, though."

I told her, "It doesn't matter," even though it did. I thought that maybe Greely would like me again if I gave him something to do for Christmas.

achy feet
achy feet

When my dad was still around, we'd buy our Christmas tree from the Lion's Club. They sold them on York Road, near Towson State College, in a vacant lot beside an old fire station. I remember how after we decided on one, usually based on price, the old men who took the money and rubbed their hands over blackened barrels with fires popping and sputtering in them passed our tree through an orange hoop that bound the limbs in a plastic net so it wasn't so hard to move around. Then they lugged it out to our car and jammed it into our trunk. At home, we always put the tree up by the front window in the living room, so that everyone passing by would see it.

We did all sorts of things every year, like caroling with the neighbors, marching into the nicest sections of Rodger's Forge, carrying candles that dripped wax onto our hands. Just a week or two after Thanksgiving, my dad always rummaged around in the garage looking for the red all-weather bow he wired to the grill of his car. I remember fires in the fireplace and seasonal stuff cluttering the shelves in our refrigerator, shiny beer cans with holly leaves drawn on the side, cookies, eggnog, and cola. For some reason, we were more of a family during the holidays than any other time. So, the first Christmas season my dad was gone was strange, and even though it was sometimes okay, it was also pretty sad.

Halfway through December, my mom toted home a fake tree from work. Junie had gotten about ten of them in the summer, and my mom had bought the last one. They appeared to be dying. They only stood about two and a half feet high, and their limbs were made of shredded green tissue paper wrapped around coat-hanger wire. All we could fit on ours was one string of twenty-five blinking lights and a few silver balls. I didn't hate it, but I was sad that we didn't head out to the Lion's Club lot, to the old men earning money for blind kids. The fake tree, sitting in my mom's bay window on a box with a green blanket hung over it, reminded me of a monument. It meant that things were becoming permanently different, that we were starting new, worse traditions. It meant that if my dad did return one day, we'd all know that Christmas had been ruined.

We didn't put a wreath on the cloudy red front door downstairs or decorate around the fireplace because we didn't have one. We didn't go downtown to see the boats parading around the harbor all decorated with lights or go caroling with the neighbors. Christmastime was so unrecognizable that I had to remind my mom to buy eggnog, something that she had done every year since before I could remember, something that we could still do, even in our Charles Village apartment. I didn't drink it because it tasted sour in my mouth, but I liked to spot it in the refrigerator, yellow in a big plastic milk jug. It reminded me that it was the holiday season. The problem was, my mom worried that it would go to waste since my dad wasn't around to glug it down, so whenever Howard came over, I poured him a tall glass. He didn't seem to mind. Then, about two weeks before Christmas, I placed one outside my mom's closed door. I hated to think about what they were doing, so I didn't call out, tell them it was there. Instead, I just left the eggnog a few inches down the hall, figuring

Howard couldn't miss it that way. He didn't. When he came out, he stepped right on top of it, barefoot.

My mom called a cab, and we rushed Howard, blood seeping into a bath towel, a few blocks north to Charles Village Memorial Hospital, looming big and old over bumpy Calvert Street. Then we hung out in the emergency room, nervous and upset, while doctors cleaned and closed Howard's wounds.

I sat, embarrassed, beside my mom. She was dressed sloppily in a T-shirt and jeans. Her brown winter coat, with its collar of phony fur, was slipping off her slim body so that it piled up against the back of the soft waiting-room chair. Her eyes were blank and watery, sunken cheeks red as a piece of wrapping paper.

"I'm sorry," I told her for about the thousandth time. I was worried that she thought I'd meant to hurt Howard. "I like Howard," I said weakly. It was true, too. I was beginning to like him a lot. Right off the top of his head he could remember early events in some of my favorite comics, like how the Silver Surfer was created, and the experiment that turned the Beast blue and hairy. "I didn't want the eggnog to go to waste."

"I know," she told me softly, patting one of my legs with a hand that was stiff and cold even through my jeans, nails scratchy as rake prongs.

"He likes it."

She let her coat fall off her wiry arms, the hunk of her elbows, and the knots of her wrists. "He's been drinking it," she agreed, eyes on her hands, cuticles red from gnawing teeth.

Sad, I looked around the emergency room. It was my first time in one, but it wasn't like I'd expected. On television they were always clean, chrome so shiny that you could see yourself in it. Ours didn't have any chrome, and even though the lights were bright, the rest of the place was pretty rundown. The spongy furniture was burned through with cigarette holes, orange and brown threads separating in long gashes so that foam rubber poked through. Air vents clicked and rattled loose in the tiled ceiling, segments saggy. A dented metal bucket on the linoleum floor across the room caught a steady drip of rusty-looking water. Dust balls swayed in corners, below tiny wooden tables with ancient magazines fanned across the top. One table had a fake Christmas tree exactly like ours on it, tissue paper needles and twenty-five blinking lights. The walls were covered with smudges and pencil and pen scribbles, decorated with fading photos of Orioles baseball players. Cal Ripken had a puckered dark area below his eyes, just like my mom did that night.

The people were different, too. Their injuries didn't seem very dramatic. A tall black teenager, face like a dark hole, features hidden by the shadow of a Chicago Bulls cap, kept coughing. The older white guy beside him, a cow in a sweat suit, thumped him between the shoulder blades. A little black girl had an earache. She cupped a hand over her ear, cried in soft blurts. Her mom, old and gray as a grandmother, squeezed the girl's narrow shoulders with brown arms.

Suddenly I was enveloped by a wave of jealousy. Everyone but me had someone to tell them that things would be okay. My mom normally rubbed my back to soothe my nerves, but all she had done since we'd arrived was scratch one of my legs, back and forth, like she didn't want to do it at all. I stared at the tall coughing boy, the guy swatting him in the back, at the girl and her ancient mother, and I wished that someone would focus on me. I wished the little nurse behind the desk, hair tugged back so that she looked like she was going fast on a motorcycle, would come over and talk.

A half hour later, a tall doctor with a thick brown mustache rolled Howard, slumped in a wheelchair, into the waiting room. He loosely held a pair of aluminum crutches across his knees. There was a bright white sock pulled over his bandaged foot.

My mom stood up and looked at the two men.

I jumped to my feet and rushed right over. Standing beside them, arms slack, I didn't know what to say.

Howard smiled, forehead wrinkling. "It was a mistake, Sam," he said to me, then gave his glasses a quick poke.

I smiled back sheepishly, glanced over my shoulder at my mom, who was slowly making her way across the room, winter coat draped over an arm. Looking into her eyes, I worried that I had hurt her by injuring Howard. I wondered if maybe she felt like I was a nuisance in her life.

She gently stuck a hand out, and Howard took it. "How bad is it?" she asked softly.

"I'm all right," he said, lips mashing together, two wet stripes below his thin nose. He was trying to look tough and smile at the same time. One of his cement-colored hands crunched a rubber pad at the top of a crutch.

"He should stay off it for a few weeks," the doctor said, tilting his head so that it looked like he was filtering air through his mustache. "Should get those bandages changed no later than Saturday. It looks okay, but there could be some nerve damage. There's no way to tell right now. Best thing to do at this point is keep it clean and hope for the best. It's a painful injury, though. He's got twenty-eight stitches in that foot of his. When he moves it, it's gonna hurt, believe me."

I looked down at the gleaming white sock, recalling a story I'd seen on television about a guy who'd been bitten by a shark. He'd gotten something like one hundred and sixty stitches. I lifted my eyes to the doctor. "Is twenty-eight a lot?" I asked.

My mom cut in. "God, yes, Samuel. Ten stitches is a lot."

I shivered, dropped my eyes.

"Be kind to him," the doctor said, patting Howard on the shoulder. He handed my mom a list of instructions and prescriptions, black scrawls on little blue slips of paper.

She looked ashamed, took them, and crunched them into a tight front pocket.

While my mom cleaned up the hallway floor, I sat with Howard in the kitchen. He was drooped in a chair, arms resting on the enamel table-top. I could tell that he was trying not to shiver in the cold air that seeped through the wavy plywood wall. His spiky hair fluttered and goose bumps rose on the colorless, hairless snakeskin of his bare arms. I studied his face as he sucked at a can of National Premium and watched my mother work; she struggled with the slanted bristles of the broom and swabbed the floor with a mop that left worn yellow particles of itself behind. Howard reminded me of Dracula. His skin was smooth as milk and his dark hair did exactly what a vampire's hair should do: come to a point on his forehead. If not for his fairly normal teeth and taped glasses, lenses thick as a windshield, he'd have been a perfect vampire.

"Howard," I whispered.

He looked at me.

"I didn't mean for you to get hurt."

He smiled kindly. "Sam, forget about it," he said, reaching over and patting one of my small hands. "When I was your age, I dropped a hammer on my dad's head. Stuff happens, you know."

With the heel of my palm, I rubbed my cheek. "How'd you do that?" I asked.

He raised his eyebrows the same way Greely often did. "Let's see. If I remember it right, we were working on a loose gutter on the back of our place, and I think I was pounding a nail in, and the hammer just slipped, bounced on a rung of the ladder and popped him."

I snickered. I don't know why. "What did it do to him?" I asked, wanting to hear more.

"Split his forehead open." Howard drew a gash over an eye with an index finger. "Eighteen stitches."

I shook my head. "That's worse than leaving a glass in the hallway," I said.

He laughed. "Heck yeah, it is."

My mom hauled a plastic bucket of soapy water into the kitchen, heaved it up, and dumped it into the sink. She placed it in the cabinet below, then splashed her hands about under the tap water. Wiping them on a paper towel, she opened the refrigerator and got herself a beer, leaned back against the big rounded door, breathed deeply, and yanked the tab. She took a slug, closed her eyes, and took a couple more, her rubbery neck expanding and shrinking. Placing the can on the counter, she reached down and rubbed one foot at a time with her long fingers. The only casual shoes she owned were an old-lady pair with blue canvas tops and funny little stacked heels and soles that were made of rope or something. She always said that they crunched her toes, but she never got new ones.

"You should get sneakers," I said, trying to be helpful.

She glowered at me, her brow knit as hard as a seam. "And where in the world would I get the money, Samuel? Tell me, please."

I shrugged with a shiver, surprised she would talk to me that way, especially in front of Howard. Before, everything bad that had happened to us we worked through together. We were a team. But the way she acted, it seemed like our team had broken up, like we were both in it alone, trying to do something just for ourselves. It made me sick.

Swallowing, I looked out the hazy bay window and into the alley, street lights glittering on broken glass and a crushed aluminum can. I was thinking that I was breathing too fast, which I hadn't done in a while.

"Come on Maxine, what happened wasn't anyone's fault," Howard said, adjusting in one of our creaky chairs.

After a moment, during which time the refrigerator's fan kicked on, my mom murmured, "I know. I just wish it hadn't happened at all."

"Hey, me, too," he snorted. "It's my foot."

Nausea crept up and down my throat, along the soft, slick tunnel between my mouth and stomach. I watched as the reflection of my face got sweaty.

"Christmas is already hard enough without this on top of it."

Howard rolled his eyes. "It's not your job to nursemaid me. My whole family's in town. I can call someone up and they'd be happy to help."

Frustrated, my mom plopped her beer can on the counter. "Think about it, Howard. Of course it's my job. My son did this to you."

My stomach spasmed, squeezed small and hard as a golf ball. I leaped from my chair and ricocheted through the kitchen and down the hall. Bumping my way into the bathroom, I closed the door behind me, turned the lock so that no one could come in.

I dropped to the gritty floor and rested my chin on the cool lip of the toilet. After a minute, when I knew I wouldn't get sick, I turned around and focused on my spindly legs, bunched up against the yellow wall like Christmas tree limbs. Lowering myself to an elbow, I rolled onto my back, focused on the bottom part of the sink, on the crusty drainpipe where it made a deep dip, then came back up and disappeared into a cut hole in the wall. I closed my eyes and felt guilt wash over me.

My mom knocked on the door, called to me in her worried voice. "Samuel?"

Opening my eyes, I looked past the sink at the ceiling with its fat bands of wallpaper covered over with paint and a spot of water damage that resembled a blurry drawing, a pressed flower.

"Yeah," I moaned.

"What're you doing in there?"

"Going to the bathroom."

"You're taking a long time. You think you'll come out when you're done?"

"I guess."

"I'm sorry about what I said, sweetheart. Okay? I didn't mean to upset you. Why don't you come out so that we can talk?"

"I'm going to the bathroom," I told her again.

"Okay," she said.

I waited a minute. "Mom."

"Yeah."

"I didn't mean to hurt Howard."

"I know. I shouldn't have implied that you did."

"Um, what does that mean?"

"Imply?"

"Yeah."

"Insinuate. Suggest. I didn't mean to suggest that you did."

"But I did," I said.

"Not intentionally. Come out, okay? We'll talk about it."

The Monday after Howard cut his foot, I asked Greely to go shopping with me on Greenmount Avenue. I needed to get to Economy Shoes so that I could buy my mother her Christmas present, a soft pair of sneakers. Since he'd told me we could only do things together a few days a week, I'd come to realize that he still liked me, that he was the same old Greely. I didn't understand what he was trying to accomplish, but I'd accepted his decision in the same hesitant way I'd accepted my bedroom. I didn't have a choice. That my mom had agreed with his decision was kind of confusing, though. She was usually pretty normal when she wasn't upset over something. Actually, I began to think that they were both a little weird.

The sun was out, and seagulls, hanging low and flat as oyster shells in the smooth sky, were drifting across its roundness. It was only about three o'clock, but it got dark so early that by the time I arrived home, unless I took the bus, it was dusky, that funny blue color just before nighttime. To save daylight, Greely and I went ahead and caught the Forty-two Downtown with all the students from the Upper Charles Village area. Even though I'd started to enjoy the walk, I was happy enough to board a creaky bus. It was cold out, a burning chill that made my face hurt, like someone was pushing a piece of metal, hard as a side-view mirror, against my forehead.

We stopped by my apartment so that I could take a pair of my mother's shoes and show them to a clerk. Howard was asleep in the closet, television on, bandaged foot propped up, a depressing soap opera blaring. We watched this lady in a cocktail dress whisper something to an old man in a tuxedo before I crept back to my mom's room and dropped her fancy plastic heels into a grocery bag. Skulking out, I showed them to Greely, who was admiring the apartment, looking it over. He nodded and we left, closing the paneled door as gently as we could on our way down the steps to the dark foyer with its bulb light.

"Your place is nice," he told me when we were outside. His breath hovered around his face, a thin cloud of fumes in the biting air.

I thought about what he'd said. "It's not so bad," I agreed, after a few seconds, because sometimes the place seemed okay, even good. I pulled the heavy front door shut. We stood for a moment by the friendly green metal chairs on the porch. Then we trudged down the steps and onto the sidewalk, blocks of cement pushed up by roots from trees that no longer looked like wood but were good for swinging. "You should have seen our old house."

Greely zipped up his thin coat, blew onto his big, hard hands. "Sam, it ain't like that apartment you're in right now is awful. You should see where I live."

"It's worse than our place?"

"You ain't kidding," he said.

At Economy Shoes, I presented my mom's shiny heels to the towering manager, a black guy with a mop of curly wet-looking hair. After looking at my mom's shoes, the guy told me that all of the popular women's sneakers would fit her. He also showed me a pile of shoes on a wobbly card table in the back. They were on sale for half price because one from each pair had supposedly faded slightly in an old window display. Picking through the knotted heap, I located some yellow leather high-tops in my mother's size. Greely and I put them on the floor in front of us and studied each. You could barely tell which one had been sunburned except for where the yellow rubber soles had grayed a bit around a toe.

"They look fine to me," I said.

"Don't look faded, if that's what you mean." Greely rubbed at his coarse chin. His short fat whiskers scraped loudly under his dry finger pads. "The thing I'm wondering is, does your mom like yellow sneakers?"

I picked them up and examined each closely. They weren't exactly bright yellow. They were about the same shade as slightly dried mustard. I ran my fingers across the soft dyed leather, the spongy ribbed ankle supports. I thought that they might make her feel younger. She sometimes said that Howard made her feel old. I nodded my head. "I think she'd like them," I said to Greely.

He tilted his head, opened his eyes even wider, so that there was so much white around his pupils that they looked flat, a smooth white sock. "You're sure?"

I nodded proudly. "Yeah," I said.

At the counter, I counted out bills from the wad of cash I'd earned working at Junie's, laid them in a stack on the manager's small, tan palm. Before tapping the amount into the register, he mumbled, "You can't return these. They're on sale." His voice echoed in his lungs, rumbled about in the hard-as-concrete tunnel of his windpipe, broke from his mouth as if amplified.

"Okay," I told him, because I knew they were the ones.

Out on freezing Greenmount, hauling a gigantic white bag of shoes around, I was nervous that someone would try to rob me. I held on to the sack with both hands, toted it in front of me like a bucket of wet sand. I watched everyone who passed, twisting my head around and monitoring their backs as they grew smaller on the brownish sidewalks and streets, among blowing bulk mail. I was most worried about gunmen. The thought of them terrified me, someone sneaking up from behind one of the lampposts that was decorated kindly with a wire and cellophane Christmas candle. In that kind of weather, anyone could hide a gun. I imagined them stuffed up a bunchy coat sleeve, strapped over a shoulder, jammed into the top of a pair of loose pants. Mist billowed from my lungs, hung in front of my eyes.

"Whatcha say, Sam?" Greely held a glass door open for me. The smell of greasy food poured out in an invisible vapor, a puff of perfume.

I realized we were standing in front of the Little Tavern. I couldn't even remember crossing the street. I breathed in the perfect vapors, slipped in under his arm. We walked down the length of counter and took the last two stools. There was only one other customer in the place, and he was asleep, gurgling thick bubbles into the plaid sleeve of his moth-bitten coat, fingers twitching. I put the bag of shoes in front of me, on the ledge below my feet.

"You nervous out there?" Greely asked as he squinted at the menu board above the grill.

"I guess," I confessed, embarrassed.

His eyes rotated down toward me. He poked out his big bottom lip, mouth deep and empty as an ashtray. "Maybe you shoulda been. I don't know. Greenmount's definitely got itself a reputation, and it ain't altogether undeserved." He pushed his hat around, looked down at a bashed thumbnail the size of a quarter, and dropped his hand. "Good thing to know is that most of the crime round here takes place after dark. Most everyone you saw out there was a law-abiding citizen. Probably all of 'em was. What we got here on Greenmount is a case where a few people are making everyone look bad. There ain't many crooks, but they're loud and stupid as dirt; and everyone hears about them. All the newspapers focus on 'em 'cause normal people is boring news. It's like a conspiracy, the way the reporters tell it. Folks in this community is just as scared to walk the streets at night as everyone else, just as scared at night as you are. Wasn't so long ago that it wasn't like this."

I chewed at the inside of my mouth, yanked at the soft skin the same way I had the last time I'd sat with Greely in the Little Tavern. "Sometimes I hear gunfire coming from here," I informed him.

Greely's lips wrapped tightly around his teeth. "Yeah, I know," he grumbled. "That's the way it is now."

Behind the counter, a little black woman, the cook, a midget in a white apron, walked over with a sorry-looking writing pad. Her butt was large, and her thick legs were bowed out as if her upper body weighed tons and her knees were giving way. "Thought that was you, Greely. Who's yer friend?" she asked in a soft, sweet voice.

"Sam. Lives right down the street."

"Hello, Sam," she said. Standing on her toes, she extended flat, greasy brown fingers. "You keeping Mr. Clemons in line?"

As we shook, I nodded self-consciously. Her hand squeezed down like a waffle slathered with a layer of butter. It was so gross that when we let go, I secretly wiped my palm and knuckles across my pant legs.

"Well, good. He's a nice man. I like to see him with somebody for a change. He comes in here and sits all night by himself. It's the saddest thing I ever saw."

Greely rolled his eyes toward the ceiling. "Don't talk like that, Rose," he said. "You going to make Sam think I'm lonely or something."

"Don't want him to know the truth about you?"

It was the first time I'd ever seen Greely look even slightly embarrassed. He shook his head, slowly, as if he was amazed. "Came in here for a cup of coffee and a soda. Didn't think we'd get hassled or nothing, or we'd have gone somewhere else."

"You ever been somewhere else, Greely?" she mocked him, flouncing around and picking up a thick white china coffee cup, a big chip missing around the lip. She stretched to reach a murky, stained pot with silver duct tape around the handle, and filled the cup to the top. Then she rose on her toes again and strained to slip the glass pot back on its old warmer.

"She's a crazy woman," Greely whispered to me, loud enough so that Rose, who was watching us as she filled a red plastic soda cup near the register, could hear.

"Heard that," she informed him, and the guy who was sleeping with his head propped on his arms almost woke up. He moved his mouth around and started to snore softly.

Waddling back down the counter, Rose slid my Coke and Greely's coffee in front of us with the tips of her fingers. Both cups glistened with oil from her hands. "You want something to eat?" she asked Greely.

"No," he said in his funny, smothered voice.

"You pouting?" she asked him.

"Please, Rose. You trying to destroy Sam's opinion of me?"

I peered down at my soda. My stomach turned. There was a small piece of mushy bread floating in it.

"I'm doing no such thing. Just making conversation." Leaning back against the grill, Rose's face and neck looked funny, drooped, the hard lines flattened away.

Greely picked up his coffee cup, plopped it right back down with a clomp. "Rose, you got something on your hands? Cup is greasier than normal."

She looked down at her worn fingers, brought them up close to her face, curled up her thin lips. She pushed away from the grill with her behind, reached up and snatched my Coke and Greely's coffee, spilling some on the counter and plunging them into what sounded like a tub of water under the ledge. She examined her apron and lime green polyester pants, cuffs practically rolled up to her knees. "Just tossed a tub of bad butter out. Must have gotten it all over myself or something." She looked up at us and laughed. "Thought everything felt slippery."

Greely snickered as he sopped up the separate puddles of Coke and coffee with a wad of napkins he'd pulled from a dispenser. "Hard to tell since it's all so greasy, anyway."

She waved a hand at him, took a few steps down the counter and opened a white door with her bulky elbows.

"Rose."

She stopped. I could see the toilet behind her, a hardened gray string mop propped in a corner, around twenty old air fresheners stuck to a plywood wall. "Yeah?"

"Got some on your head, too." Greely lifted his hat, wiped across his brow with the sleeve of an arm.

She nodded, let the door pull shut behind her.

"Mirror's above the sink," he explained to me. "She can't hardly see herself it's so high. Top of that, her eyes are going." He got up and moseyed slowly past the bathroom and behind the counter. "I've known Rose for about"—he paused, considering as he poured himself some coffee—"somewhere round eighteen years. Met her in nineteen seventy, her first day on the job here." He plopped the battered cup in front of where he'd been sitting, wiped his hands on a rag. Coffee sloshed back and forth.

Greely walked down to the end of the counter and pulled a big waxed paper cup from the top of a stack. He pushed it against the soda dispenser lever and filled it. Shuffling back, he trudged past the bathroom again and plopped onto his stool, which let out a burst of air, then set my drink down in front of me. Smiling, he said, "This one won't have a bread surprise in it."

I stifled a laugh.

"I worked with Rose's first husband, Glen Mitts. We tarred roofs together. Don't know her second husband real well, though. They met at her church."

We sat quiet for a minute as Rose splashed around in the bathroom.

"Whatcha thinking, Sam?" Greely asked.

I leaned over with my hands curled together against my mouth. "Is she a midget?"

He shook his head, face and cheeks like gnawed wood. "She says she's a dwarf," he whispered. "Midgets look like normal people, only smaller. Dwarfs look different. They're heavier looking, like she is." He latched his lips on to the rim of his coffee cup, sucked in a gulp. His frail legs hung limp off the squishy orange pad of the stool, two cooked noodles in worn blue pants. He hunched his shoulders high, so that the flimsy collar of his jacket covered a bony lump on the back of his nearly bald head.

"How'd she get married, then?"

He laughed. "It ain't illegal, Sam. You got someone as nice as Rose, and even though she's a dwarf, a lot of old men with any sense are going to like her. At my age, looks don't matter so much. Heck, if you want to know the truth, ten years ago, after Glenn died, I considered asking her to marry me. I thought about doing it every day for years. They slipped by, and I was too late."

I liked that idea, that it didn't matter so much how you looked as long as you were nice.

Rose opened the bathroom door, waddled out like Coach Murtleson at school, a chicken with its head hanging forward, butt pointing up in the opposite direction.

"You don't look so greasy anymore," Greely told her.

Embarrassed, she grinned so wide that the corners of her lips disappeared beneath the frames of her glasses. "Glad it was you in here and not someone else." She leaned back against the old grill. "If my cataracts weren't so bad, I'd have noticed I had something on my hands." She cast a glance at the sleeping man. His snoring sounded like a distant car. She looked back at us.

"How late they got you working alone, Rose?"

"Till eight."

Greely dropped a hand to the counter. "That boss of yours has no sense."

"Rhonda quit," she informed him. "We're short-handed."

"I'll come back after I take Sam home."

She rolled her foggy eyes. "That ain't necessary, Greely. I got Dwayne to watch me." She pointed at the sleeping guy.

"I'm coming back," Greely told her.

Rose breathed out, sagged forward, acting like he'd worn her out. "If you do, I'll make you something free."

"Suit yourself," he said, and took a sip of coffee. He watched her over the rough edge of his cup, which looked tiny the way he held it between his two hands. "By the way, I won't be around for Christmas this year."

She tilted her head and looked at him from the corner of her eyes.

"Sam invited me over to his place for dinner."

Her mouth dropped slightly, then formed into a big smile. "You did? Well, that's awfully nice," she said.

The muscles in my shoulders went weak.

"A real Christmas dinner. I don't think Greely's had one of those in quite some time," said Rose.

I tried to smile back, but I couldn't. I looked down at the dirty black rubber mats on the floor behind the counter, food mashed into the pattern. Rose's tan orthopedic shoes milled about kindly on top of them. "It won't be so nice," I said, thinking about it. "Not like when my dad was around. He made it fun." I watched her feet shift, her pants wrinkle around her stubby legs, the bulges of her knees.

"Where's your dad?" she asked me softly.

"Gone," I mumbled, eyes still rooting around on the floor.

"Where'd he go?"

I imagined his tombstone with nothing drawn or written on it. "Nobody knows," I murmured.

"That's awful."

"That's what I think."

Rose was quiet for a minute. She adjusted against the grill. "Greely ever tell you his story about disappearing?"

I didn't know what she was talking about.

Rose squinted at Greely. "God gives people second chances."

Greely leaned over and placed a hand gently across my shoulders, pulled me against his musty coat. "Maybe I can do some good," he told her. "Maybe I can make just a little amends."

forgetting
forgetting

On Christmas day, cold and gray, the sky as flat and low as the underside of a table, my mom and I carried all of our presents out to Howard's car and put them into his crumpled trunk, clamped it shut with the colorful bungee cord he wrapped across the top to keep it from popping up in traffic. He'd driven over after breakfast at his parents' place, foot still bandaged, tucked gently into one of his father's big white walking shoes so that he could work the gas pedal. I climbed into the back seat while my mom went back up to our apartment to get the dish we were taking to Ditch and Junie's, a large pan of puréed sweet potatoes covered in a layer of melted white marshmallows. Sitting there with Howard, I noticed that he smelled like eggs and butter and cigarettes, the way he always did when he spent time at his parents' place. Their home must smell like the Little Tavern.

"What'd you get?" I asked him, scooting up between his tan bucket seats, dotted by crescent-moon stains, jealous that he'd already opened some presents.

He lifted a plaid scarf, wrapped around his neck about ten times. "This," he said, "and a ratchet set."

"That's it?"

"My sister gave me a juicer." He shrugged, the thick shoulders of his winter coat rising up as if they were filling with air.

"A juicer. What's that for?" I glanced at the steps wishing that my mom would hurry up.

"It turns vegetables into a drink, like carrot juice or something."

"Carrot juice. Gross," I groaned, wrapping my hands across my stomach, making a face. "Who wants that?"

He shook his head, laughed. "She thought I did."

I flopped back against the seat, bounced. "You wondering what I got you?"

He watched me in the rear-view mirror, glasses reflecting the cracked black dashboard, the speedometer that didn't work, pointer hanging limp against the zero even when Howard was speeding, a fender-bender magnet. He never caused them, but for some reason, people were constantly running into his car, crashing into it like a stunt vehicle. Funny thing, too, in the giant truck he drove for work, he never had any trouble. "I didn't think you'd gotten me anything."

"I did."

"Well, I got you something, too."

I had already figured that he had. He might not have expected to get a gift from me, but I'd taken it for granted that he'd get me one. "What?" I asked.

"You'll find out in about an hour."

I kicked the bottom of his seat. Seams were splitting, and sheets of cottony stuffing were hanging out in snowy clumps. "You feel that?"

"Yeah."

"Your seat's falling apart back here."

"This car's falling apart," he told me.

"It's because everyone runs into it."

"I guess," he said.

"The car my dad drove at work looked like this one."

"The model, you mean?"

"No, it was dented all over, too."

He nodded, watched me in the rear-view mirror, a tiny movie screen. "You guys talk about your dad this morning?"

An electric feeling buzzed my shoulders. "No."

He twisted around, put out a hand so that I would give him five.

I slapped it.

"It's a hard Christmas for you and your mom, what with your father gone. I know that. But it's been nice for me. You guys have gotten to be like family real fast."

I managed a weak nod, my lips curling up the way paper does when it's heated. I felt guilty for liking Howard, my dad's replacement. Part of the problem was, I still couldn't remember how my father had looked. Sometimes when I thought about him, Howard's face appeared, floated like a ghost's. I needed just one picture to remember my dad by. The thing is, my mother had put them all away, and I wasn't sure I could ask her for any. I worried I'd upset her, especially after the way she'd looked that night in the emergency room, let down with me, face as floppy and lifeless as a pancake.

I turned my head and watched my mother skip down the cement front steps in a pair of flat black shoes that couldn't have been very comfortable. Behind her, our downstairs neighbor, a skinny old lady librarian at the Enoch Pratt Free Library downtown, waved to me, her beige plastic blinds rolled open for the first time I could remember. I waved back, wondering if she was all alone. As far as I knew, she was. I didn't think she was all that nice, anyway. Even though I always said something to her when we saw each other in the dim downstairs hallway, sometimes she didn't say anything back. Sometimes she just looked at me in this strange way, like her tongue and eyeballs were loose in her skull. That gave me the creeps.

My mom climbed into the car. "Who you waving to, Samuel?" she asked, scooting Howard's aluminum crutches around to make room.

[151]

"Mrs. Lacy," I whispered, still watching her watch us.

My mom turned her head, caught sight of our neighbor, and waved, too. "I thought you didn't like her."

"I don't think she likes me," I said in a hush.

Howard kissed my mother's cheek and slid his car into gear. I watched Mrs. Lacy till we turned the corner onto Thirty-second Street, drifted past the empty parking lot dotted with parking meters, stubby and forgotten as lost dogs. We rumbled by Harry Little's Pizza and the feminist bookstore, stopped in front of the Little Tavern. As we waited at the light, I looked at the moving, tilting shadows behind the steamy windows. I couldn't make out who was working the counter, but the place looked caught up in celebration.

Howard turned onto Greenmount, and we headed up the road to pick up Greely.

We bounced by lines of storefront churches, faded yellow poster-board signs in their windows, their pastors' names over the doors, tiny square letters carved onto plastic plaques like you'd see on a businessman's desk. Some of the churches were packed with people, others empty, doors closed. There was Wing Li's Carry-Out and the New Rex Liquor Store, one of the best-looking buildings on that portion of Greenmount before it turned into York Road and suddenly got nice. At the thirty-nine-hundred block, by Marcel's Afro Hut Barber Shop, with its window air conditioner poking out of a hole in the wall, Howard hit a blinker and drifted onto Devin Lane. Slowly we drove down between two lines of rowhouses, wood boards slipping off window frames like flaky skin, shingles worn into giant blackened slabs, brick and Formstone walls covered with graffiti. Windows were broken, and frayed curtains drifted out, fluttering as if driven by fans. Garbage spilled off porches and into the street like mudslides. A tricycle sat turned over in a gutter. One okay-looking house had lights decorating the front porch, and two others that were in pretty good shape had wreaths on their doors. At the end of the block, Greely stood on the corner, puffed up in about ten layers of clothes, a few gifts under one arm.

"He lives here?" I whispered, feeling sad for him as he limped around to my mother's side of the car. No wonder he'd thought our apartment was nice.

"Hello, Greely," my mom said as she opened her door.

Greely bent down. "Maxine," he mumbled thickly. "Merry Christmas."

Howard leaned over, clattered his crutches with an elbow, stuck his hand out. "I'm Howard," he said, "a friend of Sam's mother."

"Well, I hear a lot about you," Greely told him, shaking his hand. "I appreciate you picking me up."

"It's nothing," Howard said. "On the way."

Greely turned his head, smiled at me, and my mom nearly snapped his jaw shut with a shoulder as she hopped out of the car and told him she would ride in back so that he would have legroom.

"That ain't necessary."

"Greely," she scolded him, holding her Pyrex dish of sweet potatoes in the crooks of her arms, toothpicks keeping the plastic wrap from settling down on top of the foamy marshmallows. She slipped into the back, bounced down beside me. Her earrings, silver disks, shook, and her knees, two knots the size of coffee cups, touched the back of the front seat.

Greely clambered in, moved the seat forward so that his legs folded tightly against the dashboard and Howard's crutches touched the ceiling. "You got room?" he asked.

"Plenty," my mom told him.

"It's not a long drive," Howard notified Greely, turned the car around, and rolled back up the road.

I tapped Greely on an arm. "Which place do you live in?"

He looked at me over a shoulder. "On the corner, to the left."

I spun around, peered out the window along with my mom. The place he was talking about wasn't as bad as some, but it wasn't great, either. The porch was slanted away, like it was about to roll into the cross street, and the Formstone was that cheap kind, so sharp that it looked more like gray bricks than big rocks. The downstairs windows, larger than the front door, had long bars running down in front of them, too narrow for a small kid to slide through. As we sped away, though, what caught my eye more than anything else was the front door. It was brown metal. By the knob, it was scratched and dented so deeply that something big must have crashed into it.

"What happened to your door?" I asked, as Howard lurched onto Greenmount and started north.

"Police thought my downstairs neighbor was selling dope."

Excited, I said, "Was he?"

"Naw, Sam. That guy is so harmless. I ain't kidding. All he cares about is his cats. The man has two, Missus and Beemus. Nearly every penny he earns he spends on them. Buys scratch posts and catnip and stuff. The police just messed up. That's all. They broke down the door, nearly scared me to death, 'cause at the time, I was upstairs reading the paper. They grabbed William and carried him downtown, ransacked his apartment. They apologized, but they didn't help him pick up the mess they made, and they didn't replace the front door, neither."

"That's an awful story, Greely," my mom said.

"Happens every day," Howard informed her.

"You right about that."

"Did they hurt his cats?" I asked.

"Naw."

I sat back, imagining Missus and Beemus cowering in a corner. "That must have made him feel a little better."

"Guess it did," Greely said. He lifted his hands to show me that he didn't know for sure.

"How long have you lived there?" Howard asked, tapping the heat control on the dash with the pad of a thumb.

"On Devin Lane? Least twenty years. So long that I was there when that street looked as good as any place in this city. It had kids all over it, families of folks. Back then, around this time of year, that block would have been lit up, Christmas trees in windows and all sorts of things." He rubbed his dry palms up and down on his fancy pants, brown corduroys with wide, deep ridges and only one stain on a knee.

I sat forward, rested my elbows across the two front seats. "Whose presents are those?" I pointed to the ones on Greely's lap.

"Guess, Sam," he said.

"Mine?"

"Two of 'em."

"Who's the other for?"

"Everyone else," he told me.

"You mean, along with me?"

He shook his head. "Sam, you can't have everything. Somebody else's got to get something."

I smiled. "I guess," I said.

My mom poked my side, sunk her finger into the sensitive area above my belt, so that I jumped. "You guess," she teased me. "Boy, you're a selfish kid."

Ten to fifteen minutes later, Howard accelerated through a dusty-looking yellow light and onto Harford Road, where we rattled past a Murry's meat store, the 7-Eleven, and the television repair shop, slowed, and turned onto the Gordons' street, clacked up toward their place, by twig-covered lawns and monstrous worn houses. As we passed by the home that had burned down, I saw that it was getting repaired. There were stacks of bony-looking boards out front, a port-o-john on the side lawn, between a black charred-looking thing that had been a couch and piles of shingles. There was also a giant green Dumpster, long and narrow as a tractor-trailer, filled with smaller pieces of crunchy-looking furniture.

At the Gordons' place, we scurried from the battered car. I went around back and unhooked the bungee cord from the trunk. Howard swayed on his silvery crutches by the driver's-side door, a big dent in it, a little green Allstate sticker on the edge of the crease. My mom stood by Greely. She was saying stuff to him, and he was nodding his head. He looked funny, and I realized that he'd left his Chevron cap at home.

"What?" I asked them.

My mom walked over and grabbed a few boxes. She couldn't hold very much because one hand was occupied with the dish of puréed sweet potatoes. "I was just reminding him that it's going to be a little awkward with Ditch at first."

My eyes got big. "You never told me to tell him that."

She nodded her head. "Junie and I called Greely at school last week. We wanted him to know what he was getting into." She raised her eyebrows, turned, and followed Howard toward the rundown front porch.

My jaw nearly dropped. I moaned and leaned against the cold metal trunk, stared into it like it was a big squarish mouth, the jaws of a whale or something, with presents and a jack on its tongue.

Greely came over to help me. "This is some kind of house," he said.

I didn't reply.

He picked up a few packages from off the spare tire, held them in his arms. "You guys are loaded up back here."

"Not like when my dad was around," I told him.

He shook his big domed head, a gray color, the color of clouds, with velvety hair underneath. "You're lucky, Sam. Some people don't get nothing."

I peered at his weird face. "Did my mom make you nervous about meeting Ditch?"

He shook his head, squished his lips together, flat as they would go. Even still, they were bigger than my mom's when she held them normal, and she's got big lips. "Naw. I've met a lot of people in my time."

"Ditch'll like you because he likes me."

"We'll find out," he said, seeming to consider something. "Anyway, I don't care so much, long as he's respectful. He got a problem with me, well—" He stopped.

"Well, what?"

Greely rubbed the back of a finger across his chin. "Well, it don't matter, Sam. We're gonna have fun, you and me."

I smiled nervously. "Don't say something mean, huh?"

He chuckled. "Naw, Sam, I won't," he promised.

Ditch, tall and lean and fragile-looking, towered over Greely. The scene reminded me of a flagpole with a truck parked beside it. What struck me was that Greely could've broken Ditch into tiny parts, like a pencil. My mom introduced them, and they shook hands.

"You're a friend of Sam's from school?"

Greely nodded. "Yes, sir," he said softly, his voice like a slow, moaning engine.

"You keep the bullies off of 'im?"

"Just sometimes."

"His father always worried about him going to a city school."

"Can be rough," Greely said. "Hampden ain't exactly welcoming to outsiders, either. But I got a feeling Sam can handle hisself."

"I got the same feeling," Ditch mumbled.

Greely looked around, placed his big hands on his hips. "You and your wife really got a nice house here, Mr. Gordon."

"We like it."

"You collect rugs or something?"

[157]

Ditch shrugged. "We got a lot of 'em."

Greely rose on his toes. "Feels like I got three under my feet."

"Probably do."

He nodded. "Well, it's a nice feeling. I got a rug in my place, but it's hard and rough as a rock. Mostly, though, I just got wood floors."

"My wife likes softness under her feet," Ditch said.

We sat in the living room, the television turned to *Geraldo*, whose face was thin, his wiry hair brushed back across his head. He was wearing a fancy green suit that never wrinkled, even around his underarms. I could tell what he would look like as an old man. It was his nose. An old Cuban guy my father had worked with had had one just like it.

"Who's next?" my mother asked after Junie had opened a box from Ditch.

I turned. "You," I said, jumping up from the floor and stepping over a sweater that Junie and Ditch had bought me, wide red-and-white stripes, COCA-COLA printed in the middle of it. I picked up my mom's parcel of shoes from under the Gordons' phony towering tree and carried it over to her. The wrapping job wasn't all that nice, crinkled and uneven, but I figured she'd forget about that when she saw what was inside. Sitting back down, I smiled nervously to Greely, who was hunkered in one of the Gordons' wing chairs.

Howard lifted his head to watch my mother's progress. "Big box, Maxine," he said, casting a quick glance at me, grinning so that his glasses rose on his face.

My mom cut the tape with a sharp fingernail, pulled the paper off in one tug. When she realized what the box contained, she looked at me as if she was completely amazed, opened the top, and stared down at her yellow leather high-tops, tucked among sheets of white tissue paper.

"Do you like them?" I asked, excited.

She pulled them out, looked them over carefully, the yellow laces, everything; then said she loved them, like they were the best gift she'd ever gotten.

"They're so your feet won't hurt anymore," I told her, watching the way her face moved. "Put 'em on."

"Right now?" she asked.

"I bet they're more comfortable than those," I said, pointing to her little black flats.

She kicked her shoes off and pushed her feet into the sneakers. "They're the right size," she told me. She laced them up, and her feet were the brightest things in the room, even brighter than the flames crackling in the fireplace. "They're very soft."

"They look cool," I told her, feeling great, like I'd pulled off something wonderful.

Junie cleared her throat, agreed.

"He thought they'd make you look and feel younger," Greely told my mom.

She smiled. "Do they do it, Howard?"

He tapped his glasses against his face, nodded his head. "By about ten years," he said seriously, studying them by leaning forward in his chair.

My mom stood up to give me a hug.

"Your feet won't hurt anymore," I informed her, feeling magical, climbing off the floor.

After she let me go, she said, "I've got two things for you. One's boring. One's not. Which one do you want to open first?"

"I guess the one that's not."

She located a big gift among the others, and in an instant, I had it unwrapped. A G.I. Joe desert war cruiser, displayed dramatically in a colorful box, was strapped into place by two thick rubber bands. For a minute or two, I was stunned. I gawked at it through the plastic

window, smiling like a total idiot. It was awesome. I'd seen it adver-
tised on television once or twice, but I'd never imagined that I would
own one, bristling with fragile plastic weapons, capable of appearing
to really hover, with five seats and a little rocket scooter thing that
clicked onto the side.

"This is perfect," I told her.

"Is that the one you wanted?"

"It's better," I said.

Ditch opened a box from Junie with two plaid shirts in it, held
them up for examination, then draped them over the back of the chair
he was in.

Greely tore into his present from me, a black plastic wallet, shiny
on the outside, dull on the inside. It was supposed to look and feel
like snakeskin, and it kind of did. What I liked the most about it,
though, was the half-hidden flap it had for storing a special key.

Greely gave me the football we always tossed around and an all-in-
one encyclopedia, the size of a fat dictionary, heavy as a bucket of
water, with a series of color pictures every fifty or sixty pages.

"It's 'cause you always want to know so much," he said, smiling.
His teeth looked like a disorganized row of trees.

"That's a sweet gift," my mom told him.

From her chair, Junie looked over my skinny shoulder. "That's a
whole set of encyclopedias in one book?"

"It's condensed," Greely mumbled. "I seen it recently and thought
of Sam."

"Does it have the stuff you talk about in it?" I asked as I flipped
through the pages so fast they were blurry.

Greely leaned forward. "Has like twelve pages on World War II and
a bunch of stuff on the Civil Rights movement, but that's scattered all
about. You got to poke through to find that kind of thing."

"You fight in the war?" Ditch, who'd been quiet all morning,
asked Greely.

"Three years," Greely told him.

Ditch lifted his cigarette to his pale lips, oozed them around the butt. "I flew over Europe during the war. Was a tail gunner on a B-17."

"Braver than me."

"Just where I ended up. I would have gotten out if they'd have let me."

Greely nodded, hunched his shoulders up under his nice blue shirt. It had someone else's initials on the breast pocket. "I was on foot or bouncing around in the back of a truck. Fought in North Africa and Europe."

"Fight at the Battle of the Bulge?"

"We came up from Italy."

"Our bomber squadron was one of the first to get through."

Junie handed Ditch one of his gifts. "You can talk later, hon," she said. "We got work to do."

I closed the encyclopedia and thanked Greely.

He smiled wide, and a relaxed look settled across his face.

Howard gimped forward, picked a flat bag out from under the tree and handed it to me. I tore it open carefully because I knew it was filled with comic books. I spread them out on the floor, jerked my head up. "Number ninety-four X-Men!"

He shrugged. "It's the one where they introduce Wolverine, Storm, and Colossus."

I brought it up close to my face. The plastic bag it was in grew steamy against my warm exhales. "I can't believe you gave me all these," I exclaimed, putting number ninety-four X-Men down, scanning other old issues of my favorite comic books. There was even a twelve-cent Fantastic Four.

I got up and got him his present, this traveling mug with a Velcro bottom. It had a little drawing of a coffee cup and a piece of toast on it.

"I can really use this," he told me.

I fell to my knees, happy. "It's not just for coffee. It'll keep soda cold, too."

After Christmas dinner, I sat in the kitchen with my mom, Howard, and Junie. They sipped on this foamy drink that Greely had brought, the gift that hadn't been for me. Everyone looked tired, especially Junie. Her elbows were on the tabletop, and saggy skin flooded down around the bend in her arms. Beneath her platinum-blond hair, gray roots framed her slack face, cheeks puffy, as if filled with soft ointment.

In the living room, a fire was blazing. Ditch and Greely sat in front of it and talked about the war. My mom had told me to leave them alone, so I'd helped with the Christmas dinner cleanup, which had taken nearly an hour. Finally, everything was done. Grease-burned pots and scorched, bent pans were drying in the rack, slow drips falling off of them like they were melting. The washer was sloshing about, too, squirting thin streams of hot water all over the Gordons' fine china and forks and spoons, clicking on and off. At some point, Greely and I were supposed to go out front and toss the football, but he couldn't budge from the living room, with Ditch sitting on him like he was.

"Whatcha thinking about, Samuel?" Junie asked in a tired voice.

I shrugged.

"You like that sweater we got you, hon?"

"Yeah," I told her, trying to look like I did. And I did, a little. I was just a little worried that it would make me stick out at school, which was the very last thing I wanted to do. "I like the neck."

"It's a nice neck," she agreed. "It's Coca-Cola brand. The lady at the department store said it was high fashion with teenagers." She drained her little rounded glass, then poured some more of Greely's gift into it. The stuff looked like a milk shake.

My mom put a freezing-cold hand on top of one of mine, squeezed gently. "It's been a good day, hasn't it?"

She was right. I mean, I wasn't sure, but it might have been the first completely good day since my dad left. If it had been me, though, I wouldn't have said anything. My mom and I were going in two different directions. She'd gotten so that she liked to speak up if she thought things were nice, as if talking about it cemented it down or something. But if I even admitted to having fun, it reminded me that I was forgetting about my dad. When I was happy, I couldn't think about him. It was that simple. His memory made me sad.

We drove home after dark, the low clouds breaking up, big twinkling stars glowing bright, as if holes in the cold sky. The streets were nearly empty, even in the bad sections of town. And the city looked pretty, with its long blocks of rowhouses, all the different types, some without porches, some that were three stories high, some that were skinny and others that were as wide as mansions. In certain sections of town, they were all covered with Formstone. In others, they were plastered with bricks or shingles or a combination of all three things, so they appeared as patched together as monsters. But there was something about all of them, something old and kind, something nice about the way they related to the street, the sky, the people.

On Greenmount Avenue, a dog raced across a wrecked sidewalk, legs moving like twirling fan blades. As he went, he kicked up a balled-up napkin, intent, like he was rushing an important message to someone.

Howard slowed and turned onto Devin Lane.

We rolled down Greely's nearly lightless neighborhood, came to a stop at the end of the block. I felt bad that Greely lived there, of all places in Baltimore. I knew there were worse areas, like places on the west side of the city, where more than half the shootings took place, but there were also places that were a lot better, places where someone as nice as he was deserved to live. Even Charles Village was a big step up.

"Greely," I said from the back seat. "You wish Ditch had liked you right away?"

He shrugged, twisted around, and looked at me, eyes like two soft glowing yo-yos. "That kind of thing don't matter to me too much anymore, Sam. That's all about arrogance, and arrogance can put you in a bad place. When I was a young man, I used to be that way. I'd consider jacking up a man for his attitude. I never wanted to be nice to people who weren't already nice to me. What the heck, huh? I learned it don't do no good. It don't make life any better, and most of the time, it makes it worse. Now, I figure, I'll come to folks to find out if they're any good. If they aren't, I can deal with that, too."

I stared at him, thinking he was brilliant.

He opened the door, gave it a shove, and climbed out. Leaning over, he withdrew the wallet I'd given him from a front pants pocket. "This is nice," he told me.

I told him that I liked the encyclopedia, too.

He smiled.

"Thanks for coming, Greely," my mom said, sliding out from the back seat.

"It was my pleasure." He shook her hand by holding it with both of his.

Howard leaned over, lowered his head so that he could see Greely under the roof of the car. "It's been a pleasure, Greely. We'll see you around?"

"I guess you will," he agreed, steam billowing from his mouth. He shoved his new wallet back into a deep, fuzzy pocket, shivered a little. "Let me get inside," he said, and tilted his head to tell us goodbye. He crossed around behind the car, tapped on the mashed trunk twice, and headed slowly toward the front steps of his sad-looking apartment. He started up, glanced back, and watching him, I suddenly thought he was the most handsome man I'd ever seen, in a strange way, beautiful.

fish boy

fish boy

It snowed and iced a thousand times by Valentine's Day. The skies were always cold and dreary with dark clouds rolling above Baltimore at all hours. It was like getting stood on by a big person who couldn't talk. It was smothering. The brightness of Christmas on the Gordons' bouncy floor of stacked Oriental carpets dwindled and dissolved till it seemed like a moment from way back in my past, when all of my memories were kept like post cards in my head instead of in words and sentences, and in moving, flickering pictures. I felt like I was slowly turning into a ghost from lack of light. There was nothing to do in weather like that. Greely and I gave up throwing the football, because it was either sloppy and muddy in Wyman Park or frozen hard, a lumpy ice rink with tufts of brown grass sprouting out of it. About two or three times a week, he just stayed at school, decided to spend the night on the soiled blue couch in the basement storage room. He told me, tired and miserable-looking, that his apartment was "too cold for human inhabitance." What he meant was it was just too cold, which I figured out by asking.

People around the neighborhood were fussing all the time. Most everyone just gave up trying to act cheerful. All morning, they hacked at their sidewalks, covered over in giant flat ice cubes, and chipped away at the bumpy windshields on their cars. Their eyes and mouths were always squeezed small in frustration, like the puny faces on my G.I. Joe action figures. If it was windy out, the few bare trees in Charles Village swayed and snapped, ready to topple at any minute. And when they did, they shattered against the ground as if they were made of cheap thin glass.

Maybe because everyone else looked so uncomfortable, or maybe because it was in my blood to get down during the winter, I got moody, too. I could never get enough sleep, even when I slept extra. It got so that sometimes I didn't even want to get up in the morning.

A week after Valentine's Day, school closed early for about the tenth time since the beginning of January. It was only around two o'clock in the afternoon, but outside it looked like it was night. It was the kind of weather my father had hated. He'd always worried about dying in snowstorms, sliding off the highway in his BG&E car. He'd talked about snow like it hovered over the city just to do him in. So it kind of scared me a bit. As a matter of fact, a few years before, I'd begun to think that the winter was plotting to take my dad away. The truth is, something was plotting, but it wasn't the winter.

I caught the Forty-two Downtown with about twenty other students. We bumped and rumbled along in the city bus toward the Rotunda, the grayness of Hampden drifting by the creaking windows, car lights shining tired beams, drivers with round zombie-eyes. Everything looked grim, as if the sun had disappeared for good behind the bone-colored clouds, as if it were stuck on the other side of the world.

At my stop on St. Paul Street, a man with a stocking cap, rolled up and slung on his head like a dog dish, gave the bell a ring, and I jumped down after him, making my way across the road to the stores. Tiny ice pellets bounced off my warm, smoking head and stuck to strands of my hair. I walked the way I did on the beach. I dragged my feet, dug ruts into the rough quilt of sleet. I liked doing that. It brightened me. Below the windows of the closed bank, a sopping newspaper was smothered and hidden under granules of ice, a little raised area with outlines. Its look bothered me, but it took me a minute to figure out why. When I did, I wished I hadn't. It reminded me of my dad, how he might have looked hidden in the dirt, his giant body stretched out, a buried log. Behind the skinny arched bones of my chest, a muscle grew tight. I yanked my eyes away and trotted nervously up the sidewalk, past the video store and the speed-reading school, right up to the half-hidden mat in front of Junie's.

Shuffling into the store, I nearly tripped over Ditch, who was lying in the middle of the aisle, working on a wobbly bedding-plant rack, twisting shiny new screws into the corners. His long legs jutted out, pipe cleaners that had been twisted too many times. "Sam," he said, peering up at me from behind a bunch of white and green leaves.

"Hey, Ditch."

"Whatcha think of the storm? Ugly, ain't it?"

I nodded.

"They're saying it's gonna get worse 'fore it gets better. Gonna snow all night, least eight inches." He climbed to his knees, gave the rickety rack a test shake, so that I saw his weird fingernails, wavy pieces of shell glimmering under the fluorescent lights. He stood up, looking like a beanstalk the way he rose, as if his head might go right through the scratchy ceiling tiles and into the clouds.

I smiled at him as well as I could and headed for the checkout counter, where my mom was sitting, reading over a list of receipts, gnawing on the tip of a pencil.

"Your hair's all wet," she informed me.

I reached up and touched the top of my head, and dribbles of water ran down the curves of my face.

"Buster, you got plans for the day?"

"Uh-uh," I murmured. I felt kind of crummy.

"You okay?"

"I guess."

She put down her pencil. It was wet and crunched with teeth marks. It rolled across the pad she was using to write numbers all over, stopped at a wad of cash-register receipts, compressed into tight curls by rubber bands. She studied my face and asked me if I was lonely or something.

"Maybe," I told her, because I couldn't admit it outright.

"Well, this weather can do that," she said.

I nodded, put my books on the counter.

"Junie and Ditch are heading home in like a half-hour. If you want, you can stay here with me, keep me entertained." She paused. "You could go up the street and get us some cards to play with or something?"

I slumped forward, grinning because I liked the idea, even if card games with my mom weren't all that much fun. Sometimes, it was just nice to do something together. "If you want me to."

"Sure, I do," she said, and reached a hand into the pocket of her loose smock, withdrew a few dollars, crunched into balls. "Here you go," she told me, and smoothed them out as well as she could on the counter, so that they looked like wide strips of bacon. "Go get yourself a Coke and me a coffee, too."

I picked up the dollar bills and pushed them into a pocket of my stiff jeans, like canvas they were so new. "You want regular cards or ones with a picture on them?"

"A nice picture," she said. "Something bright."

I nodded. "You want a big coffee?"

"Medium's okay," she said.

Excited, I turned and shambled down the wet aisle, pushed the front door open.

Ditch moseyed after me. In the storm, he lit a cigarette and stood looking around without saying anything. That was the way he went about conversations, I'd come to realize, nonchalant, so I stood there, too. After a minute, he reached over and squeezed one of my shoulders, blew smoke sideways out of his mouth. "Sorry to hear yer feeling low, Sam," he said.

My face warmed in the cold air. I dropped my eyes and looked down at the faded knees of his pants.

"You know, crummy weather like this makes a lot of folks feel down." He ran a hand through his coarse gray hair, and ice crystals fell against the collar of his jacket.

"That's what mom said," I told him softly. I bit at my lip. "Does it bother you?"

He took a long drag on his cigarette, so that the tip glowed. "Sure," he said, smoke curling like a snake from his mouth.

"Junie, too?"

"She's got Hummels to keep her busy. She gets lost in 'em."

I nodded.

He glanced off toward St. Paul Street, covered in white, hard tire-tracks cutting through it, heading toward downtown, the tall buildings and narrow sloping streets. Off in the distance, behind spitting sleet, a blue police light flashed against the walls of pretty three- and four-story rowhouses. Ditch took some more puffs on his cigarette, then pivoted and pointed at me with it. "Bet you want to get yerself a comic book?" he declared.

"I got all my favorites already," I admitted in an embarrassed voice.

Pulling out a cottony dollar and sticking it into one of my coat pockets, he muttered, "Then go explore. Get one you ain't never gotten before. What's life all about, anyway?"

Snow started mixing with the tumbling sleet. It fluttered between the hard droplets, like someone had cut open a pillow. Ditch reached over and shook one of my shoulders again, dropped his cigarette, and snuffed it with a heel of his shabby leather boots. "Go on," he said. "I'm heading back inside. It's just about as miserable as it can get out here."

"Thanks," I said, throat stinging with good feelings for him.

"For the dollar? You're always welcome, Sam," he said as he banged his way through the door.

Turning, I tromped up the slippery sidewalk, steam puffing out of my mouth. At the Dime Store, I pulled the cold door open and entered along the low candy counter. As usual, the place was a shambles, shelves dark with dust, smothered by forgotten items changing in their packages. The floor was a checkerboard linoleum, white and blue, dotted with swirls of in-between colors. There were little patties of mud all over it, triangular pieces from off the soles of work boots and sneakers and such. The way it always looked, I figured it must have been years since anyone had cleaned the place. It reminded me of something from the past. Even the tall cashier looked antique. She had a bundle of blond hair twisted up on her small head like a serving of soft ice cream, and when she spoke, half the words pushed through her narrow nostrils in funny squeaks and vibrations. I asked her where the playing cards were located, and she pointed me to a shelf between old plastic buckets and air fresheners.

I went ahead and picked out a pack with a painting of a saggy-skinned bulldog on the front. He was wearing a brown fur coat, the kind that old-fashioned rich guys sport in movies, and a bow tie. I liked the picture because he appeared so funny and self-conscious, as if he was embarrassed by his nice clothes. On my way to the counter, I stopped by an old comic-book rack and decided on getting *The Micronauts* with Ditch's dollar. It was about tiny space-travelers from another universe.

Outside, the sleet had turned mostly to powdery, spinning snow, the kind that shoots around in all directions. It shooshed down the front of my nylon jacket, stuck to the soft clear hairs on the backs of my hands and fingers. As I opened the glass doors to the Waverly Deli, a gush of heat splashed against me. All year round, the place was like a sauna. I blamed the bright yellow lights on the ceiling, where long fluorescent tubes flickered and hummed like big power lines. They gave the Formica counters and chrome surfaces a searing orange tint.

I filled a Styrofoam cup with soda and watched the cook, a strong-looking black woman, salt down a shiny batch of French fries, then start scooping them into little white bags. Since she was busy, I took the opportunity to slurp on my Dr Pepper, then top it off again. When my dad was feeling good, he'd always gotten himself a little extra. He said that places made so much money on their fountain drinks that it was okay.

When I got back to the store, Junie and Ditch were getting ready to leave for home. "Awful out there, hon?" Junie asked me, squeezing into her ankle-length purple coat, covered in puffy squares of insulation. The belt cut into her stomach like she'd swallowed a basket of soft clothes.

"It feels like the North Pole," I told her.

"Oh, Lord." Junie looked at Ditch, stomping her red rubber boots.

"We'll get home," he muttered.

She peered up at the ceiling and mouthed a prayer. When she was done, she dropped her eyes onto me. "Well, Samuel, hon, there'll be no school tomorrow. You can bet on that," she said.

"I guess," I mumbled.

"It don't take guessing," she declared, then located a crinkly plastic rain cover in her pocket and strapped it over her bushel of hair, flaming red from a brand-new dye job. "Now, you watch out for your mom in this mess," she instructed me.

"I will," I said weakly.

After they were gone, I took off my heavy coat and stuck it behind the counter, jamming it into a space beside a jumble of store bags. I put the coffee cup down by the register and took a sip of my fizzy soda, so carbonated that it made my nose burn.

My mom picked up the cards I'd gotten and looked over the picture. "A dog in a fancy jacket."

Suddenly, I was embarrassed.

"Looks like he swallowed a canary."

I leaned over and studied the painting. "What does that mean?"

"It means, he looks like he knows something we don't."

"Like what?" I asked.

"Like maybe he just bit the painter or something."

I smiled. "You think?"

"Sure I do."

I had to crack up imagining that, the dog snipping the painter.

We played boring Go Fish till nearly closing. It was boring because, as usual, my mom won practically every game. She was good with cards. Back in Rodger's Forge, she had played Solitaire every night, set up in the big, square kitchen as the dishwasher churned and squirted. My dad had hated it. He'd thought she was just trying to avoid him, but I never did. She really liked playing. It was the only time she ever got cutthroat and shady. It started the minute a single card slid across her long fingers. That's why she said she never gambled for money. She was worried that she'd go crazy, spend every last penny. I couldn't imagine her being so reckless, though. She was always careful with cash, even before we were broke.

Outside, it was still snowing and icing like mad. The wind had picked up, and big gusts shook the store windows so that they popped and shivered. Reflections moved up and down, stretched away into bright, globby blurs. The tall, crusty iron streetlights, bulbs glowing, appeared fogged in by churning white specks. And even though I was tired of that kind of weather, it was pretty to see, and it grabbed my heart.

At five o'clock, my mom stuck the cash-register money into the safe, and we left, headed for the WaWa convenience store to get supplies. As we kicked along through the storm, I dragged my feet the way I enjoyed. She pulled on a pair of floppy green gardening gloves, decorated with little lines across the knuckles, the tips mashed because they were too long. Our stumbling feet splashed up dusty rooster tails, and the sharp, cold wind blasted our faces, leaving our cheeks and ears frozen and achy. To stay warm, I jumped around, ran and slid on the ice, coated in a powdery white.

The WaWa was located beneath the corner of a big building. From a distance, it looked like the old apartment had scooted onto the store in an earthquake, shook and groaned and swamped the place. I felt sorry for the WaWa, because no matter how shiny the chrome trim and door handles were, how bright the place was, the milky windows above, and the leaning building itself, made it seem older. Also, for some reason, homeless people liked to gather out in front of it when the weather wasn't horrible. They begged for money at the entrance and made me guilty feeling when I walked out glugging a soda and chomping on a piece of candy.

That night it was different, though. There was no one out front, and the store, which was usually almost empty, was hopping with crazy customers, dripping-wet people with their bright winter coats unzipped down the front. Two beefy cabdrivers leaned against the speckled coffee counter, blabbing, bending the thin wooden surface, as at least five Hopkins students, one with a Mohawk, milled around between the scratched metal shelves.

I stumbled after my mom as she walked about the store gathering up supplies, cans of Hormel chili, milk, eggs, and two packages of cookies. On our way to the counter, I spotted a tin of sweet rolls and showed them to her.

"You want 'em?"

"No," she told me, tired.

[174]

"But they're good for breakfast," I argued.

"We've got how many boxes of cereal?"

"None of it's the kind that I like, though," I said coyly.

"It's the sweet rolls or these," she told me, indicating the two big packages of duplex cookies. "Take your pick, but we can't get them both."

"Why not?" I asked.

"Samuel, this is all I've got," she said, and showed me a ten-dollar bill, pinched between two of her fingers.

"That's all?"

"Ten dollars."

"The cookies," I decided.

A few minutes later, we shuffled beneath the concrete-looking trees of our dark neighborhood, snow bombing down on us, dousing our heads and shoulders with white. Lazy, I dragged the heavy, plastic grocery bag behind me. It slithered along like an ice block with a rope tied around it. Meanwhile, my mom, who was following a few yards back, let hers clank dully against one of her legs. The wind started to swirl, filled my ears, and it took me a minute to realize that I was walking alone. I turned, and my mom was down the block, half-hidden in the snowy dark between streetlamps. A man in a coat stood beside her, talking, shaking his arms to emphasize whatever he was saying. The hairs on my neck rose, pricked like ants swarming across my collar. Slowly, I started back to see what was going on.

My mom's sack of groceries was in a clump by her yellow sneakers. Her thin garden gloves were cast in the snow beside it, like two bobbing cans twirling down the Jones Falls. Bug-eyed, she searched madly for something in her linty coat pockets.

"Mom," I called as I got closer. "Who's he?"

She jerked around. "Just a friend," she said in a shaky voice, almost a bird whistle.

I got closer and closer, still dragging the bag behind me.

From a pocket inside her coat, my mom located some money and gave it to the man.

"You told me you only had ten dollars," I said in a trembling voice.

The guy in the jacket twisted his head around and glowered at me. He was wild-looking and burning angry. Steam floated above his shoulders. Slabs of hair were plastered like sopping dishcloths to his ugly crater face. Glassy sweat rolled into his eyes, made him blink. It even dripped off of his nose. When the stony trees shook, spots of fiery light moved across him. That's when I spotted the little gun he was holding, so small that it looked like a silver toy. He had it pointed in my direction.

"Shad up!" he hissed.

My hand released my sack of groceries and it slid in the rolling breeze like my mom's. I tried to yell, but I couldn't. Instead, I stared at the man, wobbled, dropped to my knees, and collapsed into the cold snow. Nearly useless, a fish on ice, I stared up silently, took everything in, a slow-motion event that etched itself onto the film of my brain.

The mugger turned back to my mom, reached over, and tore her watch, which was always needing batteries, right off her skinny wrist. He yelled at her, his mouth so big and wide that it looked like a cartoon, but she didn't have anything else to give him. Squatting, he searched our groceries, pulled out the colorful packages of duplex cookies. He tucked them under an arm, sprang up, and crashed into my mom's shoulder, knocked her over and ran down the middle of the road toward St. Paul Street.

When the guy had turned the corner, my mom called for help. She crawled over to where I was lying, on my side, useless, and kept calling, so that her shaking voice rang in my ears. A front porch light popped on, then others up and down Thirty-second Street. Doors flew open and people scurried down their slick rowhouse steps over to where we were flopping about in the road.

"We've been mugged," my mom, sobbing, told a man.

"I called the police," he promised, reaching down to help us to our feet. Suddenly, all around us, the street swirled with people. A black lady broke from the crowd and draped soft blankets over our backs. Mine smelled of mildew, but it kept me warm, made me feel better as my side thawed.

The blue lights of a police car flashed off of Greenmount Avenue and roared down Thirty-second Street, through the deep snow, pushing it to the side. The officer threw his door open and climbed out. His wipers scraped the slush to the edges of his windshield, and his headlights lit up the crowd, shivering and hunched.

"Everyone all right?" he asked.

The crowd backed away so that he could see us.

"You all right, ma'am?"

"Yeah," my mom mumbled.

"Yer sure?"

"Uh-huh," she moaned.

"What happened?"

She took a fluttery breath. "Me and my son got mugged."

The officer withdrew a pad from his coat and instructed her to describe the man.

"He was a tall white guy," she said in a jumpy voice.

"How tall do you think, ma'am?"

"Just tall," she said. "Kind of skinny."

"Can you remember anything else? Anything at all?"

She shook her head.

"Think," he told her softly.

She tried to, but she couldn't. She shook her head again. "It happened too fast. He had a gun, and I worried. He held it right against me, not six inches away except when he looked over at my son." Tears rushed down her cheeks.

"What'd he take?"

[177]

She slumped forward, felt in her pockets. "All my money,"—she wiped at her nose with a sleeve—"my watch and . . . and two packages of cookies."

The officer shook his head and wrote it all on his pad, then squatted down so that his wide behind sunk into the snow, so that he looked me straight in the eyes. His brown face was heavy, and his nose was broad, the shape of a pie wedge. He took off his hat, let it hang loosely in one of his plump hands. "What's your name, son?" he asked me, eyebrows pinched together.

"Sam," I mumbled.

"Can you tell me anything?"

"Yeah," I muttered.

"All right," he said, nodding his head.

So I gave him the man's exact description, talked about his flat belly, his longish brown hair, sweaty and pasted to him. I told him about the man's jacket, the bent silver buckle and the torn pocket with red stuffing poking out. I described things I didn't even know I'd seen. One of his hands had a flower tattooed on it. I could see it clearly. One of the man's eyebrows drooped forward, sagged like it was slipping off his head, down one side of his bumpy face. I told him about the man's boots and his baggy green army pants. I recalled everything, rambled on till there wasn't anything more to tell.

"You're positive about all this stuff?" the officer asked me when I was done.

"Yes, sir," I whispered without looking at him. I was kind of mortified that the reason I'd seen so much was because I'd been lying on my side, eyes wide, staring up at the guy.

"You got a good memory," he informed me, rubbed my wet head with a hand, and stood. He called the man's description in on a little black walkie-talkie that was clipped to the shoulder of his coat. There was static, like on my dad's old CB in his messy BG&E car. He clipped the radio back onto his round shoulder and closed his pad.

"Ma'am," he said to my mother, "normally we'd ask you to ride around in the car. We spot a lot of muggers that way, but we got a real good description, and it's an ugly night. Why don't I just take you home?"

My mom nodded her head.

The lady took back the soft blankets she'd slid onto our shoulders. "You'll be okay," she said to my mom. "Happened to me last fall, and I don't even think about it atoll no more, you know. Too many good people in the world to let the bad ones set you off."

I dragged the two bags of groceries over to the police car. The engine was rumbling softly, wipers squeaking. People wished us well as we climbed across the back seat, along the slick blue vinyl where they normally put criminals. I stared at my mom's bony face, and I felt terrible and chicken, as unsuperhero-like as anyone could possibly be.

The officer turned his squad car around and drove us slowly home, through the falling slivers of snow.

When I woke up the next day, a Friday, the sun was up and the world was covered in a blanket of white. I gazed out of my hazy bedroom window, sealed behind its rusty grate, feeling hollow and puny. I was a complete wimp, and I'd proved it.

Howard was out of town, and my mom had phoned the Gordons after the policeman had dropped us off. She'd been kind of upset, stuttering and all, so in the middle of the storm, Junie and Ditch had climbed back into their van and spun and slid their way slowly over from Hamilton. Ditch was snoring in my bed, head tilted back across my pillow, a wrinkled foot sticking out from under the sheets. His cigarette breath filled my room. I could hear Junie rummaging around in the chilly kitchen, clanking metal pans and talking to herself as she got things ready for breakfast.

The soft, bent roofs on the rowhouses across the alley looked padded, puffed up and soft. Ice clung to the brick walls. Broad

[179]

odd-shaped fragments of shiny glass glittered beautifully in the sun. An old tire in the yard across from ours was a powdered doughnut, the old car radiator beside it a pastry. Everything appeared so kind and nice when it really wasn't at all. The area was unsafe, dangerous even. On one side there was Greenmount, gunfire and drug addicts, on the other muggers and more guns. Guns were all over the place, blasting like dog barks into the night. Baltimore was swimming in them. And in the middle of it all, my mom and me, both unarmed. I didn't want it to be that way, though. I was the man of the house. In my father's absence, in Howard's absence, I was supposed to watch out for my mother. I wanted to, and I wished more than anything that I had done something brave the night before, dashed across the snow and disarmed the guy by delivering a wicked karate chop to his wrist. I imagined doing it, and it wasn't even that hard. The puny handgun just popped right out of his hand, flew into the air, and landed in mine. Then I held it on him till the police arrived.

Miserable, I turned away from the window and walked across my old sleeping bag, a knot on the floor, and out of my miniature room, turned the corner, and went into the cold kitchen, where I was surprised to see my mom sitting in the breezy bay window, yammering with Junie. To be honest, I'd kind of expected her to hide in her room for days, till she was a brittle white ghost again, the way she'd done when we'd first moved.

My mom looked at me. "Some night."

I was so surprised she was all right, I just stared back.

"You doing okay, Samuel?"

"I guess," I mumbled after a moment.

"Talked to Howard this morning. He'll be back tomorrow. He was worried about you. You should have heard how worried he was."

I nodded.

She studied my slack face. "Oh, honey, what're you thinking?"

"Nothing."

"You've got to talk to me. You said you would."

I looked down at the floor, swallowed. "I just wish I had done something. I was thinking that I could have chopped his arm maybe."

"The mugger's?"

I nodded.

"Lord," Junie said, poking at bubbling eggs with a half-melted plastic spatula. "Thought we'd discussed that last night."

"But I fainted."

"It was scary."

"I wish he'd shot me."

"No, you don't," my mom said.

"Not to death or anything. Just enough so that I had an excuse for lying on the ground." I walked over and sat across from her, stared at the crack beneath the windowsill, wide enough now to be a mail slot, except for it was on the second floor, facing the alley, and pretty blue ice had sealed most of it shut.

"You know what?" my mom asked.

"No," I mumbled.

"Next time you want sweet rolls, you can have them. No self-respecting mugger would steal sweet rolls."

I looked up at her, saw that she was joking. "I don't know about that," I told her, feeling a bit better.

My mom shrugged, moved painfully in her chair. She was sore for almost an entire week.

the measure of a kid
the measure of a kid

Greely's strong face was slack, craggy cheeks soft as raw ground beef. He pulled his Chevron hat off and rubbed his face with an arm, rolled his cue-ball eyes, tracing-paper-thin lids shrinking back into his head. "Some weekend, eh, Sam," he muttered, plopping his cap on the table. "I didn't get home till yesterday afternoon. Our friend, Nurse Jones, came and got me, delivered me straight to my front door. I was going crazy in this school by myself. Thought I might start talking to the mice, the way it was looking. And wouldn't you know it, when I did get home, all the pipes'd burst. Soon as it warms up, that house is going to spring leaks all over the place. You should see the radiator in my room. Got a hunk of ice sticking out of a seam. It never did work that well, banged and all that. But it sure won't ever work now. Had to dress in four layers of clothes and wrap myself in every single blanket I got, just to sleep, 'cause a house without heat is colder than the coldest night. Now I got to find me a new place to live. Twenty years, and I'm done with Devin Lane. Downstairs neighbor, William, he is, too. He's taking Missus and Beemus somewhere else. Our landlord don't have an ounce of human decency. All night I was awake. Laid there shivering and shaking and cursing his sorry name. Feel like breaking that man's neck, if you want to know the truth."

I peeled the soggy bun of my hamburger back and slathered it with ketchup from out of a squeeze tube. Looking up at Greely, I asked, "Why'd your pipes burst?"

"Froze inside," he told me, shaking his big head. He pinched a few napkins off his tray and unraveled the little squares into bigger squares. "Water swells up when it freezes, so if it's stuck in a pipe, the pipe breaks like it's made of china or something. It's an awful sight, too. I seen it crack pipes right down the middle, big iron fittings fat as two of my arms."

I took a hunk out of my hamburger, chewed, mouth full and cheeks stretchy.

"Gonna choke if you eat that way all the time."

"I won't," I told him, gobs of bread sticking to the sides of my teeth.

"Anyway," he muttered, picking up his fork and digging around the pile of orange spaghetti on his tray, "those pipes froze 'cause we didn't have no heat. If the landlord had gotten the heat working right, those pipes woulda been fine. He didn't listen, though, 'cause it was just us, me and William, making demands on him. That's what he thought. Now he needs to put all new plumbing in that place, and he ain't going to do it. I know he ain't. He's going to be cheap and come up with some sorry way to patch it, or he's just going to slap boards up in the windows and let the place rot." He stared right at me, frustrated.

"Guess what, Greely?" I said softly.

"What?" he asked, voice so heavy and muffled it sounded like he was talking into the arm of a sweatshirt. He lifted his fork to his giant lips.

"Thursday night my mom and I got mugged on the way home from Junie's store."

He put his fork down. "Damn," he declared. "Right in the middle of the storm?"

[183]

I nodded.

"You guys all right?"

I pulled my mouth to one side, said, "My mom's voice was shaky afterward."

"It's an awful thing to go through."

I nodded again, throat getting tight, so that it felt bound by scratchy strands of twine.

"How 'bout you, Sam? You all right?"

I studied the selections on my beige plastic lunch tray, hunks of swampy food and the oiliest French fries possible. My face burned red, and a chill went up my back. "I guess I'm fine," I said, embarrassed. I leaned forward. Checking around for other students, I whispered, "I think I fainted or something." My mouth got thick, like there was a batch of powdery cement in it, slowly hardening till I couldn't move my jaw.

Greely sighed, his cheeks stretching with air. After a moment or two of staring off into nowhere, he leaned forward and tapped one of my hands with a finger. "Sam," he said, and took a deep breath, a big inhale, "blacking out ain't nothing. It ain't. I know it feels bad, but when everything is said and done, it don't matter at all." He peered into my eyes. "You want to know something I ain't ever told anybody? I fainted once, when I was still young and living in Atlanta. 'Cept the difference is, I was an adult." He put a stiffened knobby finger to his wet lips, looked off toward the empty section of the cafeteria, plastic chairs turned upside down, hung on the sides of tables. "It was a terrible thing, and part of why I moved to Baltimore. But I know now, it wasn't nothing. It was the smallest part of everything."

I dropped my eyes away from his and poked at a withered wedge of cabbage on my tray, pushed it over with the blunt points of my fork. The way it landed, *splat* in its water, I thought about Greely tumbling onto his big side, a man without any wrinkles, and arms so strong he could have lifted my dad up over his head. I mumbled, "What made you faint?"

He kept his finger against his mouth, barely open. "Fear and worry, Sam," he grumbled roughly into a knuckle. "Just like you."

I asked, "What was so scary?"

His finger bent, so that it looked like a bumpy question mark. "You really want to know?"

I nodded.

"The neighborhood I lived in. It was so sorry and broken down. And rain was beating against it. I was thinking about the bad way I lived. It was all that. You know what I mean?"

I sort of did. When my mom and I had first moved into Charles Village, it had appeared so dreary, like we were crashing through Baltimore to the very bottom of the basement, into the dark hopelessness of slum life that the *Sun* paper sometimes printed pictures of on the front page. I knew it wasn't the same, that his neighborhood probably really was a slum. But I understood just a little, and it wasn't a good feeling at all.

"Right then and there, I knew that I was always going to be poor. And worse than anything else, it seemed like it was my family's fault. I was always worrying about them, and they was drowning me, and I was strangling. I blamed it on them, I was so hopeless and lost and scared. The most scared man in the world." He drooped forward, looked at me, eyes big, a dying bird with its dark shiny pupils turning dusty blue. "Next thing I know, I'm at the bottom of the steps and looking straight up at the rain. I fainted. I was so down about that. For a time, that faint drove me mad." He picked up his fork and started eating again, shoveling food into his circling mouth.

I watched him; and the way he ate, I could tell he didn't want to think about it. He'd already said enough to help me, though. He was a strong old man, brave enough to have fought in World War II, and just the fact that he'd fainted once made me feel better. Maybe everyone fainted, but no one ever discussed it.

I picked up my floppy hamburger and gnawed at the side, jammed a couple of fries between my grinders. I swallowed. "I guess I just wish I'd done something instead of flop on the ground. You should have seen my mom. She was so upset that Ditch and Junie drove over in the middle of the storm. It took them more than an hour, too."

Greely took a sip of iced tea, a cloud of sugar, a watery dust storm, swirling around the bottom of the tall, spotted glass. "He have a gun?"

"A little one," I explained. "I think it might have been a phony."

Greely shook his head. "Well, I hate to let you in on this secret, Sam, but you're just a kid. Whatcha going to do against somebody with a gun? It might have been phony, and it might not have been. If it wasn't, well, a gun's a gun, and you ain't Superman."

"I wish I was," I told him quietly, and took the last bit of burger and shoved it into my mouth, then washed my gums with milk. After a minute, I muttered, "Greely?"

"Yeah, Sam," he said, fork loaded with food.

"Why'd fainting make you come to Baltimore?"

He stared right at me, eyeballs flitting about in his head. "I'll tell you sometime," he said.

"Does it make you feel bad?" I asked.

"Sam," he said deeply, "it can make me feel real bad. Not the fainting or anything, just the fact I'm here." Lifting a big hand, a ragged brown baseball glove, he rubbed his face like he was tired and trying to relax.

Then I remembered his crumbling apartment and all of its frozen pipes. "So where are you going to live now that your pipes have all froze?" I asked.

He shook his head. "Don't know for sure. Got to find a place. But Nurse Jones is going to put me up for a while. They got an extra room in their basement. She and her husband, Ray, said I could stay there till I find me a new apartment. But I'll be out by late next week. I'll get me a newspaper every day till I am. And you know what, I'm finally gonna live somewhere decent, too, where I can go out and see a neighborhood and not a wreck."

When school let out that day, Howard was waiting for me in the snowy, grooved street leading up to Falls Road. He was leaning against his dented car, engine puffing a squiggly, drifting shaft of smoke high into the sky. "Sam!" he called, shifting his feet, laced into boots, brown as knots of wood, to keep warm.

I jumped off the icy curb, hurried across the slippery road. "Why'd you come get me?" I asked, excited.

"Because we're going downtown," he said, leaning over and taking some of my books. He held them under an arm and bounced around the way a boxer dances with his shadow. He was trying to keep warm.

"Why's that?"

"Because the police think they got the guy who mugged you and your mom."

I squinted my eyes down on him like I was a gunfighter on a Saturday afternoon Western.

"They want you to pick him out of a lineup, like on television." He smiled, face fogged in by a cloud of steam, thick as syrup, rolling from his cold nostrils. "You're going to sort of be a hero."

I blinked at him and unsquinted. My stomach rumbled. I swallowed, and halfway down, a burning gas bubble caught my spit and brought it back up, made me burp. I'd always wanted to be a hero, but a hero like the kind I read about in comic books. I wanted a special power.

"Guess what else? They say he might have shot somebody last night, right over on Greenmount."

"He shot someone?" I asked, icy terror knotting up my back.

"Not for sure, but he might have. That's why I drove your mom down there this morning. She couldn't ID him, though, not absolutely, so the guy in charge of the investigation wanted you to come take a look."

All of my strength began whooshing out of me, like I was a rubber ball with a big dog bite in it. "His gun was real?"

"That's what the police said." Howard shivered in the cold air.

"We could be dead," I said distantly.

"Only if he'd pulled the trigger," he joked.

I glanced up at Howard's face, pale and still perfect for Dracula's. "What if he'd shot Mom?"

He squeezed his mouth together, into a blistery bump, then released it. "Don't think like that, Sam."

"It could have happened."

Howard glanced across the road, took in the horde of kids making their way up the icy hill, glanced back. "Teachers always told me that there's a big difference between 'could' and 'did.'"

My achy, cold hands felt like thousand-pound weights roped to the ends of my arms.

"What's thinking about it going to do for you, anyway? You should just be glad it didn't happen."

I nodded weakly.

He studied my face, sucked a cheek under his teeth. "I know it was scary, but you got to let things go. That's what getting older teaches you." He stooped a little so that he could see my eyes under the shallow ridge of my forehead. "Hey, you know what I'm thinking?"

I shook my head.

He pivoted and opened the driver's-side door, gouged and warped, wrinkled like splashed water. "That maybe after we're done at the police station, me and you could go over and get a snack at the Inner Harbor or Little Italy or something. How does that suit you?"

I liked the idea, nodded agreeably. Then I tried to let go of the guy with the gun, push him from my mind, just like Howard told me to do, like an adult.

"I figure, either way, we've got to go, so we might as well have fun afterward."

"That's what I think, too," I said, trying to sound bold. I trudged around the rickety, slanted front bumper, yanked open the creaky passenger's-side door and settled myself onto the seat.

Howard climbed in, started the car.

We drove slowly up the little hill to Falls Road, where we sat at the stoplight, rumbling in place. We were there for about a minute, shimmying like a gag gift, when someone hurled an icy hard snowball at the car. It banged loudly against the plastic grill.

"Can you believe that?" Howard asked me. "There must have been a rock in that thing."

I could believe it, but I told him that I couldn't. I didn't want to appear smart-alecky or something.

The light turned green, and Howard babied his car into a grinding gear. The engine moaned, and we shimmied around the corner, then whistled down the long hill toward the Jones Falls Expressway.

I watched the snow-trimmed trees flicker by, the rundown row-homes of Hampden, crunched and squeezed together, old broken washers and dryers and ovens and hot-water heaters and bathtubs and refrigerators, pushed out like water from a twisted rag. We tore up the ramp and onto the expressway, drifted along the snaking, rolling, raised cement road toward the tall buildings in the distance, the clouds above, gigantic slate islands dangling dangerously over Baltimore. Cast in yellow from the sun, they looked like they were on fire deep inside, popping with lava. I glanced around as we went, as the mound of Druid Hill Park disappeared behind a swooping overpass and the salty roadway climbed. In less than a minute, I spotted

[189]

the fancy antique rowhomes of Bolton Hill, where a lot of rich people lived. The tall buildings bristled with stone balconies and turrets and bright marble steps and wide windows covered in intricate black iron grills that looked more like decorations than security bars. The homes in Bolton Hill were like castles, big and ancient and beautiful. Decked in lacy snow, they resembled one of those perfect miniature landscapes in a snow globe.

The road dipped slowly away, and a rise grew beside it. On top of it was a nice old-fashioned brown building, part of the Maryland Institute College of Art, a place my mom had wanted to go, back when she was in high school. Her parents were opposed to that kind of study, though, so instead, she'd spent two years at a university in New Jersey, then quit to get married, which was something else they were against.

The car dropped into a rut below the city's bumpy streets. We passed the blocky, shimmering train station, stone decorations and sculptures stuck all over it, then under a series of rusty metal bridges— Charles Street, St. Paul, and Calvert—blue-and-yellow paint curling off. We curved north of downtown toward the east, where Ditch had worked at Bethlehem Steel, where the blackened stone jail poked up from the low streets of a bad neighborhood, a mountain trimmed with barbed wire.

I looked over at Howard and asked, "What would you have done if we'd been shot?"

Howard shook his head. "I'd have been lost, Sam."

We rose again, clattered in a slow arc back toward the south, beside the middle part of Baltimore, the worn brick area, covered with all sizes of buildings, and the clean Washington Monument looming straight up from the center of a traffic circle on Charles Street, a stone rocket ship pointing toward the cloudy sky.

"Would you have cried?" I asked.

He looked at me from the corners of his eyes. "Yeah," he said. "A whole lot. I'm not your father, and I'm not trying to be, but I care about you two. You know that?"

I didn't say anything, but I was glad he would. I'd have cried if he'd gotten shot. Silently, I watched as the newest part of the city got closer, buildings that were tall and modern, slick with glimmering metal and mirrored windows. Behind them was the harbor, empty and cold, green water sloshing about in the wind, sea gulls, streaks of white, soaring sideways. On the other side of the expressway was the Shot Tower, where they'd made bullets or something in the old days. It looked like a giant, brick smokestack.

We barreled down an off ramp and into the heart of the city, passed by squarish mounds of snow that had been pushed into gutters, compressed chunks bigger than lunch boxes spilling onto the broad sidewalks. Howard turned the wheel, and we bounced beneath this tall building with golden windows, drifted into a dark parking garage, and stopped at a black-and-white-striped gate.

An officer stepped out of a trailer. He wore a thick blue coat, the fuzzy collar tilted up against his floppy white ears. There was a bright red rash on his neck, a line of welts that disappeared under his dark shirt like a strip of Velcro. "Can I help you, sir?" he asked Howard.

Howard rested a hand on the rolled-down window. "We've got an appointment with Detective Addler."

"And what're your names?"

"Howard Ivanesavich and Sam Webber."

The guy went back to his trailer as fumes of burnt gasoline and oil seeped in through Howard's open window. When the policeman came back, he waved a hand so that he could breathe, instructed us to park on the third level, to take the elevator down to the lobby.

Howard shifted into gear and the car jumped, nearly crashing through the rising gate. Then we started up the ramp, muffler rattling so hard that it sounded like we were dragging a bunch of crumpled tin cans.

Detective Addler was only a little taller than Rose from the Little Tavern. He was skinnier, though, so puny that he didn't look like he had any muscles. Even though his hands stuck out at his cuffs, his arms were small enough to make his shirtsleeves look empty. I figured that he made up for being weak, with intelligence, because he had a smart face, like he could figure out the hardest mystery without a pencil. His nose was big and yellow and looked like an eagle's beak. On top of it, he propped a pair of small round glasses, the kind that college professors on TV glimmer through, eyes shrunken to the size of raisins. And just like most smart men, he had barely any hair. There was a smooth circle of brushed brown stalks starting at one tiny ear and ending at the other, but that was it. The skin on top of his head was sleek and shiny, splotched with one big mole, a blood-red bump, as if his brain was so giant it was coming out of a crack.

At first I liked him because he was tough. Talking to me before the lineup, he seemed like the toughest man I'd ever met, and it wasn't just the black gun on his belt. His voice was smooth and deep, a movie star's, even though it sometimes wavered and cracked into a high squawk, a strange hiccup that never snapped his confidence. The entire time I was there, he had a thick white coffee mug, sometimes empty, sometimes full, dangling on the tip of a slim finger. On another, he wore a fat gold ring, threatening as brass knuckles, some kind of long letters chiseled across the flat oval part. He hitched up his shiny brown polyester pants like a cowboy and ambled around smartly as he explained what I was supposed to do when the curtain was pulled back.

"I've worked a thousand of these cases, Sam, and I know that it can be scary for people to pick someone out of a lineup. First of all, they aren't sure that the accused can't see them through the glass, which I can assure you he can't. Then they worry about picking the wrong person because the events around the confrontation, the contact with the perpetrator, all took place so fast. But I'll tell you something I've learned from twenty years on the force: deep inside, you'll know who it is. I promise you that, Sam. That face is seared into your head somewhere, and you just got to search around till you find it." He placed his coffee mug against his bottom lip and took a gurgly slurp. Slowly, he made his way over to the closed curtain, covered with a bright sunflower pattern. He took a straightened finger and pushed it aside, let it swing back into place.

"Any questions, Sam?" he asked me.

I twisted around and looked over the bump of my shoulder at him, standing there as flat as a fly strip. "Howard told me he might have shot someone?" I spun forward and sat nervously in my wobbly wood chair, my feet a couple of inches off the floor, hands in a loose sweaty ball in front of me.

Detective Addler ambled across the room, black-and-white cowboy boots echoing off the rutted linoleum floor. He settled into the cracked plastic seat in front of me, leaned back, took another gulp of his coffee, and a chunky gold cufflink flashed in my eyes. "Well, we can't say for sure. I mean, he probably did, but he isn't guilty until someone proves he is, in a court of law. I think he did it, though, because the guy who was shot thinks he did it, and about three other people say they saw him do it. That's good enough for me, and usually that's good enough for a jury. We got you here to pile up some of the charges against the guy, to hang you over his head when he claims to be a model citizen. Heck, Sam, if you want to know the truth, we probably won't need you at all." He leaned over and jiggled his empty coffee mug in front of him. "When I put them away, I like to put them away, see. That's the thing."

I nodded, then asked, "Where'd he shoot the guy?"

"You mean where on the man's body? Shot him in the side." He reached over and poked me under the ribs. "Right there."

"Man," I whispered, because Detective Addler's icy finger felt like a bullet.

"Few inches in any direction, and the guy's goose would have been cooked, there's no doubt about that." Detective Addler pulled one of his bony legs atop the other, so that the underside of a cowboy boot, including the stacked heel, faced me. Stroking a knee, he glanced over my head at the floral curtain on the wall and checked his watch.

"Detective Addler?"

"Yeah?" he said.

"On television, the crooks always know who tells on them." My chair creaked as I adjusted in it. I was so uncomfortable in my own skin that I couldn't stay still. I wished like mad I was a braver person.

"The guy can't see you. He can't even hear you. It's that simple. How's he going to know?" Detective Addler asked, voice breaking off into a high hiccup. For emphasis, he lifted his small shoulders, from tip to tip, about a foot.

"But on television, they do," I told him, the words floating from my mouth. I hadn't wanted to say it, but it had come out, anyway.

"That's make-believe, Sam." He dropped the one bony leg off of the other, leaned forward so that his warm wet coffee and chewing-gum breath beat against my face. "I'm not trying to say that this isn't kind of a scary thing to do, because it is. What I'm asking of you is to be brave, not turn your back. That's the measure of a man, even when he's still a kid. The measure of a person is what he does that he doesn't know for sure he can do."

Detective Addler raised his eyebrows so that they edged toward the red spot on his head. It tugged downward toward them. "You want to know something? I bet it's more scary in your imagination than in real life. In real life, Sam, the guy's just a big idiot who doesn't even care who puts him away. Even if I went down to his jail cell and gave him your name and address, he wouldn't care. He's a junkie, and those are the facts of it. He's just dumb."

I nodded, and a feeling of pride washed over me. I was glad to sit so close to Detective Addler. I was sure that he was the toughest guy I'd ever met, even tougher than Greely, and I knew, deep in my heart, that he'd never fainted, not once. And more than anything, I wished that some of his toughness would float from the brown-speckled lip of his coffee mug through the air and into me.

Tilting my head away, I whispered, "Do you know karate or something?"

"What?"

"Do you know karate or something?"

"Sam," he said, "is there a reason for this question?"

I nodded my head.

"What is it?"

My hands were sweating even worse than they had been. They felt oiled up, shellacked with a whole tub of Vaseline. I rubbed them against each other, two slimy fish slipping around on a newspaper. All I wanted to know was how he could be so tough when he was so weak-looking, but I gave up. "I don't know," I mumbled.

"Fine," he said, rocking to his feet and ambling around the empty room. For the first time, I noticed that his cowboy boots were tilted so far forward that he looked like he might crash into one of the walls.

A few minutes later, there was a tap from behind the curtain.

"You ready, Sam?"

I looked at him, feeling my heart squeeze down in my chest. "He can't see me?" I asked one last time, hands knotted together.

Detective Addler closed his shrunken eyes, opened them. "Not at all."

I made my way over to the curtain.

Before stepping up beside me, Detective Addler went to the door and called a couple of other people into the room with us, a muscular black man in a suit and tie, and a regular officer. Then Detective Addler reminded me to give it a few moments if I didn't recognize anyone at first. He pushed down on a button by a little speaker on the wall and told someone that he was going to open the curtain, which he did, in one quick yank.

I tottered at the sight of all those criminals looking out at me, mean, wild faces, killers with evil hearts, the type of people who'd kidnap someone for no reason, torture them for fun.

"Watch, Sam," Detective Addler said, his voice breaking again. He waved his hand in front of the window. Not one thug responded. "Can't see you at all."

I nodded, gazed through the glass at the lineup, and there he was, the second person in on the left. He wasn't sweating like he had been, and he wasn't wearing the same clothes, but his eyes were just as cruel, one of them framed by that limp brow, sagged like it was sliding off his painted-brick forehead. I remembered the longish brown hair swinging about that night, a grimy strip of soggy threads, dull and salty, weighted down, strung across his cheeks. But more than anything else, there was the flower tattoo, sickly blue, tapped into the back of a veiny hand, around bony knuckles. It stared me smack in the eyes, glowed and beat like a heart. The palm of that same hand had held the silver gun. The shoulder had bashed into my mom, run her over like a football player. I was furious to see it all again. Like trickling water, I felt meanness fill my spaces.

I pointed at him.

"Whoa, Sam. Slow down," Detective Addler said. "You've got to be sure. Remember, a few days have passed, and jumping at the first guy ain't taking the necessary precautions. Your emotions might be cluttering up your thoughts. You got to let your brain breathe."

"But that's him," I said.

Detective Addler shook his head, then rocked forward onto the sharp toes of his Western boots, pushed down on the microphone button, told "number two" to turn sideways.

Our mugger turned.

"Still?" Detective Addler asked, biting at his lip like he wished it was my head.

I never worried that he was the wrong guy. I knew he was our mugger, but I wondered if he wasn't the person Detective Addler was hoping I'd pick. I hesitated, then, gritting my teeth, mouth puffed defiantly beneath my nose, I pointed at him again.

"Sam, one last time. Look hard. You make a mistake now, and nobody's served. You sure that's him?"

Nodding my head, I tried not to care if I'd let him down.

Detective Addler's face broke into a big smile, a huge, ugly grin. He reached up to the microphone and instructed someone to hold the guy I'd picked. "Couldn't throw you, Sam, that's good. That's real good. That'll help me when I bring this incident up to the state's attorney." He shut the curtain, walked across the room. He asked the guys who'd been watching if I was a brave kid; they said I was, then left.

Standing there, feet apart, the yellow walls jumped at me, hollered in my head. I was dark and angry inside. My white hands were trembling. I zeroed in on Detective Addler, pacing, rubbing a finger across his miniature chin. "Why'd you act like I was picking the wrong person?" I asked him.

He crossed his nothing arms, the white coffee cup still stuck on a finger. "Wanted to make sure. He's an ugly guy. Kind of stands out in a crowd."

I turned around and looked at the sunflower curtain. "It wasn't a very nice thing to do."

"Yeah, maybe, but that's the way I work, Sam. It's the way I get things done."

He opened the door and led me back to where Howard was sitting. On the way, he blabbered to me, and I could tell he was trying to get back into my good graces, but I wanted nothing to do with him. I didn't say a word. I acted like his voice didn't pass into my ears. After that, I only heard from him one more time. A phone call. He told me that the guy'd gotten fifteen years in jail, and that he'd be in there for at least five.

Howard and I went for a snack at the Inner Harbor tourist area, which was centered around these two fancy metal buildings that looked like permanent circus tents with bright blue sloped metal roofs and huge gleaming windows. They were located on the brick docks along the squared-off end of the Patapsco River, by skyscrapers so tall that they sometimes disappeared into the clouds. In the summertime, the place felt like a carnival. It filled with tourists from all over the world. Once, when my dad and I were down there on a Saturday in the middle of July or August, I heard these two guys speaking a foreign language. We couldn't understand them at all, and we tried. It was like being in another country. But on that freezing cold day with Howard, the area was empty except for employees. All of the cashiers at the tourist shops and the fast-food counters in both buildings yawned and read magazines, bored out of their minds. I couldn't help but feel sorry for them; I hated it when things were like that.

Howard and I got soft ice cream at a place that used a special machine to mix smashed stuff in with it. We got Oreos in ours, and they served it to us in waffle cones that were a little scorched along the edges. We ate the ice cream with long plastic spoons, wandered about the nearly empty aisles, then sat at a table by a bunch of colossal windows that overlooked the harbor. Straight across the rough water from us was the steep slope of Federal Hill, covered in a shimmering layer of brownish snow. It reminded me of pictures I'd seen of exploded volcanoes.

Howard leaned back, facing the window. "When I was about how old you are, me and my dad would walk all of the way over here from Canton and sled down that hill."

I stared over at it, at the busy road that cut around the broad square bottom, then hooked off toward south Baltimore, the big loading docks, and the Domino's Sugar factory. "Weren't you scared of getting run over or something?"

He smiled. "Naw. We went off the other side, where it's not so steep and they close the street."

I nodded, imagining Howard shooting down a gentle slope, a kid with a sharp widow's peak and glasses so heavy that they left dents on his nose. "I wish me and my dad had done stuff like that."

Howard lapped at the side of his drooling cone. "Maybe next time it snows, me and you'll come down."

I smiled, adjusted in my chair. I imagined taking the hill, moving so fast that my lips stretched back, ears pushed toward the rear of my neck.

We sat, quiet, for a few minutes, slurped at our ice creams as they turned to liquid and dripped from the folded bottoms of our cones. Howard crunched into his, chewed, and swallowed. "Your mom's going to be real proud of you for what you did today, Sam."

"The guy couldn't see me or anything," I told Howard.

"Yeah, I know, but if you watch enough television, it always seems like they find out who snitched on them."

My heart tightened into a stone.

Howard took another bite of his cone, left a tooth-shaped dent in the side. "When my mom was mugged," he told me, chewing, "she decided that she never wanted to leave the house. My dad had to drag her through the front door to get her outside again." He poked at his

[199]

glasses with a pinkie. "The thing is, nothing good ever comes out of something like this. Nothing. All I can say is at least everyone's okay."

I flashed my tongue across my sticky lips, thought about what Howard had said, and decided that, actually, something good might have come from getting mugged. I had learned that I preferred the kind of people who faint once or twice in their lives to those who don't, and that our new neighbors in Charles Village took up for one another, came to the rescue. It seemed like important stuff to know, just a bad way to find out.

I glanced out the window, across the whooshing, sloshing water. Beyond a faint ghost of myself, the sky was turning a cold, dark red, changing slowly, then quickly, into a winter night, and I knew I was going to be all right, that my mom and I would be all right. I could feel it somewhere deep inside, along the bones of my back, in the flat space above my chest, and in the strips of muscle that connect my arms to my body. There was a warmth, like an electric blanket buzzing against me.

the place you are at
the place you are at

The Little Tavern's gigantic windows were all steamy. Warm drips rolled down them as if we were inside a greenhouse. Turning in circles on my squeaky padded stool, I couldn't see through the glass at all. Rose was working behind the counter, fixing Greely his dinner, a stack of crispy pancakes and a watery bowl of coleslaw. We were the only ones in there, taking up the orange counter.

"Sam," Rose said to me, standing on a blue plastic milk crate, working the griddle, "where you been hiding at for the last couple weeks?"

I gnawed on the tip of my straw, then told her, "Junie's. They're getting ready for the spring and all."

Rose shook her large head. "Spring couldn't come soon enough for me."

"Sam ain't no polar bear himself," Greely informed her, blowing at his black thick coffee. "Bad weather bothers him some."

"My dad was that way, too," I told them in a soft mumble.

"How's that, hon?" Rose asked me, peeking over her shoulder, wide and square as a block of wood.

"He just kind of was," I muttered. I stared at her normal-sized body, balanced atop those short wobbly legs. I thought back to my dad, how at different times throughout the year, he'd seemed to worry at twice the rate he normally did, which was a whole lot, anyway. The thing is, after Christmas he was always predictable: he got tired. From January through February, he did a lot less of everything. I remember how he'd pull into the garage behind the house and sit in his car with the engine and the lights on for about ten minutes before coming inside. And when he did make it into the house, his eyes were usually deep and lost, two distant flashlights. Just catching a glimpse of them told me that he'd been thinking about problems that I couldn't imagine.

I peered at the wide hot metal surface Rose stooped over. "I remember that he never took the Christmas wreath off the front of his car till halfway through March. My mom said it was because he was too exhausted in the winter. Once, he was too tired all the way till summertime."

Rose nodded as she worked. "I got to admit, and Lord forgive me, but that bothers me. Why put a wreath on in the first place if you're just gonna leave it there till Easter? It don't make any sense." She slipped one of the crispy pancakes onto a chipped china platter, sides gray from rubbing between others in the big stacks below the counter. "But I guess you're right. It's got something to do with the way people feel inside."

"Course it does," Greely muttered. "Don't take a doctor to see there was something wrong with the way he was feeling." He adjusted his Chevron cap, slanted it to one side so that it just touched a curled ear. "Back in Atlanta, I had this neighbor, a nice old man, who didn't rise out of bed for nearly three months. Just laid there. His son had got killed in Korea, but Korea might as well have done *him* in, too. You could smell him through the window between our homes, it got so bad, 'cause he didn't even get up to go to the bathroom. It was sadness that did it, made him weak as a kitten." Greely licked a finger and pulled some napkins from a dispenser. "Sadness does things to people that makes broken bones look like nothing. It's got all sorts of levels, too. Can make a sane person ruin everything."

When he was done talking, I waited for a moment, then asked him what happened to his neighbor.

"Wasn't pretty, Sam. He went off to the hospital and got shock treatments. He came back better, but he never was the same."

"Shock treatments?" I whispered.

"It's when doctors shock sad people with electricity. If they do it right, it makes them feel better, snap out of it. You know?"

I thought about the time I'd shocked myself while plugging a lamp into the wall. "I guess it makes them jump or something."

"Guess yer right," Greely said.

I stared into the Coke I was drinking and thought more about my father. "Maybe my dad needed shock treatments. He got sad sometimes, even when it wasn't winter."

Greely bobbed his head up and down slightly, took a sip of coffee, and set the cup on the orange counter. "I been like that, too, and I'll tell you, it's a bad way to be."

Rose clanged her metal spatula down against the grill. "Greely, Sam must get tired of all the half stuff you say to him. I know I do. You never jump in. You don't got the courage to just out and tell everything, put your cards smack on the table."

Greely glanced at me, papery eyelids fluttering he was so surprised. He looked over at Rose, his mouth slightly open. "I'm saving it for the right time," he told her.

"That's what you call what yer doing?" she asked, sliding the rest of the charred pancakes onto the platter and stepping off of the milk crate with a creaky thud.

"That's what I call it," he replied.

She stood on her toes and slid his meal in front of him, dropped to her heels, and put her stubby hands on her wide hips. Her fingers

[203]

reminded me of Vienna sausages. "If I weren't a lady, I'd wrestle you to the floor and twist you into a knot, just like you doing to him. You'd find out how uncomfortable it gets." She shook her head. "You make me crazy."

Greely picked up his fork, held it in a fist. "Rose," he murmured softly, like he felt sorry for her.

"I'd tie you up so that you couldn't yank yourself free," she declared. "See how you like that treatment."

"Twisting me up wouldn't change me," he told her.

"Probably not. Probably couldn't do it even with that stiff knee of yers. That thing wouldn't bend, not one sorry inch. I seen you try and crook it yerself, and it don't work." She raised her shoulders. "I give up."

Greely looked at me. "Should we leave, Sam? You make the call."

My face glowed with heat.

"Now look what you done, Greely; you've embarrassed Sam."

He nudged me with an elbow, mumbled, "Sorry."

"It's okay," I promised. And it was. For some reason, I liked the way they talked to each other.

"Sam," Rose said, "Yer far too nice a boy to be hanging out with this old hardhead. You know that? He's so infuriating he might just make you crazy one day."

I walked slowly through the welcoming streets of Charles Village, past wood rowhouses shifted just slightly atop their brick bases, slumping, disappearing like the first glistening dribble of melted wax from a candle. It was only two weeks before my birthday and about two weeks since the last sputtering winter storm had rolled through. There were still icy patches from it lurking in the cool shadows, but most of the snow had melted away. And everything was wet, even the concrete sidewalks, flecked with damp lacy scales of salt. March was like that, the end of winter but not quite the beginning of spring, often dark and dreary with a hint of light around six o'clock, glowing, flickering with slight warmth, the yellow from a match that looked like hope.

I stumbled along with my clammy fingers jammed in my pockets, watched my neighbors sweep their slanted, scuffed steps, their front porches, a few boards pulling up, some bending under their weight. They waved, and I waved back. I studied cars as they drifted slowly by, rolled through stop signs, brakes grinding, loud, two bricks rubbing together. The smell of breakfast drifted and mingled with the odors from the alleys. There was the sweet scent of coffee. I got whiffs of eggs cooking in pools of bacon grease. Ahead of me, an overweight old man in a billowing tan coat, yellowed in spots, staggered and struggled down the bouncy steps of his front porch. A little brown-and-white dog pulled him along. On the sidewalk, the man stopped and stood holding his stomach. He moved his mouth around, tugged on his tiny dog's leash, a loop of thread with a silver clip on the end.

The dog spotted me and pulled against the leash to get closer. I smiled. I couldn't help it. As far back as I could remember, I'd wanted a dog, a friend. Even such a small one would have been OK, its nubby tail wagging, mouth hung open and lips curled back so that needle teeth were visible, glinting white, two rows of rock shards.

The old man studied me, smiled under his mustache, so full beneath the curls of his huge hollow nostrils, soft as the black bulb of a bicycle horn. He pointed to his dog, with a battered hand, brown with bruises and sores. He leaned against the tottering rail of his steps, a couple of two-by-fours nailed together and painted green. "His name is Pepé," the man told me, his accent thick, familiar from television shows about drug dealers.

"Pepé," I said, smiling, leaning down to rub Pepé's miniature head. His ears looked like furry pointed tablespoons. "I love dogs," I told the old man.

"Most everyone loves Pepé when they get to know him." He smiled, too, then looked uncomfortable, and let out a huge fart that shook his whole body. His mouth mashed around some more, and he pointed to his lumpy rolled side. "I have a bag," he explained, except that I didn't know what he meant. "A colostomy bag," he told me, and the long mysterious word sounded perfect and beautiful the way it rolled from his narrow wrinkled lips.

"It makes you have gas?" I asked, patting the dog as it leaped against my folded knees.

"It makes it so that I can't stop the sounds."

I nodded as I scrubbed the little mutt's back, not too much larger than my hands when I knotted them together. "Why do you have a bag?" I asked softly, trying to be polite about it.

"Cancer," the old man said, shaking his big jiggly head, skin sagging in graceful puddles under his eyes and chin. "It is because of cancer."

I shivered, glanced at shorthaired Pepé as he jumped and tried to lick my face, his long snake-tongue sweeping the chilly March air. I wondered if the old man's hands were smashed-looking because of his cancer. "Is it gone now?"

"I hope," he mumbled, "but I don' know."

I stared at him, surprised. I wondered how he could just come out and say it like that. So quietly. So calmly. If I might be dying, I would scream. I never could understand how people on television just sat down calmly when their doctors told them that they weren't going to make it. The thought of dying made me want to live more than anything else.

"Are you scared?" I asked.

The old man dipped his head politely, shaking the leash in a hand blue around the fingertips. "I was scared so much before I got sick that cancer has made me better."

I bent and gave tiny Pepé a hug, squeezed his white-and-brown body against me so that he would feel secure and safe. I felt sorry for him, his father sick, maybe dying and lost, lost for good, the same way as mine.

"What's made you so scared?" I asked without looking up, eyes on the man's funny square feet, jutting out at the sides of his scuffed loafers.

"Loneliness," he answered. "I am sure of that. I never let this place become familiar." He bobbed his head forward, reminded me of a cow. "See, I was born in Cuba, and I felt that I was always a stranger in this country. You know, my wife, she understood what was necessary to take away the fears, but I never listened to what she said. When she was gone, I still did not see that she was right." He lifted his big round shoulders. "It is cancer that has made me understand how important it is to treat neighbors as family, to call the place you are at home. Cancer for me has been both awful and good. It has made me learn even better than my wife, and I loved my wife. But if you ask me why the cancer has done this, I don' know. Maybe it scared me like a car accident. Maybe it forced me to depend on strangers, to talk to people." He pointed at me with a crooked finger. "I never spoke to anyone too much before."

Pepé skittered to the curb, pulled at the leash, and stood on his hind legs, chicken wings tight as kite string. He hovered toward a rumbling, huge American car as it drifted through the neighborhood, a white guy at the wheel, thinning hair a tangle of knots, eyes deep and satisfied the way Howard's sometimes looked.

"You like Pepé?" the old Cuban man asked me, adjusting the collar of his huge overcoat, belt as long as a tattered whip, drooping closer and closer to the sidewalk.

"A lot," I said. I liked Pepé's jittery excitement and electricity, the funny way he noticed everything—leaves skittering, a crumpled Coke can rolling across the sidewalk, banging against a pebble. I'd always wanted a big dog, but Pepé was more like a shrunken person, a whole, excitable kid stuck in the tiny body of a funny-looking bowzer.

"In the city, one must own a dog, I think. People talk to you when you have a dog, but no one ever threatens you. I always told my wife not to walk at night without Pepé. Pepé watched out for her. He made sure no one troubled her. We had Julio before Pepé. Julio was bigger, a German shepherd, but Pepé does just as well. Pepé is small, but he is tough. He knows where he lives, that he lives with me and I am his home, so he will always protect me. He knew the same of my wife, and he protected her the same way, with his whole heart."

I forced a weak smile, but I really couldn't imagine that fragile Pepé would scare away a soul, not like a German shepherd would, not like old Julio. I stared at the old man, pointed. "How long have you had that?" I asked, indicating the bag he'd hinted was somewhere on his side. I searched for it, strapped there, doing something that made him unable to hold in a fart.

"Three months," he said, and moved away from the stair rail he'd been holding. He clicked his tongue for Pepé to come to him, squatted down, and that dingy coat of his flopped about his skinny ankles.

"Does it hurt?"

"No."

"What's it do?"

He smiled. "If you don' know, you don' want to know."

I nodded, feeling sorry for him. I was still curious about the bag, though. I wondered if everyone with cancer got one.

Up the glistening silvered street, a group of black boys rounded the corner of an alley, passed by a child's abandoned crib, a heap of fabric and metal beside a scratchy Formstone garage, wood doors and windows all new, trim painted a searing jumpy red. The boys were older than me by a few years, jerking and swaying, bopping rhythmically toward us as Pepé scrambled against the slim leash to get to them.

They wore fat oversize basketball shoes, glistening nylon sports jackets, logos bright as paint splotches. Their pants were worn and covered with patches.

Instantly, fear leaped into my heart, slammed through the rubbery veins in my neck. Groups of kids, especially boys, alarmed me. I worried that they were looking for someone to bang on, a smallish mark like me.

The old man smiled wide at the teenagers. His face pulled so tight that it looked like it might pop, a balloon inflated too much. He flapped his crushed hands about, motioned for the boys to come to him. "Pepé will not hurt you," he said.

But they didn't want anything to do with the little dog, smaller than most cats, a yip popping from his mouth instead of a bark. The boys strutted off the curb and onto the oil-splashed street, gave Pepé his space, as if he were a big toothy wolf.

I mumbled, "Hello," to them, but my voice barely worked. It sounded like a car engine about to conk out.

A couple of boys dipped their heads at me, one said, "Homeboy," and another laughed like I was a joke.

The old man breathed out sadly. His eyes fell to the ground, and he noticed the wrinkled belt of his coat, buckle dragging beside his exploding brown shoe. After drawing the flap of fabric up and through the baggy loops, he said, "I don' understand why blacks don' like dogs." He fixed his eyes on the boys, now halfway down the block, backs to us. "Pepé would not hurt them unless they threatened me. He is trained. I trained him myself. Unless he is provoked, he likes everybody like the way he likes you."

I looked over my shoulder, stared. "Is that true?" I asked him after a moment or two.

"What?"

"That blacks don't like dogs."

"Sure they don'."

Pepé scooted and zigged around the man, and even though the dog had frightened the boys off the sidewalk, I couldn't imagine him actually doing anything to anyone that they couldn't stop by giving their legs a hard shake or just picking him up and tossing him like a football.

"By the way, my name is Mr. Garcia," the old man said. "What is yours?"

"Sam," I mumbled. "Sam Webber."

"Well, Sam, Pepé and I are happy to meet you. It is Pepé's favorite thing to do, to meet people."

I nodded. "Sometimes, dogs don't like that."

"This is true," he agreed.

I studied Pepé, and my heart felt like it was swelling, getting bigger and bigger inside me, a dry sponge sucking up water. "You know," I said to Mr. Garcia, "if you ever feel sick or something, and you can't walk Pepé, I'll do it for you. I mean, you can just call me at Junie's Florist, if you want. You know where that is?"

"Why sure," he said. "I get my African violet food there."

"Well, that's where my mom works."

A big rattling truck scooted by, an ancient white refrigerator in the back, anchored down with chains and ropes.

"I know the proprietor, Mrs. Junie. She has been there so long, and she is very nice."

I nodded. "My mom's nice, too," I told him.

"Why sure," he said, adjusting the leash, coiling a few gentle loops across his palm.

"I'll tell her what you look like so that when you go in next time, she'll know who you are."

"That would be nice." He scratched at an ear, fuzz poking off of it, then looked at me kindly. "Sam, I hate to go, but Pepé and I are supposed to walk vigorously three times around the block before lunch. That is why I have come out. You are welcome to come if you would like. We would enjoy the company, Pepé and me." He mashed his mouth around so that I could hear the spit squeaking in his cheeks.

"I'm supposed to meet my mom," I told him, wishing I didn't have to.

He smiled, and the light wispy hairs around his deflated lips gleamed in the gray air. "We will do it some other time, Sam. And for sure, I will contact you if I cannot walk Pepé." He stuck out a bruised hand for me to shake, but I hesitated.

"My hand looks this way because of diabetes," he told me.

"Can I get it?" I whispered, embarrassed.

"No," he replied softly.

I gritted my teeth and plunged my fingers into his palm, soft and frail, dry as tracing paper.

He gave my hand a few quick shakes and let go. Then slowly, he backed away, waving to me like he was on a tall ship drifting out into the Chesapeake Bay, starting on a long trip out to the Atlantic Ocean and all the way down the coast and across to Cuba, where they make cigars. His coat billowed around him as he shuffled off.

"I hope your cancer gets better."

"I'll be fine, Sam. Have a good day."

"Bye, Mr. Garcia. Bye, Pepé," I murmured as they moved cautiously across the street, down Guilford Avenue, toward Charles Village Memorial Hospital. I watched them for a few minutes, Pepé running in circles, a shrunken pony on a rope, then I continued on to Junie's, sad for Mr. Garcia, for the way I'd nearly jumped when he'd tried to shake my hand, for the fact that he might be dying, and he was just learning to be happy.

Junie's store was hopping with all sorts of weirdos. One woman wore chunky gigantic pieces of jewelry that stretched her long ears, squeezed her neck. Another had a corkscrew hairdo, a velvety pink housecoat buttoned over a pajama top. Both of the men in the store wore battered army jackets. One had his hair slicked up like Elvis, while the other had long wide sideburns that hooked into a tangled beard. They were buying all sorts of junk—dried flowers and bulbs and ugly glass pots shaped like snuggling bears, stock cars, and starfish. Also, there was a big truck parked by the sloping sidewalk, and Ditch and Mr. Oritz were hustling to unload sacks of fertilizer from it.

I went out to the tractor trailer and stood by the gaping metal door, fastened to the silver side with rusty hinges. The guy inside tossed dusty plastic bags of fertilizer by the edge, and Ditch and Mr. Oritz threw them over their shoulders and carried them, two at a time, through the welded gate to the back of the cement pad. The bags looked light—grimy pillows filled with soft stuffing—but they weren't. Every so often, I tugged a sack off the platform and into my arms and had to hurry along as it slowly slipped from my grip. As far back as I could remember, my dad had helped Ditch unload that sort of thing. I wasn't sure, but I remembered him casually hoisting five sacks at a time onto his giant shoulders. Maybe I was just lying to myself, the same way I'd lied to Greely about my father lifting a car. I knew full well that I was starting to create stuff about my dad. He did things in my memories that I was sure he'd never actually done when he was around. I didn't care at all. The real memories hurt, while the fake ones felt fine, making the two together hard to swallow at times, but not impossible. At least there were moments when I could think about him without guilt. My head had come up with a way to do it, even if it wasn't always the way things had gone.

After about an hour, when the rush was over and the truck was gone, I sat with Junie, Ditch, and my mom inside. Everyone was relaxed, and it seemed like a good time to ask what a cancer bag was.

"There ain't no such thing, far as I've heard," Junie informed me.

"This guy I met, Mr. Garcia, he got one for his cancer."

"Who's Mr. Garcia?" my mom asked, adjusting herself on her creaky stool, the wooden top split in half so that it pinched like a crab even through pants. I'd caught the back of my leg in it years before, howled like I'd been shot.

"This man I met on my way here this morning. He's from Cuba, and he's got a cancer bag stuck on his side. It makes it so that he can't stop his gas."

"A colostomy bag?" Ditch asked.

"Is that what it sounded like, hon?" Junie wanted to know.

"Maybe," I told her.

"It's for people who can't go to the bathroom no more," Ditch said. "He might have had colon cancer or somethin'."

"He can't go to the bathroom anymore?"

"Goes into the bag," Ditch informed me.

I shook my head from side to side, feeling terrible for old Mr. Garcia. He was more broken inside than I'd ever heard of anyone being.

"If his cancer is gone," my mom said, "he can live as long as anyone else."

I peered down at my sneakers, a piece of grass jammed into a seam, poking up like a shrunken knife blade. "He said he comes in here to buy his African violet food. He's got this little dog named Pepé."

"Wait a minute, I knows who you mean, hon," Junie declared. She cast her chalky eyes at Ditch, liner flaking off in little hunks, coal chips. "He's the man with the Jack Russell."

Ditch nodded, motioned with the tip of his lit cigarette, burning unevenly; one side of the ash was closer to the filter than the other. "Had to deliver him some flowers a couple years back, right up the block on Thirty-second Street. Remember? His wife had passed away."

"Don't have any recollection," she mumbled.

"That's him," I said. "That's the man—Mr. Garcia. I think he's trying to make a lot of friends because he's lonely or something, and that's what his wife told him to do, before she died. He said that meeting people is Pepé's favorite thing to do, but I think he likes it, too. I think he wants to meet everyone. When these black guys walked by, he wanted them to stop and talk and pat Pepé, but they scooted around us because they must have been nervous about Pepé biting or something. He wouldn't have, though. Mr. Garcia trained him. Mr. Garcia thinks that blacks are scared of dogs, but I don't know about that. I'm gonna ask Greely on Monday." I looked at my mom. "I told him that if he can't walk Pepé ever, I would do it. So he might call here, okay?"

"That's fine," she told me, untying her smock. She bundled it up into a red ball and stowed it under the old counter.

Ditch shook his head, laughed to himself. Smoke coiled from his mouth like dingy cloth, twirled between the cracks separating his teeth. "Sam," he said, "don't go asking Greely about niggers and dogs. Dogs scare the pants off 'em for some reason. Everyone knows that."

Niggers. The word got me like a punch to the stomach. I hadn't heard him say it in so long that I'd thought he'd stopped. I dropped my eyes to the floor, couldn't get myself to look back up at Ditch, nice Ditch, who could sometimes be so horrible, who could unknowingly say things that were just as cruel as the cruelest things that could be said. I glanced at my mom, pleaded with her to speak up, but she didn't. She said that we were heading off to lunch, that we'd be back in a half-hour.

When we were outside, walking up the sidewalk toward the Waverly Deli, I asked, "Why didn't you say something? You told me you would."

She breathed out gently. "I couldn't, Samuel. I like Ditch too much." She glanced over at me, caught my eyes. "I know he doesn't mean it the way it sounds."

"That doesn't matter, Mom," I said, waving my hands, taking big steps, and stomping my feet.

She held the glass door, blurred with fingerprints, open for me, and I squeezed in around her hip bones.

When we sat down, I ate my St. Pauly without saying anything, dragged the soft doughy English muffin through the clear grease on my round paper plate. I jammed the sandwich into my mouth, stared above one of my mom's shoulders toward the messy back of the dining room, where bright lights flickered over the deli counter. It was trimmed with flimsy wood panels, occupied by a tall narrow man with a paper hat on. He was slapping together sandwiches.

My mom pulled off hunks of chewy corned beef from between the bread, pushed them into her mouth with a skinny finger. After sucking them down, she squeezed a tiny napkin beside her plate. That's the way she always ate her corned beef sandwiches, and, somehow, she still liked them.

"He wouldn't say it around Greely, you know," my mom assured me out of nowhere.

I finished my St. Pauly, took a sip of my Coke, perfectly sweet and thick, all syrup. I thought about Ditch, saw his stretched-out body, face slashed with wrinkles. Before my dad had disappeared, I'd been scared of him. He'd been too mysterious for me, something to avoid, like the Bermuda Triangle. But in the saddest moments of my whole life, he'd changed, cushioned my gloom with his stick body, with his funny, awkward kindness, and I'd kind of started to love him for that, to worry about his achy knees and his slipping heart. I never wanted it to stop beating. I knew Ditch, and even if he said *nigger* a thousand times, he was a good person doing something wrong, not a bad person acting normal.

I glanced at my mom, dropped my eyes. "I could maybe tell him I don't like it?"

My mom squeezed at her napkin. "Maybe. I think it would proba-bly be better than me telling him for you."

I sucked on my bottom lip, soft as a boneless finger, rolled it between my teeth. "The thing is, I don't want to make him sad or any-thing."

"He doesn't want to make you sad, either," she said.

"I know." I sighed.

My mom finished her sandwich, swigged at her dark iced tea. Some splashed down her windpipe, and she started coughing.

I put a sour look on my face. "I hate that."

"Me . . . too," she said between watery hacks.

When she was better, I asked, "Did Dad say that kind of thing?"

"You mean, what Ditch said?"

"Yeah."

She nodded uncomfortably.

I looked back down at my greasy plate. "I wish he hadn't," I told her, trying to get an image of him in my head. His face was washed away like chalk marks on a wet sidewalk. As usual, thinking that got me a little rattled, a little lonely, and a little lost.

We walked slowly back to Junie's, the sky surrendering warm drops of water that splattered against the concrete. Cars whipped through the light at Thirty-first Street and St. Paul. It turned yellow, and engines roared and brakes screeched. The air smelled of flowery detergent floating up from the Laundromat down the block. We passed a man who was trying to sell a half-used bucket of exterior house paint, a rickety stepladder, and an ancient blue lawnmower, shriveled bits of weeds stuck all over it. At Junie's, we trotted up the steps and slid into the store, cowbells clonking in our wake. There were a couple of people inside milling about, and Junie stood by the line of refrigerators, talking to someone about how to make a rose last. Her hair was platinum blond again, and on top of that, she'd got-

[216]

ten it chemically straightened. It looked phony. Her face appeared pushed down from the top, square and compact as a box. Ditch seemed to think that it looked good, though. He was constantly commenting about it, whistling and making her blush, which was a funny thing to see, those melting cheeks flushing bright red. I'd never seen her do it before. I hadn't even thought that she could.

Ditch stood behind the counter, chewing on a hangnail. He raised his eyebrows at us. "How was lunch?" he asked.

"Okay," my mom said.

I stood in front of the checkout counter, leaned my knees against it. "Ditch?" I mumbled nervously, my heart pounding against my ribcage, pushing blood all through me, hard and fast.

"Yeah, Sam?"

"Can I tell you something?"

"Go ahead."

"Ah, maybe we can go outside for me to do it?"

"Sure," he said.

We went on through the side door and stood among the fertilizer bags and bedding plants. Ditch drew out a pack of Winstons from his baggy pocket, pulled a cigarette from the soft container, and stuck it on his lip. Cupping his lighter the way he always did, he lit it.

"I . . . I wish you wouldn't say *nigger* anymore," I whispered. "I . . . I kind of don't think it's right."

He looked at me. "You mean earlier, when we were talking about dogs?"

I nodded, neck stiff.

He glanced up at the side of the brick building. His eyes slowly wandered back to me. "Sam, I say it, but I don't mean it about good blacks, people like Greely."

I nodded. "Maybe it's just kind of mean to say at all. And the thing is, you're not mean. You're one of the nicest people I ever met."

He lifted his shoulders. "They call each other niggers half the time. You gotta notice."

I wiped my sticky lips with the back of my hand. I didn't know how to explain what Greely had told me.

Ditch sucked in on the wet filter of his cigarette, a dozen scratchy lines, shallow creeks, cutting outward from his mouth. "Said it all my life, Sam, and sometimes I mean it and sometimes I don't. I'm a city boy, old Baltimore boy, and you ain't seen what I've seen, nice neighborhoods changed when blacks moved in, changed so that they ain't safe no more. Friends of mine've lost their shirts, everything, nearly. Blacks moved into their neighborhoods and they couldn't get nothin' for their house no more. Nothin'. They was good folks, too. See, Baltimore used to be somethin', but it ain't no more, and sometimes I blame the blacks. Not all of them, just some of them. The bad ones. Those are the ones I call niggers."

I wiped at my lips again, licked them. "The thing is, Greely's been telling me about this thing called the Civil Rights movement and all of the reasons why it started. He remembers hearing things that he says were terrible, but that doesn't stop him from giving people a chance. He said he's forgiven, mostly because he had to. But it doesn't seem like he had to to me. It seems like he just did. Sometimes I think about that, and I think maybe everybody should be that way. You know?"

Ditch took a big, callused hand, rough and wooden, and cupped it sweetly across the back of my head. "You're a good guy, Sam. As it stands, I'm afraid you might be a bit better than me. I mean, I could stop sayin' it, but that don't mean I'd stop thinkin' it."

I looked up at him, way up into his tired eyes. "I wonder, if you stop saying it, maybe you'll stop thinking it as much?"

He took a draw on his cigarette, and the ash glowed. He breathed out, shook his head from side to side. "Wouldn't bet on it," he mumbled.

[218]

We stood there for a minute, cars and trucks banging down wide St. Paul Street, framed with old rowhomes whiskery with detail, gleaming like a photo from Europe, reminding me of pictures in my encyclopedia.

"Maybe, Sam," he said.

the softest heart

the softest heart

On the day that I turned twelve, I got up alone, took a shower, and fixed myself three slices of bread, all of which were turned a crispy black by our malfunctioning toaster. It was a school day, a Friday, and when I was finished with breakfast, I plopped my plate, speckled with jelly, into the sink and went back to my room, where I sat slumped amid the thin, twisted sheets of my bed and tied my sneakers to my feet. In past years, on past birthdays, my dad had gotten up with me, slung me over his bulky shoulders, and carried me to the table for breakfast. I missed him. I actually allowed myself to, and his absence hurt like a terrible, deep gash.

I sat in my warm room that morning, and my father's face grew clear in my thoughts for the first time in almost half a year, clear even though I'd been sure it was gone, drifted away to some unreachable corner of my brain. He was driving his BG&E car, shoving down Roy Rogers cheeseburgers and slurping on a Dr Pepper, his favorite soft drink. He smiled at me. He'd always had a good smile, too. It had made me sure that everything was going to be OK, even when he had trouble getting from the garage to the house at night. "Dad," I wanted to tell him, "I miss you so much that sometimes I can't even think about you." But I didn't say anything.

It was in March that my father had usually, finally, pulled out of his winter doldrums. For most of my life, it had been a pretty good month, what with my birthday to celebrate and basketball squawking on the television nearly all of the time, too. My father's mood usually began its slow rise, so that he would eventually pass right by being normal and do unexpected things, like arrive home with a car full of presents for me and mom. Sometimes, he drifted from one mood to the other within the same week. But he'd always, eventually, come back. Whatever way he felt wouldn't last. He was kind of like a yo-yo, bounced up and down several times in a year. But I'd gotten used to it. I'd even started remembering little events by thinking back to the way he'd been at the time. The thing is, when he was feeling good, he was feeling perfect, and I missed that. The best birthday present I could ever have gotten would have been him walking through the front door, not dead, without amnesia, and ready to make friends with all of our new friends. He would have to do that or it wouldn't be so nice. He would have to like everyone without being jealous—which he'd sometimes had trouble doing—just as we'd have to forgive him for disappearing.

Climbing from my bed, I slipped into my new spring coat, a dusty brown jacket that my mom had gotten at the Goodwill on Greenmount Avenue. I went to the window, which was coated with a dry film, and looked out on the alley, the big crunched garbage cans, metal and plastic. In one neighbor's yard, there were dozens of mildewy leather women's shoes in a wide box. Ours was nearly spotless—clean and open. I stood there for a few minutes, remembering the day that Ditch and I had cleaned up the backyard. That had been nice. I never would've guessed, but it had been.

When I turned around, my mom was standing there, propped like a board in the doorway, looking at me. Her slim rope arms were wrapped snugly across her waist, and she wore shabby shorts and a wrinkled T-shirt with a stain the shape of a tear on the stomach. "Happy Birthday," she said to me softly, eyes narrow, two sleepy slits.

"Thanks," I smiled weakly, still wishing for my father.

"I'm sorry about not getting up with you. I set the alarm, but it didn't go off."

"That's okay," I whispered, even though I'd been feeling crummy about it. I picked up my books and tucked them under a scrawny arm, against my poking, curved ribcage.

"We're going to have fun tonight — a nice quiet evening, just you, me, and Howard."

I nodded my head. I told her, "That'll be great," but I didn't feel very enthusiastic. The last thing I wanted was a quiet evening. As a matter of fact, the whole idea seemed crazy to me, to have a night like a thousand other nights, when a birthday was a good excuse to do something completely different.

"You need lunch money?"

"I guess," I said from deep in my narrow throat.

I followed her into the kitchen, where a cool breeze rushed through the big crack below the bay window and swirled — an invisible tornado — by the sink and the stove, causing the paper towels to flutter on their rack. My mom shivered as she searched her purse, slung over the back of a wobbly chair. She gave me three crumpled dollars and two quarters. "Happy Birthday," she said again, dropping the roll onto my wet palm. "I gave you extra in case you want a Coke or something on the way home."

"Thanks," I said, grinning weakly again. I really did appreciate the bonus.

It was a cool day, and I stopped outside the front door and zipped up my coat, stared out at Charles Village between the two square pillars that held up the mostly useless porch roof. During bad rainstorms, water poured through the empty light-bulb socket on the ceiling, splashed down like it was a malfunctioning showerhead. But if it was sprinkling out, or just raining lightly, it was the best place to sit. In the fall, my mom and I had used it a few times, rocked in front of our downstairs neighbor's bedroom windows and watched Baltimore grow dark, the flat rooftops across the street flickering yellow in the dying sun or shining like china in a damp drizzle. After our closet, the porch was my second-favorite thing about our apartment. The wood had grown soft and friendly, smelled slightly of decay. The rails that surrounded it were made up of big brown rungs, like bowling pins. But that morning, the porch was different, lonelier than normal, and I couldn't figure out why. It wasn't the day or anything. Orange spots of light dotted the streets and sidewalks, and the sky was dusty gray, brushed by a hint of pale blue, the nicest weather we'd had in months.

I stumbled down the front steps and onto the sidewalk, square cement slabs slanted at funny angles, icebergs battering against each other on a clogged river. The trimmed trees looked like giant chrome tools. Across the street, every rowhouse was missing something— pieces of wood, patches of shingles, or slabs of Formstone. But most all of them were well kept, clean. On Thirty-second Street, trucks and cars rolled slowly past. Their sounds reminded me of a hurt person, of an old lady with a sprained ankle and fingers bent up by arthritis. I kind of moaned, too, but on the inside. In a soothing sort of way, I felt hurt, sorry for myself, a little frustrated.

I drifted slowly down the sidewalk as if pushed by the wind, across busy St. Paul Street and over one block to Charles, where no one cared or even wondered what I was doing when I stood alone by a tree, because I always stood by myself, daydreaming all sorts of big and small things.

* * *

Greely was the only person at school who knew that I was turning twelve. The thing is, even if the whole school had been told, it wouldn't have mattered. My classes had changed in February, but I was still a loner, separated from most everyone because I was too smart and couldn't help it. The nice thing about the switch was that my new teachers were friendlier, knew I could remember most anything they said, except for numbers. The bad thing was that my classmates were mostly worse. Even most of the girls seemed dangerous. Up the aisle from me in math, this one girl cussed and threatened people, like a boy. She even did it right in the middle of class as she tore a fat comb through her blond curls. And every day there was more and more of her. She was pregnant, and her stomach bulged till it touched the front of her scuffed, flat desk. I avoided her as much as I could. I didn't even glance at her when she flew into tirades, scratched someone beside her, or banged her lardy hands against her cheeks and into the dents around her droopy eyes. She was just one of about ten insane students in each of my classes, and not nearly the worst. So I always kept my mouth shut, even when I wanted to shout out loud that I wasn't as boring as everyone thought, even when I wanted everyone to know that it was my birthday.

Sitting in a class before lunch, I looked forward to seeing Greely. I even started to feel better thinking about it. I knew that he'd treat me special even if no one else did.

I got to the cafeteria first, settled myself at our regular table, and waited. When Greely tramped in, he flapped one huge leathery hand, like a mitten, at me, went right on by, picked a big fiberglass lunch tray out of a tall stack, and disappeared behind the wall that separated the lunch line from the dining area. Through the opening, a door surrounded by steam, I watched his dark reflection bend across the chrome surfaces till it disappeared, and I knew he'd forgotten.

I was crushed. I gnawed on the chewy edge of a taco, oil dribbling through the bottom. When Greely sat down, I glanced up, looked into his eyes, two enamel balls oiled with cola, wonderful to watch because they moved so smoothly together. I asked him what he was doing after school, tried desperately to spark his feeble memory.

"Going to look at a television. Man in the neighborhood is advertising one on trees and poles up and down the block. Says it's a nice color model that's cable ready and everything. Called him yesterday, and he told me he'd sell it cheap. His son just bought him one of those giant-size models that takes up nearly half a living room."

"That's what you're doing, getting a TV?" I said, throat tight.

"Maybe getting one. I got to look at it first." He made a funny face like he smelled something bad.

"You aren't doing anything else?"

He lifted his big shoulders. "That's all I was planning, 'cept for if I buy it, then I got to get it home somehow." He smiled. "You know what, Sam? I ain't never had a nice television before. I was always 'fraid someone'd steal it in my old place. Don't think I got to worry about that no more." His fingers twitched, latched onto his fork. A week before, he'd settled into a basement apartment in Waverly, right near Memorial Stadium. "Sam, I shoulda moved off of Devin Lane a long time ago. It was like I was frozen in place."

I nodded, dropped my hands off of the sticky table, left my spoon, a harpoon, poking out of an ice-cream-scoop serving of mashed potatoes.

"Somethin' wrong?" Greely asked, tearing a hunk out of a roll he was using to sop up lumpy brown gravy.

"No," I mumbled softly.

"Well, why you look that way, then?"

I stared straight at him, exasperated. "Remember? I told you all week."

He stared back at me, face blank. He shook his head, wiped at his lips with a crumpled napkin.

"It's my birthday," I told him.

"Naw, it isn't."

"Yeah, it is."

His acne-scarred cheeks drooped like a bulldog's. A few of his crooked bottom teeth poked between his lips, toward his nose. "I been so busy, Sam. God, I'm sorry. Totally slipped my mind." He studied me. "Don't know what to say. I mean, maybe we could meet at the Little Tavern tomorrow or the next day. I'll get you breakfast or a hamburger or somethin'."

"I'm working at Junie's," I murmured to him.

"I'm gonna make it up to you," he said.

"That's all right," I told him, feeling sorry for myself. I was thinking that as close as Greely sometimes seemed to being like a father, he wasn't. No one could ever replace my real dad, who always remembered my birthday and how old I was. He'd always made it nice.

Greely put his fork down, tapped my hand. "I'm awfully sorry, Sam."

I looked at him as if he were a thousand miles away.

He stared back for a minute or two, took some bites of food, then shook his head from side to side. "Don't mean to change the subject, 'cause I know yer upset, and you got a right to be, but I keep catching a funny scent." He waved a hand in front of his nose, twisted his face into a rag knot.

"Don't know what it is," I muttered softly.

Greely nodded. "Sam," he said, fanning the air. "Just slipped my mind. I'm sorry."

When the bell rang and school was over, I walked slowly to my locker, took out my secondhand coat and slid it over my shoulders. I tucked a couple of books under one arm, got rid of a few, and slammed the skinny metal door shut with a foot. I turned, rickety and motorized feeling, and fell into the jumpy flow of students heading down the steps. My pointed chin was stuck against the hard plate of my chest, and my eyes flickered across each tile as they disappeared under my toes. I tried to count them but kept losing track. Throughout the echoing hallways and tile-covered stairwells, there were all sorts of shouts and howls due to the fact that it was the beginning of the weekend. Normally, I'd have been all relaxed smiles, but I told myself that I didn't care much about a couple of days off. I tried not to care about anything, not even my birthday, not even the fact that it didn't mean anything to all of the people that it should have meant something to. My body, with all its slim bones, hummed with a tuning-fork dullness, like I was falling through space, through layers of soft blankets that brushed my face and neck as I shot by.

On the first floor, I made my way to the big front doors by the office, followed a pack of perfumed girls outside onto the broad white steps in front of the school. The sun was out, shining dully, throwing a thin yellow tinge across the wet parking lot, breaking against cars and the chalky white rowhomes along Thirty-sixth Street. It was cold enough so that when I exhaled, I could see my breath, a foggy cloud bank that billowed out from the back of my throat, disappeared into the heavy air. I clomped along the sidewalk and headed toward Falls Road. At the top of the hill, I crossed the street with everyone else and packed in around the blue bench with "Baltimore, the City That Reads" written across the bumpy wood slats—painted more than a hundred times, I thought.

I stood there for nearly a half-hour, and a couple of creaky city buses came and went, spewed dark, spinning clouds behind them as they headed north, skirted the tall trees of Roland Park, and bounced off toward the county. Finally the Forty-two Downtown teetered up the hill and stopped at the crumbling, windy corner. Brakes screeched, and a wave of smelly heat beat against me. The driver, who had a blob for a nose, so smashed to one side that the tip almost touched a cheek, leaned way out and shouted that he could only take four riders, that the bus was full. His face was like getting cracked by a whip. It woke me up. Even before the last word had passed his tongue, I was rushing forward. I wanted to make the bus. I felt like I deserved it. I stumbled, though, and bounced off of a big girl's hard butt, spilled my books to the ground. I dropped to my knees and scooped my stuff into a pile as fast as I could. But by the time I'd collected it all from under everyone's stomping feet, the Forty-two Downtown was on its way, the engine grinding and tugging, spilling black bursts against the steel-gray road.

I kicked at a crack, pounded it with a dirty toe. Everything bad that could happen had happened, I thought. It could only get better. I spun around, flailing my arms and my books, and walked over to the blue bench, felt everyone's eyes on me, like I was some kind of failed circus act, like I'd fallen off the back of a prancing zebra. I sat in a lump, stared across the street at a check-cashing place that had a shiny green awning above the door. It was the only new thing I could see in all of Hampden. I thought that it might be the only new thing in all of Baltimore.

I considered pushing off the bench and walking home, shuffling through the broken-down neighborhood and up past the Rotunda. I wasn't in any kind of rush. My mom was at work, and Howard wasn't coming over till five o'clock, meaning my birthday celebration, as boring as it was going to be, wasn't officially starting for a couple hours. I didn't, though. I don't know why. I watched pigeons flutter their tattered bodies across the sky as if someone had thrown them, a flock of unraveling softballs. I watched the crowd in front of me push and laugh and gnaw on chewy candy they'd bought or stolen from the 7-Eleven. Buses came and went, and kids disappeared, and others wandered up the hill, smoking and cussing and acting cool. Someone flung a rock and it bounced off the sidewalk and hit the wooden slat beside one of my arms. Across the street, people scampered in and out of the check-cashing store. Behind me, cars ground to a stop in the 7-Eleven parking lot. I took it all in quietly. For some reason, it even made me feel a little bit better. It was dingy but alive, like a small carnival. In some ways, I actually liked Hampden. Then someone blew sour breath and cigarette smoke into my face, made me cough and sputter.

I looked to see who was harassing me and nearly jumped. Newt Novacek leered in my face, dull yellow teeth grinning right at me. Jolted to action, I scurried to my feet, tried to catch my breath as it flew out of me in one big clunk. My lungs shrunk to the size of light bulbs, got rid of every particle of smoggy Baltimore air.

"Think I fergot ya?" Newt asked, a cigarette stump in his mouth. He shook his dented face as if he felt sorry for me, but I knew he didn't. "Singing a differnt tune raht now, huh?"

I couldn't talk.

"I'm gonna hurt ya," Newt told me.

The crowd on the corner jostled about with excitement. People pushed and elbowed to get a good view, formed a ring around me so that I couldn't run. A couple of kids yelled down the hill to the dropouts at the community center. "Gonna be a fight!" they hollered, and the older guys quit their rough game of basketball and came running, tore between honking motorists, brakes howling, to make it before they missed anything good.

"Where's yer nigger friend now?" Newt asked me when the audience was large enough. He laughed like he'd told a great joke.

My hands began shaking, tittering like two wind-up toys. I glanced around, praying that I'd spot Greely among the crowd, but his funny, carved face wasn't there. I was on my own, completely, a situation I'd wondered about since the very day that my father had disappeared, for months and months.

"Yer perverts, ain't ya? You an' the janider."

I shook my head, heard people laugh.

"Punch him," someone called to Newt.

Newt jiggled around the bench with his huge soft chest puffed out, as if he was about to do something bold and dangerous instead of simple and cowardly. He ambled over to where I stood and shoved me with his wide swollen gut, a gut that was hard as a Superball in some spots and soft as a bag of hot jelly in others. There was a hunk of flesh missing where his bellybutton whirled in toward his guts, a crater that was soft around the rim, that glommed against me so that I nearly gagged on it. I even hoped that I would. It was like getting kissed by an overgrown slug draped by a greasy scarf. And I wanted to barf, but I couldn't.

Newt rammed me a few times that way, smoking casually as he worked. Then he slapped me across a cheek with a grimy hand, and even though it didn't hurt that much, I nearly fell down from humiliation.

When the crowd saw me wobble, they hooted and hollered like they were at a heavyweight prizefight. People cashing checks across the street and guys hustling into the 7-Eleven for coffee stood and watched.

Words finally flew out of my mouth. "I don't want to fight, Newt," I hollered.

Everyone scoffed, considered me a coward, a chicken with a tiny little heart, muscles of paper.

"The reason is, it's my birthday," I tried to explain to Newt, hoping he'd take that into account.

"Got a gift for ya," he said, and licked his lips the way Elvis did in those movies when he was young.

"Hit him, Newt," a girl howled, all excited.

Newt exhaled cigarette smoke and slapped me across the face again, harder this time, so that my jaw throbbed and my skin tingled painfully, tightening under my eye. He rushed forward and crashed against me with his stomach, steamrollered me till I fell backward, landed on my behind. My books pounded to the pavement for the second time that day.

"Ya think yer so hot, but ya ain't nothin'," Newt informed me. "Yer like a little girl. Where's yer little dress, little girl?"

The crowd laughed.

Someone said that it wasn't a fair fight, but he didn't try to stop it.

I squirmed to my knees, dizzy and scared. I could barely catch my breath. I made one more attempt to put a stop to the slaughter. Gritting my teeth for show, eyes slit tight, I declared, "I know karate."

Everyone laughed.

Newt shimmied forward and stepped on some of my fingers, ground them with the gritty sole of his brown scummy sneaker. "Somebody should git ya a doll-baby, one of them ones that pees all over itself."

Ha-ha-ha rushed through my ears.

I yanked my fingers free.

"Naw, ya don't," Newt said, and tried to mash my other hand with the same foot.

I saw it coming, though, yanked it away in time. I shook with anger and embarrassment, rose to my knees. When Newt tried to bump me over with a leg, I grabbed his dirt-smeared jeans in my hands and shoved him away. "Stop!" I shouted.

The crowd *eew*ed.

"Punk!" Newt spat. He twisted his body back, cocked an arm, and threw a punch at me.

I tried to duck, but his gigantic knuckles clubbed my lumpy skull. A ragged fingernail dug into one of my ears, and the whole side of my head exploded into sharp and dull pains, throbbed and burned all the way down my neck to my collarbone. Holding my bleeding ear, I glowered at him and screamed, "You're a butt."

When he smiled, I cracked. I lunged forward and clawed at one of his fat legs as hard as I could, so that he recoiled in shock. Then I reached beside one of my knees and snatched up a big book, hurled it at him so that it flew through the air in a perfect arc, slammed into his side, and crashed to the ground. Superhero drawings spilled out, drifted back and forth till they landed softly on the dry cement.

Newt felt the sore spot on his ribs with some pudgy fingers. He pushed and grimaced, leveled his gaze, and rushed me.

Awkwardly, I crawled out of his way, squashed one of my hands with one of my knees. Somehow, though, I stood up.

Newt spun around. A hunk of ash from his dwindling cigarette rolled down the oily front of his black heavy-metal T-shirt. He was mad, furious. I could see it in his dull eyes, in his lopsided face. I was mad, too, crazy mad at Newt the bully, Newt, who reminded me of the worst thing about my father, his terrible school years. Trembling, a wild boy, I ran at him, lowered my head, and collided with his belly. It was like running full steam into a tree. I ricocheted off, *eep*ed in pain, and fell in a lump to the ground. I curled into a ball with my hands wrapped around my head. I ached all over. I closed my eyes, and I gave up, waiting for him to pummel me. I waited and waited for what seemed like hours but was really only seconds, and nothing happened. Eventually, I rolled onto my scraped sore hands, my banged knees, and looked up.

Newt was half on his back, propped up on an elbow. He was desperately searching for his lost breath. The bent stub of his cigarette smoldered on the ground by his feet, and drool painted the corner of his mouth. He actually looked beaten, like a picture in a comic book.

"It ain't over," someone called. "Git up!"

"Git up!" squawked in my ears.

"It's finished," declared a high school dropout from the community center. He came over and helped me to my feet, brushed loads of sand and dirt off the back of my used coat. "Y'all right?" he asked.

I nodded my bleary head.

He gathered my books and papers together, handed them to me. "Wasn't a fair fight, shorty," he told me, "but ya did all right."

The crowd broke up and got interested in other things. They were disappointed that it had ended so fast. I could see it on their moon-pie faces. "Everyone's a jerk," I muttered, wiping at my swollen eye, puckered with liquid, like I was peeping from behind a mud puddle.

"They was just having fun," the guy said, and shrugged.

Cautiously, I looked over at Newt again, still on his side in the patchy strip of grass between the sidewalk and the road. He noticed me and flopped over to his stomach, which rocked about like water.

"I don't like to fight," I whispered.

"Takes gettin' used to," the big kid told me.

But I knew that I never would like it. I wasn't a fighter. I wasn't like Greely or Detective Addler or my father had been. I was just a kid, and that's nearly all I wanted to be. I wanted to have what I had when I wasn't overwhelmed at school or clogged-up feeling at home. I didn't want to make people feel any worse than they already did, to make sadness or humiliation for anyone, even terrible Newt.

"Got a basketball game to go play," the guy told me. "Don't want to lose my spot." He thumped me on my shoulder, smiled. "Name's Frazier. Always down there shooting in the afternoons."

I nodded.

He ran across the busy street, right in front of the Forty-two Downtown rumbling up the long hill from the bottom part of Falls Road, where for about a mile, it looks like a country drive cluttered with cigarette billboards, dark as twilight beneath the shadows of the Jones Falls Expressway.

The boxy city bus screeched to a stop in front of the blue MTA sign on the corner, and I staggered up the rubberized steps and down the aisle, where I bounced into a soft plastic seat. As the bus pulled away,

I watched Newt, a bulky lump, a baby whale stranded and broken in the middle of Hampden.

I got off at my regular stop. The bus groaned and drifted away, and I stood frozen in its exhaust, peered across the road at the start of my neighborhood, at Junie's and the bright line of little stores hung with chrome strips, old-fashioned signs, and faded awnings. Clouds moved in the bright sky above, raced away. I stood there for a while, and a warm feeling fizzed into my sore shoulders and throat. Battered and bruised, I felt better in Charles Village. The funny trees, the jumbled rowhomes and alleys made me comfortable, had sunk into my thin muscles, become a part of me, a nice part of me.

I rushed across the road and started into the neighborhood, along Thirty-second Street. As I went, I looked around as much as I could. It was all so normal now. I had gotten used to pale arms poking out of housecoats, potato chip bags dancing on the ground, and all of those rowhouses, endless rowhouses, some dingy with age or laziness or both, heaped with all sorts of wonderful doors and windows, others as perfect as the day they were finished. They were all practically the exact same models, but they were different, too, painted red or purple or blue or brown, clapped over with Formstone or brick or shingles or crinkled aluminum siding, a few drizzled with splats of tar or graffiti. They'd all been personalized. I hadn't seen that at first. Or, at least, I hadn't thought about it. Then I noticed the wall I was scuffing beside. I stopped and reached one of my stinging hands out and ran my fingertips across the smooth red bricks. They appeared lit from inside, each one casting the slightest glow. They were warmer than the air, and the warmth made them seem almost friendly, like Ditch's and Greely's hard hands. The wall felt alive, protective.

On Abel Avenue, I limped between parked cars and across the street, past the dusty white hot-dog truck, up the front steps, and into the apartment. Upstairs, I stood in the hallway by the bathroom, invisible fumes of Comet cleanser floating in the air. For some reason, all the threadbare curtains and blinds were drawn, blotting out nearly every bit of sunshine. Automatically, I worried that my mom was back in bed, sleeping and lost, curled into the shape of a sea horse. I felt weak with the idea. Sneaking about, I looked into her room, but it was too dark to see anything in the shadows. I fiddled for the light switch on the bumpy wall, let my fingers sweep around the blotchy plaster, searching for the little plastic plate. I heard something move behind me and jerked around. "Mom?" I rasped nervously. She didn't answer back. I stared into the shifting darkness of the kitchen.

The lights popped on and people hollered back, "Surprise!"

I blinked a few times, searched the different sets of eyes—my mom's, Junie's, Ditch's, Greely's, and Howard's—and I smiled, a deep relieved smile that tugged on every muscle in me.

My mom slipped between Ditch and Junie, scrunched over in her yellow high-tops. "Happy Birthday," she told me, wrapping a cold hand under my chin and smiling down at my face. It took her maybe five seconds to spot my shiner, my black eye that was fat and heavy as a tiny pouch. Her lips cracked open. The soft skin above her thin nose tightened into small, hurt bundles. "Somebody beat you up!" she exclaimed.

Greely, who was standing by my bedroom door with Howard, focused his gaze on me. "Somebody beat you up, Sam?"

I nodded my head, admitted the truth even though I wanted to lie.

"Was it Newt?" my mom wanted to know.

"Yeah," I admitted.

Ditch's long face went cold and stiff.

My mom closed her eyes and breathed out a tiny stream of frustrated air.

"He beat me up and all," I tried to explain with a raspy voice, "but I got him to stop. I ran into his stomach, and he couldn't breathe. He had to quit."

"You mean you got him?" Greely questioned.

"I ran into his stomach," I said, embarrassed that it sounded so stupid, not like a normal fight.

The edges of Greely's fat lips curved upward.

"Like a bull, hon?" Junie asked me seriously.

"Kind of," I answered.

"Well," she smiled, "that ain't so bad."

My mom pushed strands of hair out of my sharp face. "Why didn't you just run, sweetheart? You're a better runner than fighter. You just should've run."

"I couldn't," I told her.

She ran a thumb lightly across one of my cheeks. "Oh, Samuel, your face is all bruised, and look at your poor knuckles." Her icy hands tingled over the lumps on my skull, stopped at my blood-crusted ear, and dropped to her side. Her eyes shifted around, narrowed, and suddenly danced with a fearful anger. She swung about and marched into the kitchen, saying over her shoulder, "I'm not going to stand for this. I'm calling the principal. What're they thinking down there, mixing kids like that with good kids? It's crazy."

I rose onto the balls of my feet, lifted my hands to beg. "Mom, please don't," I said desperately.

Ditch reached from behind her and wrapped a wide hand over both of my mom's. He kept the phone from her ear and told her softly, "Don't, Maxine. Get him in trouble with the other kids if you do. That's the way it works. Anyway, the school can't do nothing to this Newt character that's worse than getting beat up."

She shook her head. "They could suspend him or something."

Greely caught her eye. He mumbled in his deep, blanketed voice. "If they suspended all the kids who got into fights, that place'd be

[236]

nearly empty. Leave well enough alone. The school don't have no power. They really don't."

"God," my mom blurted. "What kind of city do we live in? My son gets beat up, and I can't do anything about it?"

"But I'm okay, Mom," I told her. "I promise."

She curled the shiny phone against one of her shoulders. Her eyes tightened down even more, and she glowered into mine. "Samuel," she said, and I could tell that her scary anger had turned on me, "I know you had no choice in the matter, but I don't want you to be a fighter. You hear me? I don't want you to act like your dad did. He was a thug, and it wasn't a good thing. He always felt bad about that. He wished he'd been different. You understand? I won't stand for that kind of thing."

I dropped my eyes to the wood floor, the splintery planks that disappeared under the curling dull linoleum tiles, all the bounce squished out of them. "I don't like it, either," I mumbled. "I hate it, too."

"Come on, Maxine," Howard called to her in a soothing way.

She looked at him. "It just scares me," she said. "I worry."

"I don't think you have to," he explained.

A quiet moment went by. Junie winked at me, raised her eyebrows, two pencil-drawn red lines. "Well, ain't this a happy birthday. Come on, now, it's s'posed to be fun, so let's have fun. I'm telling you, Ditch and me didn't close up shop early jist to sit around and sulk." She lurched in a half circle, reached up, and rubbed both of my mom's cheeks with her palms. "They's just bumps and scratches, Maxine. He'll get over 'em. He's a good kid."

My mom's eyes loosened, and all the anger rushed out of her, left her standing in a hunch. She laughed a little, wrapped her limp arms as far around Junie as they would go, which wasn't all the way around.

"There, there, Maxine, " Junie joked, stroking my mom's hair.

"I'm sorry, Samuel," my mom told me, looking over a soft shoulder. "Like I said, I just worry for you."

I smiled shyly, relieved that she was back to her normal self. "You don't have to," I told her.

"Maybe," she murmured, shaking her head like she wasn't exactly sure. Even still, she let Junie go, and put the phone back on the hook.

Greely tromped over to where I was standing. My shoulders were bent inward, drooping like a dry weed. He shook his head and patted my skinny back, pulled me against a strong hip. *"Phew.* Sam," he mumbled, "You're something."

I smiled up at him. "You didn't forget."

"How could I? You spent the whole week reminding me about it, didn't you?"

I was embarrassed. "I thought maybe." I bit at a fingernail. "What about the TV?"

"Come on, there ain't no television. I got me one that works okay."

I sat bundled on the chilly porch with the men, bounced in one of the green rusty metal chairs. My mom and Junie were upstairs preparing dinner, frying hamburgers, boiling hot dogs, simmering beans, and stuff. It was the nicest party I could ever remember. The presents didn't even matter to me all that much. They fell from my thoughts like ideas, and I sat there mesmerized, listening to the fathers of my life talk about old Baltimore, a place that I'd never known, filled with families from all over the world, people who kept their rowhouses in sparkling shape, scrubbed their marble steps to a pale shine and washed the wood trim over in a new coat of paint every single year. Ditch reminisced about childhood, about a candy store, about greasing the streetcar tracks and window-shopping with his mom at the big department stores. He told us about playing baseball in Patterson Park, how if he hit a homer, his father, who wasn't a very friendly person normally, took the entire family for ice cream at

Macht's in Pigtown. When he was done, Greely talked about Pennsylvania Avenue and the Royal Theater, where famous black performers came and played. He said that when he got off the sooty bus from Atlanta, he went straight into the bathroom, put on a coat and tie, then hiked on down to the theater and bought a ticket. He listened to Nat King Cole sing and saw a dog show where French poodles danced to music tooted out on a slide trombone. Afterward, he went for a plate of Chinese food at the White Rice Inn. "That's when Baltimore was the place. It was the black center of the universe," he told Ditch, Howard, and me. The way they talked, it was like watching a movie.

Eventually, though, I had to go to the bathroom, and I rushed up the steps and slid through the door to our warm apartment, which was open and smelled like cooking hamburgers. My bladder was about to explode, but for some reason I stopped by the bathroom door and listened to my mom and Junie, who didn't know I was there. They spoke in whispers.

"He always did like celebrating Samuel's birthday," I heard my mom say. "I hope he feels terrible about missing this one. I really do. I hope he can't sleep for a month."

There was a pause, and Junie said, "I guess I can't hate him like I should, Maxine. You know? He was kind of like a son for Ditch and me. I mean, I never woulda guessed this running-off stuff. Never woulda. That man had the softest heart of any person I ever knowed and wouldn'a harmed no one, especially you guys, if he didn't have ta. But I think he couldn't take the responsibility no more. I think it was getting to him."

"You know what I think? We were too young when we got married. I always say it, and it's true."

"You swear to that, but Ditch and I got married when we was still in our teens."

"That was a different time, Junie. Things changed."

Junie let out this big sigh, the kind only a heavy person can make real well. "I guess you might be right. Things changed, changed for the worse, if you ask me." The hamburgers sizzled loudly. "You still think he's in Florida, hon?"

"He always liked warm weather. If I had to guess any city, I'd bet he's in Miami, amid all that glitter and glitz."

"Maybe he turned into one of them hermits and lives in a swamp?"

"Not him. He was too embarrassed about being without."

"I knows," Junie replied in a murmur. "I know he was, hon."

Neither of them said anything for a minute; then my mom mumbled softly, "Guess it's time I go get everyone."

"Guess it is. Now don't you go rushing down there looking like that, though. Take some deep breaths and get the thoughts outta your system," Junie instructed. "It don't help no one to feel hurt about it anymore."

While my mom took her breaths and cleared her head, I slid into the bathroom and pulled the door shut behind me. I crumbled onto the edge of the deep tub, my bladder poking me like the corner of a board. I was numb and hurt all the way down to my toes. Tears came gushing out of me. I forgot that I was twelve years old and trying to act more mature. Tears ran down my battered face and dripped onto my clean pants. I moaned and coughed. I felt like dying. I felt like I couldn't live anymore. Somewhere inside I'd always known that my father had chosen to leave. I'd known it, but I'd never wanted to admit it outright to myself. After hearing my mom say it, there was no way to keep it out.

There was a loud knock on the door. "Samuel?" my mom called nervously.

I couldn't talk. I couldn't get words out.

"Samuel? Please."

I rocked back and forth, nearly out of my mind with pain.

"Samuel, I want you to say something, or I'll get someone to knock down this door, I swear. Talk to me, baby."

"Mom," I blabbered in a slur, "I got to stay in here right now. I can't come to the party anymore."

the way it goes
the way it goes

In the middle of April, I recleaned the backyard, straightened the crimped wire fence so that it swung loosely from rusted pole to wooden post without any major dips or bows. I raked and swept and trimmed the grass with big scissors from Junie's, then went up and down the alley, tried to neaten it. When I was done, I lined the plastic sacks against the house's flaking brick wall because I was going to wait until garbage day before I hoisted them into the alley. I understood the city a lot better than I had.

The work took me an entire afternoon, the springtime sun warming the bones spread like roots across my bent back. I don't know what got me out there, except that Charles Village had become my neighborhood. I wanted to do something to help it look better. In my mind, I'd never really lived until I'd arrived there. At least, I'd never understood things until then. The good soft memories of Rodger's Forge were gone. I hated to think about our old neighborhood, the clean carpet-lawns, the perfect homes with their paint jobs as smooth as skin. There was nothing behind any of the prettiness, I told myself.

I forgot the old trees that reached so high into the air, that filled with leaves and shaded entire blocks from the sun like giant clean beach umbrellas. I forgot the sounds of birds, not pigeons, tweeting and kids roaring around on Big Wheels. Rodger's Forge became a dark place, black, the inside of an old chimney.

When I finished working in the yard and I was tired and faded, like after my birthday party, I sat out on the front porch and watched my neighbors roar off in their cars, flop their dusty rugs against telephone poles, or think about whatever people think about when they don't move and their eyes are open. My hands were stabbed and scraped from work, smeared with dark dirt and liquid from broken beer bottles, cola cans, and the radiator, still half filled with yellow fluid. They stung, and I bounced up and down on the front-porch chair and let them float in my lap, two blazing alarm clocks attached to my dim body.

That morning, my mom had said that she was worried about me, and I was glad. The more she worried, the better I felt. I didn't blame her for anything; I was just kind of angry inside and wanted to give some of that to someone else. When I did, some of the pressure inside me blew off, whistled away.

Across the street, an old fat man tugged a pink-and-blue striped recliner out onto his porch. He lit a stogy as fat as a hot dog and sat down and put his legs up and smiled and waved to me once with that cigar of his, a spike of shriveled brown skin rising between his fingers.

I didn't wave back. Instead, I dropped my eyes and studied my feet, my newish sneakers that were already stained and worn and unraveling around the toes. The leather looked like layers of old newspaper, spray-painted white to seem high-quality.

My throat hurt from dryness, rubbed against itself, one long sheet of sandpaper all the way down to the rubber bag of my empty stomach. The sun was low. Minute by minute it disappeared behind the bumpy outline of the row across the street. Slipping into shadows, the man's cigar glowed orange, burned like a wild eyeball. Off in the distance, I heard Howard's car with its fan belts whirling louder than the police sirens on Greenmount Avenue. It had been that way for about a month, since a sixteen-year-old kid without insurance had swiped off half the grill and bumper. Howard, like a sucker, had gone ahead and decided to live with it until the boy could afford to get it fixed. He'd told my mom that he didn't want to get the guy in trouble.

Howard chugged around the corner and parked in a space on the edge of the block. Cutting the car off, he climbed out, his pasty Dracula-face hidden until he passed from under the shadows. His long legs were all exaggerated in a tight pair of jeans that flared out just above his feet. They showed off the lumps at his knees, caps that looked like turned-over bowls. He also had on the green coat he liked to wear, the one he'd gotten free from work, with a tree patch ironed on the pocket. Howard shambled toward me slowly, his shoulders bowed down as if he had a couple of bricks on them. When he was nearly to the porch steps, the guy across the street, smoking in the easy chair, called to him.

"Hey, you mind getting that car of yers fixed?" he said in a loud-mouthed friendly way. "Woke me up a couple of weeks ago, ya know. Thought I was in the middle of some kind of air raid."

Howard stopped, put his hands on his hips. "I'm looking into it," he told the guy. "Got into an accident."

"Don't remind me about accidents," the man groaned. "I been in my fair share in this town. Got my license revoked last year, and it wasn't even my fault."

Howard shrugged, poked at his glasses, and rustled up the porch steps. "Hey, Sam. What're you doing out here?"

"Mom's still at work," I said.

"Thought you'd be inside watching television or something."

I told him in a monotone voice that I didn't like television anymore.

He nodded, sat down beside me. The chair's metal joints gave off a creak, and he put the sticky heels of his sneakers up on the rail, slid his butt forward, and slumped in the middle, like a rope bridge. I could hear him breathe, soft inhales that made his chest rise. "You've got your mom all worried, you know," he said.

"I'm doing okay." I kicked my toes against the floor and bounced madly back and forth like one of those boring supermarket rides. "Anyway, when did she tell you that? You haven't been around."

"Been working."

"Mom said you were sick."

"I guess I've been doing both."

"How can you work if you're sick?"

"What happened is, I got better and then started working."

"That doesn't make any sense."

Howard lifted his shoulders so that his green coat rose up around his droopy earlobes, touched them softly. "Life doesn't make sense, Sam." He blinked. "You don't seem very happy, that's what I want to talk about. You haven't been the same since your birthday. I'll come out and say it, everyone's worried about you, that you might be hurt for good by what you heard. I'm worried." He rubbed at his chin with a thumb and a finger, pushed it back and forth so that small dark rolls scrunched up under his bottom lip.

"Maybe I am," I said, because I didn't know.

He nodded, took off his glasses and cleaned them with the front of his flannel shirt. "Everyone liked the old Sam. People say that the new one's not as nice. Me, I don't know the new one real well, but I used to look up to the old one."

I shot a burst of air out of my nostrils. "You can't look up to me," I informed him. "I'm just a kid."

"Doesn't mean I can't look up to you."

"Yes, it does."

"Course it doesn't."

"Things don't work that way."

"You're wrong," he said matter-of-factly. He swiped his spiky dark hair with a pale hand, then by mistake, poked himself in an eyeball with the earpiece of his glasses.

"Adults can't look up to kids. The whole world knows that."

"Anybody can look up to anyone, Sam. Age doesn't matter one bit."

I looked at him for a moment, finally nodded like I got it, but I wasn't so sure he hadn't broken some rule. He was too nice a person to argue with, though.

He blinked his eyes, one red, both magnified behind his ratty glasses, lenses that were so scratched they made his pupils look fuzzy. "You wanna know why I looked up to the old Sam?"

"I guess," I said, and started swinging my feet as hard as I could.

"I looked up to him 'cause he was tough. Because he dealt with everything that happened, and it never really made him mean. It would have made me mean, I'll tell you that, what with so much of my life being stirred up and confused in such a short time, with my dad disappearing and my mom dating someone else. But once you got to know the old Sam, he was always friendly. He was a nice guy."

"I'm not as nice anymore," I told him.

"Guess not. I think it's too bad, though."

I continued to swing my feet hard, soles banging against the gray planks of the porch. Then I spit out a question that I already knew the answer to. "So have you and my mom stopped going out or something?"

Howard swallowed, cast his eyes on to the street, which glowed like steam. "I guess, maybe," he admitted weakly. "I love your mom, but she doesn't love me. That's sometimes the way it goes, Sam. You can't make someone's heart love you when it doesn't."

I swallowed. I was learning that hearing something and knowing something were different things for me. "I wish you could," I said, the sharp edge in my voice fading to a dull raspy whisper. Howard and I were friends, good friends. He was like a small piece of my father, a tiny fragment that filled part of the giant hole in me.

"I wish you could, too. I even asked her if she might change her mind, but she can't. She says we'll always be friends, though, and I believe her. That means something to me. She even told me to come by to see you anytime I want to, and I'm gonna. I'm not going to stop coming by."

"I know you will," I told him. "It'll just happen."

"Not everyone's the same, Sam."

I stopped rocking and slumped forward, dug my bony elbows into the thin cushions of my thighs. I propped up my head with my fists. "You mean you're not like my father?"

"I don't mean that, Sam. I just mean, some people might feel awkward or something coming by, but I won't. I wish your mom the best, and that's the truth, and I won't stop being her friend or your friend."

"You know what?"

"No."

"I don't need friends anymore," I told him.

"Yes, you do," he whispered back. "Everyone does."

"Not me," I decided.

He pulled his long feet off the rail, settled them straight in front of him. "Well, maybe you don't, but I know I need friends. To be honest, I was pretty lonely before I started dating your mom."

I swallowed, and it felt like there was a long nail in my throat, stuck halfway between my mouth and my gut. The last thing I wanted was for Howard to feel lonely. It wasn't right. I fastened my eyes on the cigar across the street, concentrated on it. It glowed and hovered, a tiny orange torch when the old man in the recliner sucked down smoke.

A minute or so passed that way, and a big familiar van turned the corner of Thirty-second Street. It drifted onto Abel Avenue, the engine rumbling low. Its bright headlights threw splashes of white across our neighbor's creaky porches, across assorted deck furniture, rusty paint cans, then onto and past Howard and me. The giant brown van stopped in front of our place. My mom scrambled from the back, told Ditch and Junie good night, and heaved the sliding door shut with a soft grunt.

"Hey, Sammy, Howard!" Ditch called from his open window. He lifted a marble-white hand, a cigarette trapped between his fingers, and drove slowly away. Behind him, I saw Junie in the dome light, her big lips painted purple, throwing sopping kisses as if she was a glamorous movie star. At the corner, Ditch hit the gas, and the van zoomed into the blackness of Thirty-first Street, headed toward Greenmount Avenue.

My mom, so thin and pretty, stood on the porch by the steps and asked Howard how he was.

"Okay, Maxine. Yourself?"

"Good." She adjusted a grocery bag in her hands. "Thanks for coming by."

"Anytime. Like I told Sam, we're all friends, and that isn't going to stop."

"I'm glad about that," my mom told him, and flashed us both a tired smile. "You okay, Samuel?"

I wanted to tell her that breaking up with Howard—our Howard, practically a member of our family—was wrong, that he seemed almost as important to our life as my dad had before him. But I didn't say anything.

"I guess he told you that we're not going out anymore?"

I moved my head up and down. "I wish you were."

"I'm sorry, Samuel. I know you do. I was going to talk to you about it, but I wanted you to get over this other stuff first. Guess I should have said something." She shook her head, just barely, thoughtful and worried. "Look, I'm going to let you guys talk," she murmured.

"Thanks," Howard told her.

I listened to her unlock the front door and go inside. I think I heard her shoes clomp up the steps, but I might have been imagining it like I imagined a lot of things at the time, my father hiding behind cars as I walked to the bus stop in the morning.

"Look at you, Sam. I know you're hurt, and that's good to see. As soon as someone stops feeling, what's the use? Take me for instance, huh? I'm sad, but I'm okay. I'll survive. The times we all had together were fun, but just knowing you're my friend will make me get better quicker."

"We're friends," I whispered to him.

"I'm glad."

I turned my head and looked up at him, underneath the broad edge of his glasses, into the coves of his eyes. "Nothing seems right anymore," I said faintly. "I tried to be good so that my dad would like me, but that didn't matter. Then my mom wanted me to like you, so I did, and now I can't anymore, not really. We can only be faraway friends. That's the kind of stuff I hate."

"Why can't you like me anymore, Sam?"

"I can, but I can't," I tried to explain. "You know."

"Come on," he growled playfully, and shook me back and forth in my chair.

"Stop," I said, but I didn't want him to.

"Not until you smile," he said.

I let him shake me for a little while longer. Then I told him, "Look," and made a big phony smile. The thing is, it wasn't as easy as that. I was so confused. My dad and his soft heart were still gone. He'd still left me and my mom, and it didn't make any sense. And suddenly, for no reason, my mom was sending Howard away.

* * *

By the end of April, it got so that if Greely could toss the ball anywhere close to me, I could catch it. I beat myself to a pulp pulling in passes. I hurled my puny body against the ground, tore crusty red patches across my bony elbows and knees. I wanted the football more than anything. But Greely didn't like what I was doing one bit, my new fire. Finally, after a few weeks, he got fed up one day and stopped throwing, rested the ball on his old hip, and stared across the grass at me. "You gonna stop trying to break yer neck, or are we gonna have ta stop throwing the ball together?" he asked. "I ain't gonna help you knock yerself out anymore, Sam."

"I'm just trying to get good," I told him.

"Bull, Sam. You're trying to make yourself hurt."

"I'm not."

"I ain't gonna throw it to you no more, you keep doing it." His eyebrows furrowed, hard, and I could tell he was exasperated. "Time we spend out here is s'posed to be fun."

"I'm having fun," I shot back.

"Sam, you ain't having fun doing it this way."

I crossed my arms in front of my chest and stared at him.

"It's true," he said, and tossed the ball right at me so that I had to unravel my hands fast.

I caught it and threw it back. It landed near his feet, thunked the ground. Even though I tried, I couldn't toss the ball that well.

Greely rustled over, bent slowly, painfully, and scooped it up. He straightened his bad knee, hidden in a pair of discolored green pants, then limped around to get the ache out. We weren't that far apart, and I saw him wince, his dark lips tight against his teeth. Watching him, I thought he looked so noble and strong and smart that it could knock me over. Then he jerked a hand up and gave one of his shoulders a rub, pushed at a hard muscle so that the sleeve of his thin T-shirt bunched up under his curly-haired armpit. He lurched, then flicked the ball toward me.

I went after it the same crazy way. I rushed forward and sprang into the air, trapped it between my fingers, which rammed into the ground; then I bounced onto a shoulder. I squeezed the cheap rubber football hard against me. When I stood up, I glanced over at Greely, expecting to see his forceful disapproving eyes, but they weren't angry at all. They were wide and amazed, open farther than I ever thought eyes could be.

He was on the ground, on his knees, holding his chest with his beautiful coarse brown hands. He looked confused, moaned, and pitched forward, buried his balding, blocky head into the dirt and grass of Wyman Park.

"Greely?" I called, surprised. "Greely," I barked, then trotted over nervously. "What's wrong?" I dropped to my narrow knees and rolled him over. "Greely," I shouted, then jerked back, fell onto my behind. There was blood on one of his arms, soaking the shoulder he'd been rubbing. It was on one of my hands, too. That's when I thought for sure he'd been shot.

His eyes were dazed and confused. Those lips—those big, ancient lips, cut by grooves and scars and dry at the edges—moved back and forth, shivering.

Terrified that he was dying, I took off, burned toward the line of rowhouses on the street high above the park, hit the hill, and pumped my legs. As I went, my knees knocked together painfully, two hunks of slate clacking. I felt like a bird, like a baby bird the way I scooted up that slope. My inexpensive sneakers wouldn't grip the turf, and I kept slipping, losing time, losing moments of Greely's life. I finally got to the top and stumbled across the road and up some steps and pounded and hollered at a white screen door. I couldn't catch my breath. My hand left little splats. Finally, a neighbor came out on the porch next door, looked at me suspiciously. I cried, "My friend's been shot!"

"What?" she asked, a long orange dress slithering around a muscular body, shoulders that were as wide as a suitcase.

"In the park! My friend's been shot! Please," I moaned and drooped tearfully against the stone wall that separated her porch from the one I was standing on.

"I'll call the police," she said, and spun into her home.

"Call an ambulance!" I howled. "Call a doctor!"

Through the pounding in my ears, I heard her on the phone. She explained the situation, then hung up. She came outside. "Where's your friend?" she asked.

"In the park," I sniffled.

"Show me," she said, and I took off, and she scrambled after me, barefoot, her brown toes squishing in the soft grass.

When we got to Greely, he was still on the ground. He stared up into the sky. His massive eyes were gooey, half shut. Thin, nearly clear lids were slipping over them in a sad, hopeless way.

The lady in the orange dress fell to her knees, pounded his chest with a fist.

"Stop!" I grabbed at her hand, covered in thick rings, big yellow-and-pink pieces of glass wired onto gold bands.

"He's having a heart attack," she said to me, and yanked her wrist from my grip.

Sirens floated in the air, rolled down the steep slope.

"He was shot, though," I blabbered.

"He wasn't shot! Your hand's bleeding," she snapped at me, and whacked him some more.

I looked down, and she was right; one of my knuckles was scraped. It was even stinging, but I hadn't noticed it. I stuck it in my mouth, sucked, and watched the lady start pumping on Greely's chest.

"I'm a nurse," she told me, her kinky hair shuffling in a slight breeze.

"A nurse?" I muttered.

She nodded.

Up on the hill, I saw a policeman in blue, and two paramedics pulling and pushing a little stretcher on shopping-cart wheels. I leaned over one of Greely's fine curled ears and whispered that he was going to be all right. I told him that the lady I'd found was a famous nurse, and she was pumping the life back into his old heart. I told him that she knew exactly what she was doing and that I wouldn't dive so far for the football anymore.

Junie, Ditch, and my mom took me to Alonso's for dinner that night. It was my dad's favorite restaurant because they had the biggest hamburgers in Baltimore. It was also Ditch's favorite. Outside, it was raining, and the sides of the roads were rushing with foamy water. Drips searched down the front window, glowed yellow from the letters of a neon sign. Leaning on the big black slab of a table, Ditch and Junie and my mom sipped on beers, and I slurped at a Coke in a red plastic cup, like the ones at the Little Tavern but less greasy.

Junie wiped her soft mouth with the twisted-up corner of a paper napkin and shook her head. "Sam, have Ditch and I ever told you we know a man who's had six heart attacks, and not one of them ever killed him? He shakes 'em off like they're bothersome, but not much more. His body just keeps on going, and that ain't so uncommon. People do it all the time."

I looked down at my sore knuckle, at the clean strip of gauze taped across it. I felt miserable inside.

"Sam," Ditch said, "why don't you and me talk at the bar, huh?"

I barely lifted my eyes to look at him.

"I'd like to talk," he muttered. "We'll come back when they bring out the food."

At the bar, there was the softest music playing on the jukebox, drifting back and forth. Plus, the silent television, mounted on the wall in a corner, threw the tenderest blue flickering cast across everyone. It all felt nice and comfortable, like a soft bed. No one could hurt too much in a place like that, where people were gentle and music was part of the air.

Beside me, getting comfortable on his stool, Ditch lifted some fingers and ordered another beer, then lit a cigarette. After a minute or so, he patted my head with a hand. "Sat here with yer dad more times than I can count," he mumbled to me. "I cared about him, Sam, and sometimes I feel like I failed, 'cause I knew he was hurting."

I didn't want to think about my dad.

"Feel like I owe it to him ta see ta you. But all I can think ta say, Sam, is life's gonna hurt, but ya gotta live with it. It won't be that way forever. Let me tell ya something I never tell anyone. When Junie and I was young, we wanted kids worse than anything in the world, except we weren't ever lucky enough ta have 'em. And that was back when kids meant everything. It was unheard of to be without. Anyway, for a while, we felt like we was failures, and we couldn't ever imagine that we'd feel different. But we did, eventually. We got on, and we've had pretty good lives."

He drew in on his cigarette, and his long lungs filled with smoke, rose up, and pushed against the front of his shirt. "My dad," Ditch went on, "he wasn't a nice man. You've heard me say that. He was a shouter. So when I got old enough ta make my own way, I went in the other direction and tried ta speak my mind by saying things through being quiet. Thing is, being quiet becomes kind of permanent, so that you can't speak your feelings real good, not outright. But I've been trying to be different with you and your mom, 'cause I think it's important that you guys know I care. Junie and I both do. We've been so worried that one of you is gonna slip away like your dad did. It's been hard for us, 'cause we could do more, but we don't know if we should." He wiped at the loose skin beside his nose, pushed it around like putty.

"I'm not going anywhere," I told him in a whisper.

"Sam," he muttered, "I had someone tell me once that there're a lot of ways ta leave a place, and leaving's just one of 'em." He swallowed. "What I'm trying ta work up ta is Greely. He'll be fine, absolutely fine, but on the off chance he ain't, he'd want ya to be happy. You know that, don't ya?"

I shook my head. "Yeah," I murmured into the slowness of the air and the music. But I could only think that if I died, I'd want everyone who knew me to be sad forever.

"He would. And if I go tomorrow, I'd want the same thing. Yer young and ya got a life ahead, and it's gonna be filled with a lotta happiness and some pain, but both will end and start up again, and neither'll go on forever. I can't imagine anything's gonna be much harder than this year was for ya, and up until lately, you've made it all right."

I blinked a few times, feeling ashamed of the way I'd been. "I know I've been acting funny," I said, my throat tight and small.

"Yeah," Ditch grumbled, "we all act that way sometimes." He reached across the bar and snuffed his Winston out in a heavy black ashtray, pushed the cigarette down so that the front disappeared into the gray mounds of burnt tobacco and filters. "You've been cheated. But ya got ta start getting past that, for yer own self." He turned away and lifted his beer, sipped at it, and peered up at a commercial on television.

In the air there was a different song drifting about, a woman's voice rolling gently. Behind it, I could hear rainwater splash against car tires.

"I used to be scared of you," I said to Ditch.

"I know, Sam. And I used ta be scared of you."

"You don't scare me anymore," I told him.

"Ya don't scare me, either," he mumbled back. He squeezed his lips down on a new cigarette, flicked at his Bic lighter with a thumb, and looked at me over his rutty hands, two bumpy starfish.

"Ditch, you think Greely's going to be okay?"

He got his cigarette burning red and pulled it from his mouth, held it between two fingers. "Oh, yeah. I'm confident that he ain't got no problem that can't be fixed."

shadows
shadows

The day after Greely's heart attack, I walked to school, wandered down Thirty-second Street to Charles, then followed it to University Parkway. Below the tall brick apartment buildings, I turned and stumbled along past the Johns Hopkins lacrosse field and down the long hill to the bridge over Wyman Park.

I looked down on the dark green, washed field and thought about the day before, about running up the steep slope, searching for help. My eyes drifted about and fell on the high trees that followed the creek. They were covered with new leaves that turned over in the wind like aluminum pie-plates. Their trunks were blue and smooth or brown and rough. I plopped my books on the stone rail and rose on my toes to look down on the cut in the ground where creek water swirled. At the bottom of one pool was a submerged metal porch chair. I fell to my heels and looked into the blue slightly overcast sky and breathed slowly.

I stood there for a few minutes, then slid my books off of the scratchy stone rail and headed up the hill, past the rowhomes that traced Wyman Park and the pretty well-kept edge of Roland Park.

After stumbling by the Rotunda, I turned and drifted along Roland Avenue, against the wind, toward Thirty-sixth Street, and into Hampden, tracing the route that my mom and I had taken in the early fall, on my first day of class at Robert Poole Middle School.

More old rowhomes rose up beside me, their fronts wavy, melting. Behind thin lacy curtains, lights were on, glowing white bulbs hanging from crimped cords. Shadowy people moved about, buttoning shirts and sipping from plastic cups and travel mugs. At a screen door, a rough-looking mutt barked, his jaws working up and down like a hand puppet. Excited, he stepped in place, whined. It was nice.

I'd never really been in Hampden at that time of day. I'd always taken the bus to school in the morning, and it went down Forty-first Street to Falls Road, never right through the middle of the neighborhood. There was a different feel early in the morning, a satisfied sensation, as if no one was worried about what they had.

Ahead of me, a man stood out on his stoop and stared off across the street at a rowhouse identical to his. He had a scar on his cheek— a wide, pink gash that had healed like a knot of chewing gum. He rotated his head on his thick neck and looked at me. He blinked. "These're the days, huh?" he said.

I stopped. "The days of what?" I asked, standing at the bottom of his peeling wooden steps, thin, with a swatch of crushed AstroTurf running down the center.

"Just nice days," he said.

"I guess," I mumbled, thinking of Greely's heart starving for blood.

"I been doing the same thing every morning for thirty years. That says something to me. I ain't budged."

My books weighed heavy on an arm, and I smiled at the man.

He smiled back, shrugged. He shifted about on his thick hips, and his belly stuck out.

I stumbled on, walked slowly, saw Ditch in my head and thought about what he'd meant the night before, about there being different

[258]

ways to leave a place. I thought that maybe changing into something I wasn't, an angry sort of kid, was one of them. Unlike the guy with the scar and the stomach, I'd been budging all about instead of seeing all the things I had, the people who were in my life, my comic books, our home theater. I had good things, and sometimes I just stopped seeing them, saw nothing but the low stuff. I wanted to be a better kid.

Sometimes I went to the hospital alone, and sometimes I went with my mom or Howard or Ditch and Junie. Whatever the case, that week, if I wasn't working at Junie's, I stumbled through the neighborhood and up Calvert Street after school, visited Greely in his white room at Charles Village Memorial Hospital. At first, he looked terrible, worn and exhausted and sore, like he'd been in a plane accident, but after just a few days, he seemed better. It was funny to see him in bed, though, tucked in like a baby under thin sheets, the soft part of his antique stomach poking up. I had to get special permission to visit by myself, so a nurse always led me to his room. Greely smiled at me whenever I walked in, and I smiled back, a big dumb grin that made my cheeks twitch and ache.

The days with Greely in the hospital went by slowly, the way the moon changes. While I was at school, doctors ran tests on him, poked him, squashed his arms with a blood pressure cuff, took pictures, and monitored all of the televisions he was plugged into. By the end of the week, they decided he needed to get a tiny balloon pushed through his closing veins.

"I don't understand," I said.

"The balloon just pushes all of the crud out of the way, like a bulldozer."

"That's all?"

"That's what they say," Greely told me, shrugging, crossing his big arms over his stomach.

[259]

We talked constantly. He told me about all sorts of things, and sometimes, when he was tired, he repeated himself and didn't even know it. Even though he had suction cups taped and glued all over his chest and a gentle kind of tremble to his hands, he was usually in a pretty good mood, laughing a lot and kidding me like he always did.

"You working on your catching any?"

"Ditch wants to toss with me on Saturday." I studied his face, wondered. "You don't feel bad about that, do you?"

"Sammy," he said, "I'm all torn to pieces about it."

I rolled my eyes, knew he was joking.

"So how's the old school? Holding up in my absence?"

"Yeah, I guess," I told him as I jumped up and tiptoed along a chrome rail beside his bed. Skittering off, I suddenly blurted, "Hey, you wanta know what happened yesterday?"

"Cafeteria blew up?" Greely said.

"That would've been in the papers," I informed him. "Anyway, this is even better. Mrs. Sporely said that if I keep up my grades and keep practicing drawing, after next year, she'll help me get into the high school for kids who like art. She thinks I'd do good there."

Greely rose up in his bed. "Now that ain't bad, eh, Sammy? School for the Arts; that's a fine place." He made an impressed look with his lips, pushed the bottom beyond the top, formed a plank. "My boy's a genius," he muttered. "Guess in the next few years, you'll come to be a regular Michael De Angelo or something."

I looked around the room, cranked my head back. I asked, "Who's he?"

"Most famous artist in alla Italy," he said. "Painted the ceiling where the Pope lives."

I stared at him, scratched a point on my head. "Doesn't sound like much," I mumbled, thinking he'd painted it the same way the ceilings were painted in our apartment, only real smooth or with swirls or something.

[260]

"He didn't just roll it on, Sam. He painted like a hundred famous pictures on it, and the whole time, he was upside down."

I froze. Upside down? I couldn't even imagine what that looked like. I repeated the man's name, "Michael De Angelo." I was real impressed.

Greely smiled. "Proud of you," he announced.

That's how the week passed. Greely mostly acted like his normal self, joking and clucking out big and small stories, rolls of strange information. I began to think he'd be that way till he got shipped home. But on the afternoon before his surgery, when the light outside was golden and pretty, skimming the shifty, sharp rooftops of Charles Village, he seemed different. He looked worn down again, like when he'd first arrived at the hospital. I noticed it right away, bouncing through the big wooden door with a nurse. I hovered about, quietly started to gab, tried to cheer him up with news he might have missed.

"Saw a Goodyear blimp this morning."

Greely raised his eyebrows, but he didn't care.

"Yeah, it floated off toward Memorial Stadium. Probably went right over your apartment."

"Probably did," he agreed.

"I think it was going to the Orioles game."

"Seems likely," he mumbled, looking up at the ceiling tiles.

A little while passed. I asked, "What're you thinking about?"

He lowered his eyes. "Somethin' funny."

"Like what?"

His hands shifted atop the sheets, resembled two cobras, hoods wide, slithering about. "That it's all catching up to me, Sam."

"What's catching up?" I asked, sitting down in a wood chair tucked between the bed and a heavy white curtain that separated the room in half. On the other side, by the bright window, some guy had kidney stones, which must have been kind of painful. He was groaning all the time.

"That Little Tavern diet of mine. It wasn't no good for me, I'll tell you that."

"All you ever have are pancakes."

"Naw. For years I had me hamburgers and scrapple sandwiches and toasted cheese. Man, I had me artery-clogging food for mosta my life. Shoulda known better, too, Sam. 'Bout twenty years ago, a guy died right next ta me in the Tavern. Had a heart attack so bad from his diet, all he did was chirp once and slip right away. I didn't even know it, neither, not until he fell against my shoulder, then collapsed off his stool. Gave me the creeps. Couldn't sleep a wink for a week, but I didn't stop getting bacon-and-egg breakfasts or nothing, not even later, when all the news on cholesterol was compelling and such. I went right on with my ways."

"He died chirping?" I murmured.

"Went more like, 'Urp,' and that was that."

"That's not very good," I said.

"Wouldn't have bothered me so much, 'cept I was living just like him, almost exactly. Ate there every night, like me. Also, he fell on my arm. That gave me the willies. The guy sold insurance for a living. Name was Murphybarndale."

"Murphybarndale?" I laughed. "What kind of name is that?"

"Murphybarndale was his whole name. Murphy was his first, Barndale his last."

I nodded and took a second to figure out what he meant.

"The lady working the counter, this old friend of mine, she called him Barn, but I called him his full name with a Mister on the front, when I called him anything, which wasn't much. That man was a bigot until he wanted you to buy insurance from him. You shoulda seen the way he acted in 1960, the first week that place opened ta blacks. He treated us like we was sitting in his house stealing food right off his plate or somethin'."

I nodded, shifted in my chair. The guy behind the wavy curtain moaned.

Greely also shifted about, moved his sore knee up and down. "So," he said after a minute, "they got my angioplasty scheduled for one in the afternoon. Doctor says I'll be outta here in a few days."

I nodded again. "That's what pushing the balloon through your veins is called?"

"Yeah."

I bit at a fingernail, peeled off a hard little strip, looked around the boring room. There wasn't a single picture on any of the walls, just an eyeball-searing whiteness. "Is it dangerous?"

"Naw. Think of a balloon, Sam. You ever seen a dangerous balloon?"

I shook my head.

"I think of balloons, I think back to when I lived in Atlanta. My littlest kid, she loved red ones. Man, she saw one and she had ta have one, and sometimes, I'll tell you, I didn't make enough money in a whole week for that kinda expense." He smiled, clucked his tongue. "Use ta hate balloons; now I got one gonna save my life."

I pushed my mouth full of air, so that my cheeks swelled; then I let it blow out between my stretched lips. I asked as delicately as I could, "You couldn't buy a balloon?"

Greely focused his gaze out into the middle of the room, where there wasn't anything to look at. "Couldn't get poor Margarette a balloon, Sam. It was a terrible feeling, too. I mean, I'm a vet. I had my pride, but I couldn't afford somethin' cheap like that. Ain't that pathetic, a grown man who can't buy his kid a balloon?"

I acted like it wasn't. I didn't want him to feel bad.

"She couldn't understand it, either. And I couldn't understand that. Got mad at her for it. I was a stupid man, more immature than a grown person has a right to be. Thought I could be somethin' better than I was if I didn't have ta waste my time explaining why I couldn't afford balloons or food or clothes, why I was such a dismal-feeling person. Didn't understand that everybody in the whole world thinks they're meant to be special, that their train ain't come in yet. Guess it takes age to accept that ain't never gonna happen." He shook his big head. It swayed back and forth, hung on invisible strings. "If I could go back and change the way I was, I would, Sam. That's the first thing I'd do. I'll tell you, it ain't hard to hate myself for my past, and sometimes I do. I really do." He paused, then said, "But mostly I just live with it."

Uncomfortable, I looked down at the cushions smooshing flat beneath the narrow rolls of my legs, at the scuffed tiles below my feet. One of my heels rested on a seam that shot out into the hallway, where nurses squished by in soft round-toed shoes. From the corners of my eyes, I saw Greely wince as he lifted himself.

Greely adjusted onto his side, stiff sheets rustling around him, pulling out from under the floppy slim mattress. He looked at me, his hip a steep hill. "I'm gonna tell you somethin' about me, Sam, so you know what kind of person I am if I die on the operatin' table." Some big craggy fingers flopped across the shiny steel bar that ran the length of his bed. Like a string of pipes, they dangled in front of my face. "You want the facts about me? The facts is, I ain't a real good person."

I shook my head. "Yeah you are, Greely," I assured him, ignoring as well as I could the stuff he'd just told me.

Behind the curtain, the guy with the kidney stones whined as softly as a song.

Greely lifted his head from his pillow. "I owe it to you to be honest. It's time I was."

"But I don't wanta know anything bad."

He pushed his heavy tongue around in his mouth, a wet cave. "Got to tell you, though. For my conscience. In case somethin' happens."

"You said the balloon isn't dangerous."

He nodded up and down. "And it ain't, not really. The thing is, breathing ain't normally considered dangerous, neither, but it can be. Remember how you sucked in so much air that you got yourself sick. Even routine, everyday things can mess up. That's all I mean."

"Still. You don't have to tell me," I said.

"I need to. I got a spot in me that won't come clean till I do. You're the person who's gotta know."

"No, I'm not."

"Sam," he begged, "You is."

I sat still, felt like he was holding me down, poking me with pins.

"You're the one who's gotta understand what I done in my life, the things I done that I ain't proud of."

My head raced with ways to get back to the conversation about the guy who'd died in the Little Tavern, how he'd fallen against Greely's shoulder, then fell to the floor. I wondered if his head had cracked on the tiles, sounded like a skipping golf ball.

"Sam, you know, back in the early fall, it was kind of public information that your dad had left. When Nurse Jones phoned your house, your mom just told her outright. And she also told Nurse Jones to spread the word. Guess she figured that maybe yer teachers ought to know what you were going through. Guess she thought they might watch out for you or somethin'. So when I told Nurse Jones that I'd sat with you at the Little Tavern, then asked her why you was always looking so sick, she told me. She did it for a lot of reasons. I known her for years, and she thought maybe I could help you, and you could maybe help me. And that's how I came to shift my lunch schedule round so that we could eat at the same time."

I looked up at him. "When that Murphybarndale guy fell, did his head really smack the floor, or did he just kind of sink like a pillow?"

Greely acted like he didn't hear me. "See, the truth of the matter is—"

[265]

I pushed out of the chair, stood. "I don't wanta know," I told him again.

He stopped, gawked at me. "Ya gotta," he said.

I stood still, considered all of the arguments. "I'm just a kid," I finally mumbled.

"I know, Sam. I know yer young and getting over issues, but, well . . . sometimes it's good ta see things from the other side. Fits things in place, so ta speak."

"I don't mind not having things in place," I argued.

"Maybe not," he agreed, "but here it is anyway. I—" he poked a rocky finger at his chest—"I understand the way your father felt when he left you. I understand your old man, 'cause all I can imagine is we felt similar. See, I know you know this, what with Rose lobbing hints at you all the time, but I did somethin' kinda like your father, maybe worse. I walked away from my own family in 1954. The difference was, they knew where I was going, that I was gonna work up here for a summer, 'cause decent jobs in Atlanta, they was scarce for black men, and here I had a cousin with a roofing business, coating at least ten rowhouses a week. He needed help, and I needed money, so I came. The thing that happened is, my summer turned to fall, and that turned to winter, and whenever I thought about my family, it gave me the shivers, reminded me of what it was like to be a nothing, to have nothing. I couldn't even look at their photos, read their letters, without getting that feeling, so I went and tossed them all out. Just dumped 'em. My wife and I, we talked on the phone a few times after that. I even asked her to pack everything and carry the kids on up here, knowing that she wouldn't, not with all her family from Atlanta and not a soul in Baltimore. And she begged me to come back, hollered at me that I was a sorry excuse. So I just stopped calling her. I stopped cold. When she called me, and I heard that voice, I slammed down the phone. When her letters came, I dropped them in the wastepaper basket. I erased my family from my life, and you wanta know something? For a while, I was happier for it. I was glad."

I stood quiet and confused. It seemed to me, the way he'd done it was worse than my dad's way. "You weren't happier," I informed him, trying to straighten things out, trying to defend him from himself. It sounded too awful, the way he put it.

"I was, Sam. I was happier. I didn't care what I did to my kids or my wife, neither. They coulda cried every night, and I wouldn't have wavered at all. I figured I was saving my own life, and that was reason enough to treat them poorly."

I grit my teeth, ground them the way my dad had. Behind all of that thoughtful talk and calm forgiveness, Greely was selfish, a selfish jerk. It made me sick to think of the hurt he'd caused, the cold, numbing injury, an endless rain on the people left behind. I knew exactly how it felt to be abandoned, like you couldn't live with the pain, and you had to. What could you do? "Your kids musta thought you hated them."

"It'd got so sometimes I did."

I looked right at him. "How can you say that?" I blurted.

He swallowed. "'Cause it's the truth."

"Well, it shoulda been your kids hating you," I snarled, "because you were the grownup."

He nodded in agreement. "Sometimes, Sam, grownups are like kids, just older. Sometimes, we get all lost in ourselves, our situations, too. But we got nowhere to go. Took me 'bout five years to see what I done, to see what I quit on. Oh, my. It just hit me, slammed inta me like a wrecking ball. Lost all my air. Thought I was dying of lung cancer. Instead, I was just lonely and guilty. I missed my children. But it was too late. I couldn't yank 'em round like that. No. Believe me, when my head cleared, I always wanted to make up for it, Sam. It's a terrible thing ta live with. But it's me. It's who I am, what I got to consider back on."

[267]

I murmured distantly, "You can't make up for that kind of thing." Tears slid along the pink base of my lashes. Forgiving him would be worse than forgiving my father, and I wouldn't do that.

"I know I can't," he told me in a deep raspy muffle, "but, hopefully, I can make another life or two better. I mean, I been good to you. Hopefully, I treated you right, Sam. I was just a dumb kid. Scared. Man, I lost track of everything. Didn't know whether I was coming or going. I understand how yer dad felt, like the whole world was folding in on him, trapping him in worthlessness. Wasn't nothing solid about it but the bars. Got so bad for me, I fainted. Remember? That's when it happened. I was sure my kids'd do better without me. I worried I was killing them with the way I acted. Worried that they was killing me, too. Sometimes I woke up in the night, scared I might've strangled the whole family. Sweat, Sam, I'd be drippin' in it. And my wife's understanding eyes, they sucked my anger away. Thing is, I wanted to be mean. Thought it might help me get somethin'. Without that anger, I was nothing but confused. How'm I gonna pay for this? How'm I gonna give 'em that? I worried that I was so dazed, I wouldn't recognize my break when it came. 'Cause I figured, for sure, if I did the right things, I'd get a break."

I barricaded my tears with the rounded parts of my palms, creases wet with dampness. Then I lowered my hands, glowering—just stood there with my face pinched, scowling at him with anger. "I think I'm gonna go ahead and go home," I told him softly, working not to yell again, to explode.

"Sam," Greely rolled about in his bed, springs popping and stretching. He looked at me, face muddy with pain. "Nothing gave me the right to leave. Man, I was wrong, and I've thought that a million times. I might've gone five days in all my years in Baltimore where I didn't think about my family, even when I wasn't bothered 'bout leaving 'em behind. Worst thing is, I know they probably hate me, and I deserve it. I just hope they didn't waste too much of their energy doing it. I hope they got on after a while, and I just became somethin' bad and nearly forgotten from their past. I hope they found some way ta do that."

I shivered, looking through the silvery metal bars of Greely's hospital bed, at the two pointed bumps of his feet and the bulk of his body under the sheets, at his face, wise and scratched. "I won't ever forgive my dad." I pushed at my runny nose with some knuckles.

Greely closed his eyes. He pulled a hand up from his side and rubbed his face, stretching his nose and his cheeks like a cartoon. "I seen that, Sam," he said through his stony fingers. "And I hope it don't blind you to what you got, a whole nother family who cares about you and your mom more than they care 'bout themselves. The honest to God truth is, I worry for you like you was mine."

I wormed my hands around in my dusty pockets, rolled some pennies. "But I'm not," I whispered.

"I know. I know you ain't. But I seen you mature so much since I met ya, Sam. You've done at least a lifetime's worth of growing. Yer way ahead of me when I was . . . I don't know, thirty. Still, you ain't old enough to see things from any kind of distance. I mean, I ain't learned a whole lot from getting old, but I do know that throughout yer life, you either got to forgive things or let 'em bother you till you do. Ya got to start seeing yer dad for what he was, special to you, important to you, but just a regular man. He was working his way through life, and he done good things and bad things. He was human, a bad person for leaving—but the leaving was the bad part of the act, not what he done before. I ain't never got from you that he was abusive. Matter of fact, seemed to me you idolized him at least as much as you don't like him now. What I'm saying is, that in order to get on from here, you got to try and see things as they are and were, or they gonna eat at you. You got to be real about stuff. I learned that the worst way I could, but at least I learned it."

Greely looked tired. His eyes were heavy, and tenderized circles folded under them against his cheeks.

I drifted back and forth, swaying on my ankles. I wondered how Greely could have been so selfish. It was hard for me to imagine the person I knew, my friend, doing what he'd done. He must have been trampled down, nearly dying at the time. He must've been a different person, like one of those murderers on Death Row who mends his ways, teaches people to read, carries the Bible slung in his arms, and still he's going to die for what he did.

"I ain't asking you to pardon me, Sam," he said, "'cause you ain't the one to do it. I just told you 'cause I needed to."

"I know," I answered, lifting my head a little.

"I hope so," he grumbled softly back.

I continued moving from side to side. I studied his face, him. I loved Greely like we were related, like he was the grandfather I never met. I couldn't help it. He was inside of me like Charles Village was inside of me. And the truth is, I wanted to tell him that I understood, just a little, about what he'd felt back in Atlanta. I wanted Greely to know that even if I couldn't forgive him completely, I did some. I knew there were things going on in 1954 that I couldn't understand, not yet. "Greely . . . ," I rasped, my voice weak. I didn't know how to say what I wanted to, so I told him what I felt. "Greely, I hope you don't ever die, you know, because I think now you're one of the best people in Baltimore, maybe the entire state. I think you've changed from what you were."

"Thanks, Sam," he mumbled, then closed his eyes, looking leathery and old and relieved.

I couldn't sleep that night. I stared at the ceiling, at the seams of wallpaper. Way in the distance, somewhere in the city beyond my closed window, there was a police siren screaming through the streets. I rolled, tugged my spread over a bare shoulder, and studied the Michael Jordan poster I had above my desk. He was slam dunking.

His eyes were big, and his mouth was stuck open, that tongue a pink salty eel wagging out. I looked behind him, at the players frozen in time, then at the crowd. It was a colorful blur.

My eyes fell to the gray metal desk my mom and dad had gotten for me at a used-furniture store. It was scratched and dented and getting kind of rusty. In a drawer, there was a crumpled list of every comic book I owned, a pad with drawings in it, and a giant eraser I'd gotten on a vacation in Ocean City. I thought about all of the hands that had passed across that desk, and I suddenly felt wounded from loving people. If Greely got out of the hospital OK, I'd ask him to put his hands on it, too.

the faded light of baltimore

the faded light of baltimore

On a gray day, drizzle washing down, Greely had the clogged passages of his heart cleaned. When I got out of school, my mom and I rushed over and waited for him in his room. The guy with the kidney stones was gone, and the heavy curtain was pulled back, so we spread out, flopped at least once in every chair, and stared out the big rectangular window that overlooked the smeared reddy-brownness of Charles Village. To keep me busy, my mom had bought me three magazines, plus she left the television yammering away. But I couldn't concentrate at all, not with Greely downstairs getting a balloon passed through his insides.

When we finally saw him, it was nearly supper time. He was laid out flat and groggy on a rolling bed. Two guys and a nurse wheeled him in and propped him up. As they worked, he turned his head and looked at me. He licked his lips—so dry, like rusty metal—and he told me that he was doing pretty good.

After the early game shows, we left, headed home through the rainy light as it changed into clear purple sky. Relaxed, we passed down busy Calvert Street, along the jumbled old rows, flowing crooked, a thousand different lives inside. It was like we'd never been mugged, we walked so slowly, so carelessly. We didn't say all that much, just splashed our feet through puddles and along the sidewalks. Turning onto Thirty-second Street, I leaned against my mom's hip and closed my eyes. A relieved feeling moved up my back, warmed me. And in a simple style, I forgave my father for leaving, as much as I could without forgetting what he'd done altogether. I did it by seeing him the way he'd actually been. The truth is, up until the very moment he disappeared, through his problems, he was a pretty good dad, and I'd always known that I was a lucky kid.

"You know what," I said softly, "even though he didn't say goodbye, I hope Dad's okay."

My mom settled a hand gently around me, held me as we walked home. "I hope he's okay, too," she whispered.

"You think we're gonna do better now?"

She stopped, scooted in front of me, dangled both of her thin arms around my shoulders. "I think so," she said, smiling in a way I'd forgotten she could.

Glass and metal twinkled in the delicate hazy glow of streetlights. The pretty red brick stood out against the faded light of Baltimore. "I think so, too," I told her.

A week later, Pepé became my dog. A nicely dressed black woman from a lawyer's office brought him to us, stood in the high doorway downstairs. She held Pepé in her slender arms and told me he was mine if I wanted him. She said that poor Mr. Garcia had died of cancer fifteen days before, and that he'd given Pepé to me in his will, along with $1,284.71, the entire remains of his savings, in hopes that it would cover food and veterinary bills. My mom hemmed and hawed, then let me keep him. I finally got a perfect little bowzer. He was Mr. Garcia's old best friend, and I never forgot that—those brittle hands, like a burnt and crumpled brown bag, belonged to a man who was trying so hard to make friends. I don't know why he left Pepé to me, maybe because I talked with him that day, maybe because he'd noticed how much I liked dogs, but it seemed almost natural for something nice to happen for such a sad reason. I don't know why, but, for me, good and bad things always seem to be connected together, pasted down beside each other so that one often doesn't come without the other.

My mom and I still live on Abel Avenue. I've gotten older, but I still read comic books, and I still throw the football with Greely and Ditch, rush beneath it, let it settle into my hands like a soaring bird. I haven't grown tall, yet, and I worry that I never will. I worry a good bit, but not as much as I used to. My mom says that I got that from my dad, but she doesn't have to, because I remember how he was. The nice thing is, we talk about him more than we used to. We wonder where he is and what he's doing. I think she still feels bad that he's gone. He might have had more sadness in him than a normal person, but he had more happiness, too. He had that soft heart.

I can't help wondering what he would say if he saw me now, drawing pictures of trees and buildings and all sorts of other things I'd never thought about, talking to people, laughing with new friends. I hope he'd see that I would've been okay all along, that he didn't need to fear for me so much. I hope he'd see that he could've saved more of his strength for himself and even taken a little from us, too. I think about that, and I still wish he'd come home, even if he just turned around and left again. At least he'd know that things could've been different, that we weren't trying to be selfish with him.

It's gotten so that I wouldn't change what happened, not anymore. I grew up after my father disappeared. I grew up in ways that I'm not sure I would have if he'd stayed around. We've got a different kind of family now, and they watch over my mom and me like we're special, even though we know we're not. They held us together when my father was first gone, when we were exploding apart, and they've been nearby ever since. Junie and Ditch, Greely and Howard, they've shown me that good survives in the worst times, that you have to keep going, no matter what. So I worry that we can't possibly give them enough. And, always, they promise me that they get their share. I hope they do.

Acknowledgments

Throughout my writing life, I have had the good fortune to meet and talk with wonderful and distinct individuals. It is because of them that I celebrate the great joys and unnerving sorrows of living. Sadly, without one, the other scarcely exists, or so it seems. In deference to it all, here is a very partial list of people and organizations that have helped me:

First and foremost, I thank my beautiful wife and daughter for their constant support, humor, and love. I also thank my mother, who urged me to see and experience as I do, without humiliation. Following her, there are my brother and sister, who have, at various times in our crazy lives together, carried me, themselves, and practically everything we own. I also want to recognize my stepfather, a man I am only now beginning to understand.

With apprehension (I know I will leave someone out), I want to note other very important people in the process: Thank you, Jim and Sue, for your trust. To all of my interviewees and museum coworkers, I appreciate your friendship. Specifically, I thank the Towerettes for their stories, Reverend Pettigrew for his strength, John for hiring me, Anita for reading, Dean for challenging me to think, and Mr. Webb for being, well, Mr. Webb. I am grateful to Steve for his exuberance and eye. I recognize Malcolm for his running technique. I acknowledge the Maryland State Arts Council for their financial help in dire times, and I extend great thanks to all of the librarians, schools, and publications that kept this book alive during its first fitful months. Without them, both the book and I would have surely disappeared into obscurity.

As for my current home, I can't imagine many locations in this country odd enough to provoke such contrary emotions within me. Baltimore City is a wonderful, sad place to write in, loaded with gracious, colorful, and dangerous souls, and a similar history. I have a great affection and the best hopes for it.

On the publishing end, I want to thank Bruce Bortz of Bancroft Press for ushering this book into all the right hands. I am also very thankful to have worked with editor and friend Sarah Azizi, who always believed in the story and me. Last, I'd like to thank Candlewick Press and their brilliant and kind editor Liz Bicknell. Their faith in me has rekindled quite a few nearly discarded dreams.

Without all of my friends and family, this book wouldn't have seen the light of day. Thank you all for your patience as well as your continued support.

Jonathon Scott Fuqua
Baltimore, 2001